# SECRETS IN CALUSA COVE

## EVERGLADES OVERWATCH
### BOOK ONE

ELLE JAMES

JEN TALTY

TWISTED PAGE INC

ISBN EBOOK: 978-1-62695-639-1

ISBN PRINT: 978-1-62695-655-1

# AUTHOR'S NOTE

USA Today Bestselling authors Jen Talty and Elle James join forces in an electrifying collaboration born from an author retreat in paradise. Inspired by the lush landscapes of the Florida Everglades, their latest venture blends heart-pounding suspense, sizzling romance, and gripping action. With their signature storytelling prowess, Talty and James weave a thrilling tale that will keep readers on the edge of their seats, proving that when two powerhouse authors unite, the result is pure magic.

# SECRETS IN CALUSA COVE

## EVERGLADES OVERWATCH BOOK # 1

*New York Times & USA Today*
Bestselling Author

**ELLE JAMES**

*USA Today*
Bestselling Author

**JEN TALTY**

# PROLOGUE

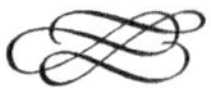



"Seriously, Dad." Audra McCain huffed as she climbed into her father's airboat in the dead of night. "I believe you, so no need to prove it to me." Only, she didn't believe. Not really. Not anymore. She'd accepted that her dad was a little left of normal long ago. His quirks—while annoying—were something she'd learned to live with because, at the end of the day, no one loved her like her daddy. He'd taught her how to survive in Calusa Cove.

Especially when the kids and their parents had started calling her a Stigini. Or an Owl Witch. At first, she hadn't known which was worse. *That,* or having a father the town considered a loon because he believed in conspiracy theories. But what difference did it make? No one but her father—not even Ken—would ever see her as a whole person.

However, just because she listened to his crazy theories didn't mean she believed a single word. Those days had died when they'd buried her mother.

Truth be told, her mama's Native American heritage, and her ties to what some confused with witchcraft, were where the rumors of Audra being an owl-like creature had started. No one understood that her mom hadn't been a witch. Her mother had been tethered to the earth, to all the elements, and believed humans needed to be spiritually grounded.

Audra's dark freckled skin and red hair resulted from her combined one-quarter Seminole and three-quarters Irish heritage, giving her a unique look. But as she'd become a teenager, that mixture had only made her feel more like an outsider.

"I want a witness, and you have that smartphone thingy to take pictures," her dad said. "Just humor your old man. Before you know it, you'll be flying the coop." He arched a brow. "You'll probably run off with that boyfriend of yours."

She cringed, remembering the fight she'd had earlier with her dad, right in the center of town for all to see, hear, and judge. The argument where she'd told her dad what a whack job he was and she wished it had been him who had died six years ago and not her sweet, kind, and loving mother. Ken had a lot to say about that.

It was rare that she and her dad fought, but when they did, the words that tumbled from her mouth were harsh and were meant to hurt.

And she'd cut him to the core. She hadn't meant to. But he'd pushed her buttons. He used the past to force her hand. To make her feel guilty for choosing something other than him. Had it only been in front of Ken, Baily, and Fletcher—it wouldn't have been as devastating. They understood the dynamic. But her dad had done it in front of half the school. It wasn't even that the entire school had heard his crazy rant because everyone knew her old man thought weird shit happened deep in the Everglades. It was a running joke, and no one believed him. Not anymore. She was just tired of being looked at as though the crazy would rub off on her.

However, everyone still enjoyed the old stories. The ones this town had been made on. The myths and legends that made people stop for a hot minute on the way to their posh vacation destination to stroll through Calusa Cove and take in one of the sights. Maybe even go on a tour of the Everglades. But no one wanted to hear this new insane crap about things that went bump in the night, about the boats carrying bad men with bad things that came and went every couple of months.

She sighed. She was stuck in this small town for so many reasons, destined to be nothing but a redhead with a mouth as fiery as her hair.

"You did bring your phone, didn't you?" her father asked, his voice laced with a sense of desperation.

"Yes, Daddy," she said softly.

It was odd that he was fixated on that. He wouldn't allow the internet in the home because someone could listen. Someone was always listening. Spying. Looking into what he was doing.

She was lucky that her dad allowed her to have a television with cable, though he did ask her to unplug every electronic device when she wasn't using it—her computer included.

He'd gone ballistic when he found out she bought a

smartphone with her own money. He demanded she power it off when she wasn't using it. Actually, he'd asked that she only use it outside, but she didn't listen. It was her only connection to the world outside of Calusa Cove.

And to her boyfriend. Though, currently, Ken was being a selfish asshole. She understood. This was Ken's opportunity to get an education. His family couldn't afford to send him to college, but the military could provide one.

Plus, his best friend was going with him—making it a no-brainer for Ken.

However, Ken failed to comprehend that he broke her heart every time he smiled and spoke gleefully about leaving Calusa Cove in the dust. Following him, even after she graduated high school, wasn't something she could just up and do. Who would watch after her old man in this backward town? For years, her father had cared for her, ensuring she had everything she needed and could fend for herself. It was her turn to take care of the man who loved her more than he loved anything.

Even his stupid conspiracy theories.

She took the ear protection her father handed her and placed it over her ears just as he reeved the engines. Raising the spotlight, she helped her dad navigate the wilds of the Everglades. They could be so beautiful and peaceful at night. The stars and the moon hung in the sky like an umbrella. The water danced as if it didn't hide death and destruction. Eyes and tails everywhere, slinking through the water, waiting for their next meal to fall in.

Audra respected the Everglades and its ecosystem. Humans might be afraid of alligators, but people were their biggest predators. Mankind destroyed more gators than there were alligator attacks. If you didn't bother them, they'd leave you alone.

Just don't go swimming with one bigger than you.

This wasn't the first time her old man had dragged her out in the middle of the night to hunt for something other than gators and snakes. The first couple of times, it had been like going on an adventure, like her and her pops were pirates searching for treasure. It had helped her cope with the death of her mom.

But nothing was going to help her dad. Without his beloved bride, he had no one to ground him—not even his precious daughter, whom he loved dearly—could do that. No, he needed his Elana.

Her dad slowed the boat as they entered Snake River, a windy, narrow section of the Everglades. It was like the water version of *Sleepy Hollow*. Dark, creepy, and with a blanket of branches, blocking the light from the bright moon.

She took off her ear protection and studied her dad's profile. He'd aged so much in the six years since her mom had died. It was as if the best part of him had left along with his wife.

He went through the motions of living. He got up and shaved, though not very well. He went to work— only his business wasn't profitable. Thankfully, the house and land were paid for. But they still barely managed to put food on the table, and Audra, at almost seventeen, was getting tired of it. She wanted more for herself.

As a small child, she'd thought she wanted to work for Parks and Rec. Or maybe Fish and Wildlife. Now, she dreamed of being a photographer and journalist to see the world through a different lens than what she'd lived.

But she couldn't leave her father.

Without her to cushion the blows, Calusa Cove would destroy him. It would eat him alive and spit out his bones.

Very few people liked her dad. Less respected him. They saw him as a crazy old man who believed in conspiracy theories.

They were right about that.

But he was also kind, loving…gentle. He knew his brain wasn't quite right. He got that. But he also knew he still had one foot firmly planted in reality.

Only, you never really knew what you were getting when you talked to her old man. It was always a mish-mash of both fantasy and reality.

"Daddy?"

"Yes, darling," her father whispered.

"I'm sorry about what I said earlier today. I didn't mean it."

"I know, pumpkin. I know," he said. "Forget about it."

"So, what are we looking for?" She leaned against her dad's arm and rested her head on his strong shoulder, the annoyance of being woken up on a school night long gone. Who cared about a stupid stats test? She wasn't going to college. And no matter how much Ken pleaded, for as long as her dad had breath, she wasn't leaving Calusa Cove.

As she stared at the lush trees hanging above while they took the last bend in Snake River, she wondered if she'd ever leave this place. What people thought of her didn't matter. The call to the Everglades was stronger.

"I've always found it interesting that we've named almost every island back here but one, though at high tide, it's not really an island, but a mush peninsula." Her dad kissed her temple. "But it's like Florida has dug its heels in and said, *We're not going to know. It's the island with no name.*"

"Well, then it kind of has a name." She smiled. "No one comes back this far or down this way much. Not even on airboats." She reached for her cell phone. No service, but she could snap pictures. "Though, Ken told me once he knew a few guys who came down from Fort Lauderdale through this section."

It had taken them two hours to get to this spot, and they had hauled ass. But she absolutely enjoyed the ride. It hadn't been too balmy—or too buggy.

Time with her dad always trumped the weird ways in which it happened.

"More people come back here than you think." He touched her hand, lifting the spotlight toward the clearing. "Some avoid it because they don't like to navigate through Snake River and Alligator Junction—especially at low tide—because too many boats have gotten plants and stuff caught in their engines."

"But that's why we have cages."

Her dad laughed. "That's for bigger debris, and we've had this conversation a million times."

"I know." She hugged his arm with her free hand. "Look at those eyes in the water over there. Got to be at least four gators just hanging out."

"This is a prime location for them," her dad said. "I knew a guy when I was in high school who came back here and wrestled three of them at once."

"I remember." Audra shivered. "Hector Mendoza. He died back here."

"No. He disappeared," her dad said, "on a night much like tonight about ten years ago. He told his wife he was going out early because he saw someone doing something fishy back here, and he never made it home. Some people believe he got eaten by an alligator. Others wonder if a swamp monster got him—or if he came face-to-face with Edgar Watson."

She laughed. "I love that tale."

"So do I, child." Her dad nodded. "However, there are some who believe that Hector was murdered back here for what he thought he saw."

She'd heard this a million times. "You're the only one who believes that." She glanced up. "Why are we out here?"

"I swear I saw something." He pushed the lever and turned the boat toward the island with no name.

At night, everything looked different in the Everglades. During the day, it was rich in vegetation. Rich in beauty. One could get lost in the decadence of it all.

Once the sun dipped below the horizon, it was like stepping onto a horror set. Cue the music for *Psycho.*

And yet, it was still the only place in the world she felt at home.

That thought made her chuckle. She'd never been anywhere else but Naples, which was a cesspool of tourists, snowbirds, and traffic.

"Give me the spotlight," her father whispered—as if someone could hear them. He scanned the mangrove, finding the tree line near a clearing about fifty feet in. "Look. There. Do you see that?"

She moved toward the bow of the boat, crawling on her hands and knees. Why? She had no idea. No one was watching. Only a fool—like her father—would be out here at three in the morning. She squinted, but sure enough, a small shack and some crates with strange markings came into view. "I need my phone."

"What the hell?" her father exclaimed. "What are you doing—"

A searing pain tore through her body from her head to her toes. It rattled her teeth. She dropped to the hull of the boat. Blinking, she pressed her hands flat on the boat's bottom, trying to push herself up, but instead, stars filled her vision.

Another sharp stab to her head. It was as if a bomb had exploded inside her brain.

And then the world simply turned… black.

* * *

*Gripping the sides of the boat, she pulled herself up. It took all the strength she had.*

*A man's muffled voice drowned in her ears. It was like*

*every sound bubbled underwater, unable to break through the throbbing in her skull.*

*A second voice. Or maybe it was the same one. She couldn't be sure. She craned her neck toward the chatter. The tone and texture of the voices were hauntingly familiar. It prickled her ears and tormented her mind. No matter how hard she tried, she couldn't place it.*

*The voice separated. Splintered into separate sounds. It was definitely two people. She knew that now. She blinked. The horrifying pain dancing on her temples made it impossible to see anything but the blackness of night.*

*Splash!*

*She leaned over and stared at the rippling water.*

*The men tossed chum overboard. She knew it was chum because she could smell the blood. Smell the raw, dead meat as it hit the brackish water.*

*She blinked.*

*Tails and eyes.*

*Eyes and tails.*

*The water flipped and flopped.*

*Mouth and teeth lurched from the waterline. Then a tail. It slapped the side of the boat.*

*More teeth.*

*Another tail. Two gators fighting over breakfast.*

*Her breath caught in her throat. Something...an arm... fingers... reached up from the murky water.*

*The sound of an engine roared in the distance.*

*Bolting upright, she screamed.*

She huffed, sucking in a deep breath. She clutched the sheets as her chest burned for more oxygen.

"Hey. It's okay. I'm right here," Ken said, taking her hand. "Same nightmare?"

"Yeah." She sighed, fluffing the pillow and sitting higher in the hospital bed. Every time she closed her eyes, it was the same. It was like her father was reaching out of the water, begging her to save him.

And she'd failed.

"Whoever clocked me—"

"Audra, you've got to stop telling that story. It makes you sound as crazy as your dad."

She pursed her lips. "Are you going to sit there and tell me the bumps on the back of my head aren't real?"

"No. But it makes more sense that it was an accident, and that's the tale you need to tell. There was damage to your dad's airboat. Before someone found you, you had to use an oar to get close to the docks. You and your dad ran into something out there, and you fell and hit your head. It's a miracle that you didn't fall into the water yourself. You go off the rails about someone trying to kill him…" Ken let the words trail off as he let out a long sigh.

Thank God. Because she would have popped him in the mouth if he'd kept talking.

But that wasn't going to stop her from laying into him either.

"Are you kidding me? Explain to me how my father got dumped into the water if he was the one driving and I was crawling on the bow of the boat?" She held up her hand. She didn't want to hear his excuses. "Also, please enlighten me how so many gators ended up swarming that boat." She cocked her head. "Because that doesn't happen unless you chum the water."

"Babe. You're basing the alligator swarm on a nightmare."

"Don't you dare 'babe' me," she mumbled. "Maybe my dream isn't completely accurate. But someone hit me over the head. I didn't fall. Why don't you believe me? You're supposed to be on my side."

"I am," Ken said. "You have to understand how crazy this sounds and how people are going to—"

A tap at the door thankfully shut him up because she couldn't listen to another word. "Come in." She adjusted her covers.

"Sorry to bother you," Chief of Police Trip Williams said, "but I need to interview you, and sorry, young man. I need to do it alone."

"No problem." Ken squeezed her hand. "I'll go get you a milkshake."

Ken and his stupid milkshakes. They didn't solve anything, and they weren't going to make their problems go away.

Trip pulled up a chair and made himself comfortable. She'd known Trip her entire life. He was a decent man who treated the people of Calusa Cove with kindness, her father included.

But sometimes Trip could be a hard-ass.

He had that hard-ass look about him right now.

Crossing his legs, he rested his hands in his lap. He gave her a weak smile.

Yeah, this wasn't going to be fun.

"There are a few things we need to clear up," Trip

said. He pulled out his notebook and tapped his finger on one of the pages. "I'm concerned about a couple of things."

"I've told you everything I remember." She rubbed the side of her head, careful not to hit the stitches. "Someone murdered my dad."

"You see, that's the problem," Trip said. "It appears the boat hit something. It appears everything's an accident."

"This was no accident, Trip. Someone—"

Trip held up his hand. "Here's the thing. I believe you when you say it wasn't an accident. However, getting anyone else to believe your story will be a struggle, and let me tell you why without you going off on me. Can you do that?"

"That depends." She cocked her head and folded her arms. She might be a teenager, but she'd never had a problem speaking her mind with adults—not even the law. "Are you going to say something that's going to piss me off?"

Trip leaned forward. "I've known you since the day you were born. When you came out with fiery red hair, I told your parents that you were going to be a pistol, and you're more like a stick of dynamite." Trip laughed. "I don't believe anything I'm about to say, but I'm the law, little girl, and I must look at every angle. So, I'm going to tell you how this will go. You'll let me haul you down to the station when they release you. You're going to get a lawyer if it goes too far, and I'll do my best to make sure it doesn't."

"You're being a jerk," she mumbled.

"I'm being the chief of police." He lowered his chin. "And right now, the town gossip is that you killed your dad, tossed his body into the Everglades, and crashed the boat on purpose so that you'd fall and hurt yourself. Then, for dramatic effect, you made sure the fuel line was damaged so the boat wouldn't be drivable. Some are even saying they heard strange noises last night. Owl noises. And that you've been practicing witchcraft." He arched a brow. "While that's all bull, there is some circumstantial evidence that points to a possible homicide, but I've got no body. And the motive? Well, it's weak. However, you opened yourself up when you threatened your dad in front of the entire town."

"I did no such thing."

Trip waggled his finger. "I don't have much to make anything stick. Nor will the State, but they will ask questions of you and everyone in this town. You know they will. Do you know what they will find?" He didn't wait for an answer. "A town full of people who remember you poking your father in the chest and telling him you wished he was dead instead of your mom." Trip dared to shrug. "Outside of talking with me, I'd stop the conspiracy theory crap. It doesn't help you. It only makes you look like you're a chip off the old man's shoulder and will add fuel to a fire you don't want to be ignited. You let me control the narrative. You let me work the accident angle. I'll handle everything else."

"You want me to sit back and say nothing? You want me to let this town believe I killed my dad?"

"That's what you heard me say?" Trip shook his

head. "No, little girl. That's not what I want you to do. I need you to let me do my job, but knowing you, you'll be out there in the middle of the night again. I can't have that. It's going to be hard. Damn hard. People will talk and whisper worse than they ever have. But only if you give them something to talk about. I'm a good cop. I know what I'm doing. Let me put this to bed so you don't have this hanging over your head for the rest of your life."

"Can I ask you a question?"

Trip nodded.

"Is your goal to prove this was an accident or that my father was murdered by someone other than me?"

Trip drew his lips into a tight line. "Your father was my friend. So was your mother. They'd want me to protect you. That's my first order of business. So, I want to direct this town into believing it was an accident. I'll continue to dig. I'll find out what really happened, but you, little girl, need to keep that big fat mouth closed."

"Screw that," Audra muttered. "Someone either took my dad or killed him. That should be your focus. I don't give a shit what people think of me. Never have. Never will."

"That's a mistake." Trip stood. "That train of thought will land you in prison for murder."

# CHAPTER 1

Dawson Ridge allowed another vehicle into the parking lot of Mitchell's Marina. He could handle the locals. They were easy. This was just another day in South Florida. However, all it took was one overly excited city slicker waving his registration out the window, yelling yeehaw, to put Dawson in a bad mood. The town hadn't wanted the challenge, and they'd fought it for two straight years, but they'd lost.

While Dawson understood the need to rid the Everglades of the invasive python, he couldn't comprehend the amount of excitement bristling in the air regarding hunting and killing massive pythons while trying not to get eaten by alligators.

He shivered while large droplets of sweat dripped from his brow.

For the first time since moving to what felt like a permanent vacation, he wanted to take an actual vacation.

He didn't care about the heat. Or the humidity. He

could even deal with damn alligators swimming in his backyard, taunting him. But he couldn't tolerate strangers coming into what he now viewed as *his* town. Mentally, he laughed at that thought. This wasn't his town, and every local let him know it. He was the interloper. The guy who'd stolen someone's job who had lived here their entire life. It didn't matter that Dawson had more experience. That experience might not have been in law enforcement, but seventeen years in the Navy—ten of them as a SEAL—was worth something.

"Good morning, Officer." A woman with long red hair stuck her head out the window.

A damn redhead.

"It's going to be a scorcher today," she said as she pushed her sunglasses to the top of her head, collecting some of that thick, lush hair and pulling it away from her face to show off her sparkling teal-green eyes.

The last thing he needed today was a distraction wrapped in the form of a sexy woman with fiery hair and freckles set against a slightly darker complexion.

"You can say that again, ma'am." He lowered his sunglasses just a smidge off the bridge of his nose. His breath caught in the center of his chest, but he told himself it was a thick clump of humidity that got stuck there like a fur ball.

Because he knew what that felt like.

Swallowing became a lesson in futility.

He'd always been a sucker for redheads, and they'd always been more trouble than they were worth.

"It's your lucky day because we just closed up. Anyone coming in now will have to park down the road." He pointed to the last spot before waving to Fletcher and Keaton, who were closing off the lot. "You can bring your registration information into Mitchell's. A woman by the name of Baily will take care of you."

"I'm surprised she's got this many boats available. I'm more surprised that Calusa Cove got so many people to sign up for the challenge. This is not the epicenter for python wrangling," the sexy woman said.

"The damn things have made their way into all sorts of places." Dawson looped his fingers into his belt. The lady had had his attention the moment she'd stuck her head out the window, but now she had his cop instincts wondering a few things—specifically, who was she, and how did she know anything about Mitchell's or Calusa Cove? "My deputies and I have been on a few snake calls that turned out to be pythons. It's not fun," he said. "Did you rent a boat?"

"No. I did rent a slip, though." The woman shook her head, leaning over the door. "Some guy named Hayes and a dockhand named Bingo directed me to the launch and said my boat would be in the slip by the time I finished my paperwork. They told me the trailer had to be left in the lot across the street."

"Hayes Bennett is a local firefighter and is a buddy of mine. Bingo works here at the marina and he's not a bad kid. You're in good hands."

"I hope so. The boat might be a rust bucket and old, but it's new to me." She nodded. "I better go—"

"As I live and breathe," Fletcher said as he marched across the pavement. "Audra? Is that really you?"

Dawson rolled the name around in his brain.

Fletcher had told many stories over the years about his hometown and the crazy people who resided in Calusa Cove.

Everyone was a character. Dawson used to understand why Fletcher and his late buddy, Ken, had wanted to get out—and stay out. That was until Dawson had moved to Calusa Cove. After that happened, he couldn't wrap his brain around why anyone would ever want to leave. All Dawson had ever wanted was to be part of something. Part of a family. Part of a town. Part of something bigger than himself. However, returning to his hometown in Western, New York when he'd left the Navy hadn't been an option. There was nothing left for him there except sadness and painful memories.

However, Dawson had taken to Calusa Cove like bees to honey. He loved almost everything about this town—the quirky people, the funky places, the smallness of it—and especially, the quietness. He loved that. When he'd first decided to come here, he'd thought he might miss the snowy winters or even the change of seasons, but he hadn't. He enjoyed the palm trees and the perpetual warmth.

Still, there were two things Dawson didn't like about his new home.

Gators and mosquitoes the size of gators.

And maybe one more thing. The lack of available single women. But Dawson had had his heart ripped out once, and he'd rather be in a place like Calusa Cove than some town where a woman could steal his soul—especially a redhead.

So why was his pulse purring like a damn kitten?

"Yeah, it's me," the pretty redhead said. "I guess I should've known that even after all these years, I wouldn't be able to fly under the radar."

"Not with that hair." Fletcher laughed, waving his finger over the top of his head. "Besides, you had to register. Everyone knows you're coming," Fletcher said. "It's been what—sixteen years since you left?"

Audra… Ken…

Dawson didn't know the entire story, but he knew enough.

"Something like that," Audra said. "Look, I'd love to sit here and shoot the breeze, but I've got to get going."

"I can't believe you came here—of all places—to do the Python Challenge." Fletcher leaned against the vehicle.

"It was time to come back." She turned, leaning across the seat. "And for more than one reason."

Dawson pushed his glasses to the top of his head and glanced around the lot. He counted fifty cars. That was five more than last year. According to Parks and Recreation records, this was the second year the challenge was open to this area. Different areas in the Everglades would get well over two hundred participants, but the reality was that less than a thousand would hunt during the ten-day challenge.

The number of pythons that would be removed would barely put a dent in the problem, but it still helped.

"I would hope the number one reason is to capture and kill the pythons," Fletcher said, "considering how your dad felt about keeping the Everglades intact. I bet he would've been out there every day trying to remove as many as he could."

"If this challenge had been going when he was alive, he'd have run it. But it's not like he wasn't wrangling snakes before he died." She lifted a large camera. "Killing pythons is one of the reasons I'm here, but I'm also here to take some pictures of the wildlife and the hunt for a collection I'm putting together and an article I'm writing on the situation."

"You should sit down with our friend Keaton Cole," Dawson said. "He's Fish and Wildlife, and he's got an opinion about the pythons and this challenge."

"Dawson's right about that." Fletcher nodded. "We're all passionate about the removal of the snakes. We're just not all thrilled about this."

"You can say that again," Dawson said under his breath. This area didn't get too many novice participants, but others did, and every year, someone got hurt. "I don't mind the professionals, but take those guys over there…" He jerked his chin toward two men leaning against a fancy foreign sports car wearing golf shirts, slacks, and god-awful shoes that some company sold for a small fortune to men like that, claiming they were "boat shoes." It was an utter disgrace—worse than those Army-grade backpacks sold online that came from China. Dawson had a bad feeling about those two and had texted Hayes and Remy to make sure they did a thorough check of their boat.

But something else about those two got under Dawson's skin. They stood out like a sore thumb, and that made him twitchy.

"Technically, I'm not a professional snake hunter, although I've done this before in a different area and grew up catching rattlers and water moccasins." Audra cocked her pretty little brow. "Do you have a problem with me?"

Dawson cleared his throat. "I guess I walked right into that one," he said softly. "I didn't mean to insult you, ma'am."

"You didn't, but keep calling me ma'am, and we'll have a problem." She laughed. "If I can wrangle an alligator, I believe I can deal with a python."

Fletcher bent over, placed both hands on his knees, and full-out laughed.

"What the hell is so funny, Fletch?" Audra narrowed her stare. "That gator might have only been four feet long, but I got him, and you were there. You lost fifty bucks that day."

"I'm sorry. I'm not laughing at the idea of you wrestling a snake—or a gator. Really, I'm not. I'm sure the fiery redhead I remember back in high school can do it all again. What I'm having a good chuckle over is you coming out of that swamp after wrestling that gator and the shirt Ken bought you—"

"Oh, buzz off," Audra mumbled. "You got to see breasts that day, even if they were itty-bitty. You should be grateful. Now get your ass the hell off my car so I can hand in my paperwork, get my boat in order, and get me some snakes."

Fletcher lifted his hands and backed away.

"Nice meeting you, Officer." She lowered her glasses

over those mesmerizing eyes that Dawson would not allow himself to be captivated by.

"Feel free to call me Dawson," he said.

She punched the gas and maneuvered her vehicle toward the last free spot in the parking lot. She slipped from the driver's side, wearing a pair of jean shorts that hung loosely from her hips, and her shirt didn't come down to meet the top of her shorts, showing off a taut midriff.

Damn. Dawson swallowed. Hard.

Flipping redheads got him every time.

And she was wearing flip-flops.

"She hasn't changed one bit, but it's going to be hard for Baily to see her," Fletcher said.

"Is that Ken's Audra?"

"One in the same."

Dawson lowered his glasses and strolled across the dirt pavement with his buddy. He snagged a water bottle from the cooler and climbed up on the picnic bench, where he could watch the marina and the parking lot. Not much happened in Calusa Cove, making his job as chief of police a relatively easy one. He loved his job. He had three deputies under him, and they were good people. Even Remy Pillar, who had been next in line to be named chief, had Dawson not shown up.

"Why were you staring at her boobs?" Dawson asked as he watched her hips sway back and forth while she marched herself from her car toward the entrance of Mitchell's Marina. She had a narrow waist, wide hips, and a round ass. "I'm sure Ken did not appreciate that."

When he'd dared to look at her breasts while chatting by her car, they were not that itty-bitty—as she'd put it. Small? Sure. They might even get lost—oh, for fuck's sake. Why the hell was Dawson even thinking about them?

She was a redhead, and he didn't do redheads.

Not to mention, if she was *the* Audra he believed her to be, she was even more off-limits.

"Do I need to be worried about you, considering you can't take your eyes off her?" Fletcher chuckled before taking a long swig of water. He sat on the table, leaned back, and stared at the sky.

"Nope. Not interested," Dawson said with about as much conviction as a kid in a candy store, dancing on his tippytoes, brimming with excitement. "But you haven't answered my question, and you know how much that pisses me off."

"For the record, I wasn't staring at any part of Audra when she wrestled that gator. That would've gotten me in too much trouble with my girlfriend at the time." Fletcher turned his head and cocked a brow. "Audra was Baily's best friend, and Ken was mine. I would've gotten the shit kicked out of me twice."

"There are lots of rumors about what happened to her old man. What do you know about that?" Instead of asking questions about the woman, he opted to discuss the mystery.

"Just the rumors."

"Are there more than the three?"

"Not that I know of." Fletcher sat tall, resting his forearms on his knees, and fiddled with the water bottle. He'd always been a contemplative man. When it came to serious matters, he took his time before he spoke. He liked to choose his words wisely, especially when dealing with matters that affected others.

Dawson had always appreciated that about Fletcher. It's one of the many reasons he'd been willing to follow him out of the Navy and to South Florida after Ken had died. But more so because where else was Dawson going to go? He had no home. No blood family. No friends outside of Fletcher, Keaton, and Hayes. They were his brothers. After his nana had died shortly after he joined the Navy, these men had taken him and made him the person he was today.

He owed them his life.

He owed Ken, too. His death was part of the reason they had come to Calusa Cove.

Dawson let out a deep breath. "No one gets into the details with me. It's just that most people believe she killed her dad. I've been told it could've been some weird witch ritual. That she's some mystical Owl Witch or some bull. Lots of strange talk, that's for sure. But what I want to know is if you'll tell me more, or do I have to start pulling your teeth, one by one?" Dawson said.

"You've got the basic idea." Fletcher nodded. "Occasionally, people wonder if it could've been someone other than Audra, and there is that one random person who might consider it an accident."

"Did you know she was coming back to town? You and Keaton had a list of participants, right?"

"I've known about her return for a while. I kept it

quiet and asked Baily not to tell anyone because I didn't want the town buzzing and coming at her before she even set foot in this parking lot."

"I think you should've told me." Dawson didn't get pissed at Fletcher often, nor did Fletcher keep things from Dawson or the rest of the team. So, Dawson was willing to reserve judgment until he had the facts.

"I thought about it, but if I had, I know you, and you would've gone down the rabbit hole," Fletcher said. "Baily also told me that Audra was a late registrant. She almost didn't make the deadline, but because of her press credentials, she would've been able to skirt that anyway."

"How do you think this town will react to her being here?"

"The rumors are already coming out of the woodwork, and it will be all this town will be able to talk about for the next ten days now that Audra is back." Fletcher jerked his chin toward Silas Monroe and his crew. "It won't be good."

Silas was a pain in the ass. He thought he knew everything and didn't take too kindly to strangers coming in and running *his* town.

That meant he didn't like Dawson, Hayes, or Keaton.

And he merely tolerated Fletcher, but only because he'd been born in Calusa Cove. Silas and others—like Baily—didn't appreciate Fletcher's return.

"And over there. Paul Massey, Dewey, they're all talking about it, too." Fletcher sighed. "I'm honestly shocked she came back."

"Should I be worried about her?"

Fletcher chuckled. "The girl I knew could hold her own."

"So, everyone in this town thinks she murdered her dad, dumped his body in the Everglades, and got away with it? That's messed up."

"She was one month shy of turning seventeen when it happened. Her dad was all she had," Fletcher said. "Ken and I were getting ready to ship off to boot camp. Ken loved Audra. Perhaps a little more than she did him, but she was always a bit of a tough read. It screwed with Ken's head for a while. He didn't know what to believe when it came to Audra. This town came after her hard. I remember late-night phone calls with Baily, which were a hot mess."

"If she had no one and was a minor, what happened? Because she was never charged." Dawson rubbed his temple. Being a small-town cop meant the puzzle pieces he had to put together weren't all that complicated. Stolen bikes. A few car thefts. The occasional boat theft. Breaking and entering. But since he knew the players and, in general, who the bad guys were, he could usually piece together what happened pretty quickly.

Drugs were big in Florida. If they were involved, he called in the local DEA agent. However, the only drug cases he'd had to deal with concerned a few dumbass kids smoking weed they usually stole from their parents' medical stash.

In the ten months he'd lived in Calusa Cove, not a single murder had occurred.

That was something.

"Oddly enough, Silas Monroe stepped in and helped

her. In Florida, a seventeen-year-old doesn't need to be emancipated. While she was sixteen when her father went missing, she turned seventeen a month later, so he took her in and offered to help her with any legal fees if that were going to be necessary."

"Why is that odd?" Dawson wanted to know more. He told himself that his badge dictated and drove this inquisition—not the sexy redhead he couldn't get out of his mind.

Nope, she had nothing to do with it because he didn't do redheads anymore.

Fletcher shrugged. "Silas and Victor were never friends. I'm not sure anyone really knows why, but their animosity started when they were kids. Some say it was over Audra's mother. Others say it was just normal male chest-pounding in a small town that couldn't handle two young men with big egos." Fletcher laughed. "And what you just witnessed was a tame version of the young girl I remember. She certainly had a way with words."

"I've got a crazy question here because you've piqued my curiosity. Do you know what Silas believes about what happened to Victor?"

"All I know is that, when it happened, he swore he didn't believe she could've hurt her father. That no matter his feelings toward Victor, Audra wasn't a killer. But his opinion changed the second she turned seventeen, and the cops couldn't keep her from leaving town. In his eyes, that made her look suspect, mostly because she just up and left. She didn't tell anyone she was leaving. Not even Baily. To my knowledge, no one has heard from Audra in years."

"Baily hasn't spoken to her?"

"Not that I know of," Fletcher said. "But Baily barely speaks to me, so I honestly don't know."

"One more question." Dawson wiggled his finger. "Do you know if either of my predecessors had a possible motive for her killing her dad?"

"That's a weird question." Fletcher jerked his head. "But yeah. She and her dad had a massive fight the day before. She said something that could've been seen as threatening," Fletcher said.

"Were you there? Did you witness that? Were you living here when he went missing? Or had you and Ken already left for boot camp?"

"Wow, that cop brain of yours is in full gear," Fletcher said. "Or are you trying to figure out if you want to entangle yourself with the redhead?" Fletcher lifted his hand. "Because if it's the latter, I might have something to say about that and not because I know you and redheads, but because I know that redhead."

Dawson chugged the last of his water before jumping off the picnic table and tossing the empty bottle in the recycle bin. If it were anyone other than Fletcher, he'd be insulted. But Dawson knew his buddy was only looking out for his best interests. Fletcher had seen him through some of his darkest hours. Fletcher was the glue that held their little group together. "I'll admit she caught my attention, but the story holds it. Now, please answer my original question, and then tell me why you're calling me off. Not that I'm going to pursue."

"All right." Fletcher laughed. "Yes. I was still living at home when Victor disappeared, and yeah, I witnessed that fight. It happened a month before Ken and I shipped off. It was a difficult time for Ken. Like I said, he was in love with Audra and was conflicted about leaving her, but he was excited about joining the Navy. At first, Audra wrote letters every day, letting him know what was going on, but a month or so in, the letters stopped. Baily informed us that she had taken off and hadn't left a forwarding address. Ken hired a private investigator. He found her once living in Virginia and paid her a visit. She told him she never wanted to see him or talk to him again. That she wanted nothing to do with anyone from Calusa Cove. Ken came back from seeing her a completely different man." Fletcher ran a hand over his face. "Ken once told me he wondered if Audra might know more about her father's death than she was letting on."

"Seriously? And he never came forward?" Of all the men Dawson had worked with, Ken had been the hardest to get to know. Dawson told himself it was because, by the time they met, Ken was a married man.

"He had nothing to go on except concern," Fletcher said. "Audra was very close to her dad, and Ken loved her enough to put up with Victor's weirdness. But that fight affected Ken. He thought Audra was out of line, and he let her know it. So, when he returned from seeing her and decided to put that part of his life behind him, I thought that was harsh. If I even brought up her name, he told me to stop. He said he was done. It was over, and he'd moved on. I had to respect that. Besides, I was dealing with my shit with Baily because we'd started to drift apart."

"I met you both two years after we all joined the Navy. Ken had already met his wife. Audra was mentioned a few times, but you warned me not to ask questions." Dawson knew there were things about his good friend Ken that he didn't know. He was okay with that. They had been through so much together. Near-death experiences. Deaths of loved ones. Deaths of brothers. SEAL training—a different kind of hell.

And then that fateful mission that had changed their lives forever.

"Ken hated coming home to Calusa Cove," Dawson said. "You had to drag him."

Fletcher nodded. "It's also one of the many reasons that Baily thinks I'm an asshole. For some reason, she likes to blame me for her brother's hatred of this town when that one was on Ken and whatever went down between him and Audra."

"Baily thinks we're all assholes," Dawson said. "Now, outside of the fact Audra is a redhead, and I don't do redheads, why else should I stay away?"

"Because I know you." Fletcher stood, stretching. "And she'll put a hole in your heart bigger than Liz did."

Dawson cringed at the name. Just hearing it was like listening to fingernails on a chalkboard. But Dawson had moved past Liz. She was in his rearview. Sure, she'd ripped his heart from his chest with her bare hands, but he'd managed to repair the damage. He wasn't so broken that he'd given up on the concept of love.

Just redheads.

Only, he really liked women with red hair and green eyes.

It sucked having a type.

"So, what you're saying is you don't like Audra," Dawson said. "Does that mean we're supposed to dislike Baily?" Dawson pointed toward the marina shop. "Because isn't she the one who broke—"

"That's the worst analogy ever, and I like Audra just fine." Fletcher folded his arms across his chest and widened his stance, daring Dawson to say otherwise. "Just not for you."

Normally, he would let it go. Baily wasn't a topic any of the guys dug too deep into. They all knew why they'd come to Calusa Cove.

To honor Ken. To help save Mitchell's Marina.

But there was more to it, even if Fletcher wasn't willing to admit it. "I don't do redheads, and I don't think this is about me anymore."

"I'm done with this discussion." Fletcher tossed his empty bottle in the recycle bin. "I've got to head over to my post. I'll see you at the end of the day." He turned and marched toward the parking lot without saying another word.

Dawson shouldn't have poked the bear. Fletcher had been carrying a torch for Baily his entire life. He'd loved her as a teenager. They'd tried to have a relationship for his first four years in the Navy.

It had failed.

They'd tried again a year later.

It became impossible after her father passed, and she took over the marina, refusing to leave Calusa Cove. But the two of them had managed to remain friendly.

Until Ken had died.

That had changed everything.

Fletcher understood, but that hadn't fixed his broken heart, and he'd never been the same.

Dawson stood there for a long moment, staring at the front door of the marina, contemplating if he should try to catch a glimpse of the sexy redhead or head to the office.

He opted for the latter, reminding himself he didn't do redheads.

His cell buzzed. He pulled it from his back pocket. "Hey, Remy, what's going on?"

"We've got a problem, Chief," his second-in-command said. "Remember the two guys with the boat shoes that rubbed you the wrong way?"

"Yeah, what about them?" Those damn shoes.

"Well, Hayes and I finished the inspection of boats, and guess what we found?"

"Do I really want to know?" Dawson rubbed the back of his neck. Of all the towns that had been opened up in the last two years for the challenge, this location was the smallest one. Most people here were passionate about removing the pythons from the Everglades. They didn't care about the prize money. They wanted the damn things gone from the ecosystem. But he'd been warned that one or two would try to slip in and do things the easy way instead of the right way.

"Dynamite." Remy laughed. "They actually have a license for the shit, but obviously that doesn't cover the removal of pythons."

"Nope, but what does the license say?" Why he asked the question, he didn't know because it didn't matter. Obtaining an explosives license with false information was a first-degree misdemeanor that came with a possible thousand-dollar fine and a year in jail. Using it made it a third-degree felony with a ten-thousand-dollar fine and potential prison time of up to five years or longer, depending on the intent.

This was not what he wanted to deal with right now. He'd rather hop on one of the airboats and check out the hunt.

Not the redhead.

At least, that's what he told himself.

"They have a federal license as a distributor, so they can be in possession of it, but there is no reason for it to be on their boat."

"You've got that right," Dawson muttered. "Where are you?"

"Dock three, slip eight."

"I'll be right there." Dawson tucked his phone in his back pocket. Time to go earn his paycheck.

# CHAPTER 2

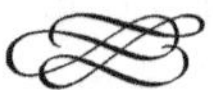

Audra paused as she strolled across the parking lot, glancing over her shoulder. Fletcher and his friend—the good-looking cop with warm, inviting eyes—had perched themselves on the picnic bench. It was strange to see Fletcher again. Weirder that he'd been so kind.

But she shouldn't allow her mind to concentrate on the other man, the sexy cop. It was a distraction she didn't need. Nor want. She'd come here to do a job. She sighed, turning her head and marching forward.

With her heart firmly planted in her throat, pulsating wildly, Audra pushed open the door of Mitchell's Marina. This used to be the place she'd come to when she'd wanted a shoulder to cry on. Or a good laugh. Or to simply sit by the water, swing her legs, and chat with her bestie.

The air-conditioning smacked her face like a frozen popsicle. She couldn't remember ever seeing this place so packed full of people.

Full of strangers and familiar faces.

Both gave her scrutinizing glares or leisurely once-overs. The innocent bystanders were about to learn about one of the town's greatest and worst legends.

She yanked her sunglasses from her face and tucked them safely in her bag while she clutched her paperwork. Sixteen years ago, she'd sworn she'd never set foot in this town again. It had taken everything from her.

Her father. Her friends. Her dignity.

It had almost taken her freedom.

Calusa Cove had been her happy place. A little slice of Florida heaven that she'd wanted to cherish for as long as she could.

Now, it represented hell.

She had no idea why she'd agreed to do this piece. She could have turned it down or begged to go to a different location. There were many to choose from. She could have let some other photographer and writer take the assignment. It didn't have to be her, even though her boss thought she was best suited for the job, and he wanted the personal angle. He wanted it told from someone who used to live there. Someone who understood the community better than most.

If only she hadn't displayed that damn picture of herself with that stupid alligator on her desk and bragged about how many pythons she'd caught the last time she'd entered the challenge, and if she'd only kept her mouth shut about Calusa Cove.

She didn't have anything to prove to anyone—yet proving herself capable of everything was all she ever did. Her father had never once believed he needed to prove himself to this town. He hadn't cared what anyone thought. But his daughter? His only child? Yeah, Audra had cared. No matter how she'd tried not to, she'd hated how people had looked at her dad.

And her.

A few people glanced in her direction. They pointed and whispered, but it was Silas and his group that decided to say her name for everyone to hear.

"Audra McCain."

The sound of Silas' voice bounced off the walls and crash-landed in her ears. It vibrated down her spine and tormented her system.

Half the room went silent.

Heads turned.

Someone dropped a knife.

The metal clanked against the floor with a thud.

"What is she doing here?" someone asked. "Isn't she the witch?"

"I can't believe she came back," another person whispered. "Lock your doors. Hide your guns. No one's safe."

She swallowed. Did everyone think she was going to go on some killing rampage?

"Well, well, well." Silas stood in front of her with a shit-eating grin. "Who let the riffraff back in?"

"Silas," she managed to croak out with a smile. She held her head high, something her father always told her to do when people looked down at her. She should be used to that in this town.

Victor McCain had always been an "odd duck." He'd been considered—by most—to be the kind of person one should shy away from. Not because he'd been dangerous but because he'd been different.

When she'd been very young, she'd had no idea what that meant.

By the time she'd turned ten—after her mom passed—she'd understood quite well that her dad was indeed a little left of normal. But he was her dad. He made her pancakes every Saturday and Sunday morning. He took her fishing. He taught her how to shoot a gun. How to skin a snake. How to remove a gator from the yard. More importantly, he'd taught her how to care for herself in all the areas that mattered.

Most of his life lessons might have been considered unconventional, but to her, they'd just been a father and daughter spending time together.

"What are you doing in Calusa Cove?" Silas inched closer. His light-blue eyes bore into her like a cattle prod. He'd aged over the last sixteen years. His hair and beard had turned white. He'd put on a few pounds and looked a little rougher around the edges.

Now, he was a man someone should shy away from. As a small child, she'd cowered around Silas. For some reason, he'd reminded her of a pirate. A scary one. And he'd constantly picked on her father, getting in his face about his run-down old shack and saying it was no place to raise a child. The fact that her old home was now a vegetable and fruit stand both broke her heart and made her insanely happy.

Now, she wasn't sure she could see that falling down structure if she had to. There would have been too many memories. Both good and bad.

"I'm here for the same reason everyone else standing in this line is." She puffed out her chest and held his steely gaze.

As hard as it was to believe, this had once been a man she'd held her faith in. She'd trusted him, even though her father had hated him—and her dad hated no one. But Silas had been the only one in this town who'd believed her story outside of Trip. He'd believed in what she might have seen. He'd asked her questions about it without judging, even offering to go out into the swamps to look at what her father had thought he'd found.

Silas had been kind. Caring. Gentle. Very different from the scary pirate of her childhood.

She'd seen a side of him that had taken her by surprise.

However, the more she'd talked about what she'd seen and what happened, the faster Silas had changed his tune. It hadn't mattered that he'd been kind about it.

*Are you sure you saw something? Or is that what your father told you he saw before he took you out there in the dark of night? You know how your father liked his stories... how his memory played tricks on him. Maybe what you recall is what he filled your brain with. You did have a concussion. It could've been an accident. You have to consider that.*

Maybe Silas hadn't believed she'd had anything to do with her father's disappearance, but it turned out he'd never actually believed her, which had destroyed her faith in Silas.

"You came back to join the hunt for pythons?" Silas looked her up and down as he sucked on a toothpick.

He leaned a little closer. "One baby gator doesn't make you a hunter, little girl."

"You don't know a thing about what I've been up to for the last sixteen years."

He arched a brow. "You're not cut out for this kind of thing. Go back to wherever you came from." He leaned closer. "You shouldn't have come back. It's been a long time, little girl, and the way you left this town only perpetuated the… rumors."

"People repeating BS lies is what perpetuates them." She swallowed her pulse. She'd never forget the night Ken had shown up at her doorstep in Virginia. She'd known the town had kept gossiping about what they believed had happened out in the swamp, but she hadn't expected Silas to be leading the charge.

Nor had she expected Ken to beg her to stop running. To stop hiding. To face everything head-on. To go home and deal with the fallout. But she couldn't. Ken should have understood that Calusa Cove was too small a town for that. Regardless of the lack of evidence, the people had made up their minds.

She had killed her father.

Ken had told her she was making a mistake. That she'd be running from this for the rest of her life. Then, he'd said the unthinkable. He'd told her those who loved her wondered if she knew something—was keeping secrets. After that statement, she'd told Ken to get out and that she never wanted to see him again. That she'd never loved him.

She'd never heard from Ken again.

Or anyone from Calusa Cove. Not even Baily.

The seed of doubt had been planted, and there was nothing she could do about it.

"Or maybe you make the good people of Calusa Cove nervous. You know what they say about your mama's people…that they practiced witchcraft." Silas arched a brow.

"My mama was no witch. Being spiritual and connected to the earth doesn't make someone a creature of the Everglades."

"Maybe not. But that doesn't stop people from talking, now does it." Silas lowered his chin. "Looks like you're up next. Good luck," Silas said. "You're going to need it, little girl." He and his crew zigzagged through the crowd and stepped outside.

Audra made her way to the counter. She sucked in a deep breath and did her best to smile at Baily, who didn't bat an eyelash. Audra didn't know what was worse. The pointing, whispering, and staring reactions —or this non-reaction from the girl who had been her best friend since birth. "Hey, Baily. How are you?"

"Doing just great," Baily said.

"Not shocked to see me?" Damn it. The last thing Audra wanted was to sound desperate.

"I accepted the online reservation for the boat slip, so I knew you were coming," Baily said. "You're lucky I had one that late in the game."

Audra pushed her papers across the counter. "I appreciate you not turning me away."

"It's just business, and it would be wrong of me to do that," Baily said with little emotion. "We do have scout snakes in the area. The GPS tracker information on those will be in the app. You should've been given that information in an email."

"I have it." Audra nodded.

"Will you be using a drone?"

"I am, and my drone information is with my paperwork." Audra stared at the person she had once told all her secrets to. Baily had been there when Audra's mother had died. She'd stood at the sad gravesite that almost no one had attended and held Audra's hand while her father cried like a baby. Baily had been one of the few people in Calusa Cove who hadn't cared that her father was the town loon.

This woman wasn't that girl. Audra didn't know who this was, and that broke her heart.

"I'm staying up the street at Harvey's Cabins. Maybe we can have a drink while I'm here," Audra said.

Baily thumbed through the papers before stamping them and filing them with the rest of the hunters'. "You know who else is back in town?"

"Fletch."

"He hates being called that," Baily said. "It's Fletcher these days." She laughed, but it wasn't a funny laugh. It was more like a sad one, and Audra knew why.

Audra reached across the counter. "I'm so sorry about Ken."

Baily jerked her hand away as if she'd been burned. "I like to continue to blame Fletcher and his friends for that."

"As in, the new cop named Dawson?" Audra's mind drifted back to the handsome man with the dreamy eyes.

"Yeah," Baily said softly. "Fletcher came back with three guys from Ken's team—Dawson, Keaton, and Hayes. They run Everglades Overwatch, an airboat touring company out of my marina. Drives me crazy that I have to see them and be reminded of what happened." She handed Audra a parking pass and a couple of stickers, along with her copy of the paperwork. "You'll find your boat at that dock, and as you can see, many hunters are using dogs. Do you have one? Because if you do, I need to know about it."

"No dog."

Baily tapped one of the stickers. "Keaton, our local Fish and Wildlife guy, wants me to ask about pairing off with another team. He mentioned he reached out in an email."

"He did, but nope, I'm staying solo."

"All right. I'll let him know I asked," Baily said. "I'll have to think about that drink."

"I know you're mad at—"

"That's not the right word." Baily sighed. "I'm angry at Fletcher and his friends. You? Well, you hurt me, and you broke my brother's heart. I'm not sure I want to go down memory lane with you."

"I don't know what Ken told you, but you know we had problems before he left for boot camp. When he found me about a year later, he..." What the hell could she say about that? Nothing. "We were kids. We can talk about all of it or not. It's up to you." She glanced over her shoulder. "But this isn't the time or place."

"Check back in when you return." Baily nodded. "Good luck."

"Thanks." Audra collected her things and made a beeline for the entrance, ignoring the stares. She pushed open the door, but before she could make it outside, she bumped right into Trinity Stevenson, of all freaking people. She blinked.

Trinity stumbled backward, not because Audra knocked her that hard, but because she was wearing two-inch heels.

"Hey, watch it," Trinity said, brushing down the front of her pretty formfitting shirt, showing off her large, perky breasts. She glanced up. "Oh my God. I can't believe my eyes." She brushed her blond locks from her face. She wore a pair of white shorts that barely covered her ass.

Well, who was Audra to talk? At least her shorts weren't tight, and she would change before entering the Everglades. She wasn't stupid.

"Trinity." Audra nodded. "It's been a long time."

"Never thought I'd see you again." Trinity folded her arms across her middle. "But snake wrangling is right up your alley."

"Is that why you're here? I can't imagine you'd want to break a nail."

Trinity laughed. "Oh, I could manage a snake if I had to, but see that pretty boat over there?" She pointed to one of the few nicer vessels in the marina. "That's my baby. I'm headed out for the day to do some deep scuba diving."

"Deep? As in past a hundred feet?" Now, that came as a shock to Audra.

Trinity was, by far, the richest girl in town. That

should have made her popular in most towns but not Calusa Cove. She was the kind of girl who never lifted a finger. She had maids and even had a driver. She told people what to do and never did a thing for herself. At least not when it came to the simple things.

"You bet." Trinity smiled. "Every chance I get. It's my happy place. But I'm on a mission. I'm looking for a boat that went down last year. My friend's little brother was the only one on it. He was lost to the sea. No one knows what happened, and my friend Mallary wants answers. I'm hoping I can give them to her."

That didn't sound like the Trinity Audra remembered. "I'm sorry for your friend's loss."

"Thank you." Trinity nodded with a mournful look.

"Must cost a pretty penny to hire a captain every time you want to go out." Audra's mouth often got her in trouble back in the day, and that comment was certainly rude, considering the confession, but Audra just couldn't help herself.

Trinity laughed. "Not when I'm the captain."

"No way. You drive that cruiser—out in the ocean— by yourself?"

"A lot has changed since you ran off in the middle of the night." Trinity leaned closer.

Here it comes—another dig about how she must have killed her father.

"I'm sorry about Ken. I know you and he were a long time ago, but I'm sure that still had to have hurt. He was a good man." Trinity squeezed her shoulder. "I understand not having friends in this town, but you can consider me one. I don't believe anything anyone has ever said about you or your dad. Get my number from Baily if you ever want to talk."

Audra opened her mouth, but nothing came out. It was rare that anyone could render her speechless, and for it to be Trinity? Well, that just made it feel like she'd stepped right into another universe.

"Hey, Trinity," Baily called. "*Princess Afloat* is gassed up and ready to go."

"Thanks, Baily." Trinity waved, then smiled. "I meant what I said, Audra. Call me. I know we weren't really friends back in high school, but we weren't enemies either. I hope you get some pythons out there. They certainly are a menace." She stepped around Audra, letting the door slam and leaving Audra outside in the hot, humid Florida air.

Well, that had been strange, to say the least.

Reaching into her bag, she pulled out her sunglasses and made her way down to the docks, doing her best not to scan the area for the sexy police officer. However, that turned out to be impossible, and her eyes found him—all of him—and he was certainly hot. She fanned herself and sighed. The last thing she needed was a man.

"Audra, wait up," a familiar voice tickled her ears. Flipping Paul Massey. Another so-called friend of her dad's who'd turned on her the second things had gotten dicey.

She paused and did a one-eighty. Over the years, she'd learned that being nice sometimes trumped being nasty. "Hi, Paul." She grinned from ear to ear. If anyone could show sarcasm through a smile, it was her. "It's so nice to see you." She dug her fingernails into her thighs, waiting for the accusations.

"I can't believe it." He took off his baseball cap and ran his fingers through his thinning hair. Paul owned the local pub—the one her father had often frequented —and Paul had been one of the few friends her dad had had in this town. They would drink dirt-cheap whiskey —the kind that made most men's guts rot—play cards and tell stories about the good old days. "You look good." He was also a lawyer. He did mostly small-town stuff. Wills, traffic tickets, and he helped the towns-people find better lawyers if they found themselves in bigger trouble. He wasn't the worst slimy lawyer in the world, but he was still an attorney.

"So do you," she said. "How are Gina and the kids?"

"Doing great. Hailey's married with two little ones of her own now. She lives in Alabama. And Benson lives in Miami. Gina and I miss them both, but they come to visit often. As a matter of fact, Benson is here doing the Python Challenge with me." Paul glanced over his shoulder. "He's around here somewhere. He came in with a few of his buddies from Miami. His friends aren't doing the challenge. They're doing some snorkeling in the area. They're keeping a boat in the big yacht marina, but I'm sure Benson would love to see you and catch up."

Yeah, right. Benson was a few years older. They hadn't traveled in the same circles, and considering he believed the worst about her, too, she doubted he wanted anything to do with her. "Wow, you're a grandpa. That's awesome." Audra shifted her weight from left to right and back again. Before her father had disappeared, Ken had talked about their future. The one where after a few years in the Navy—once he had enough money—he'd send for her. They'd get married and start a family.

Part of her had been on board with it—at least the concept of it. The only thing they hadn't agreed on was when the family part would start. He'd thought twenty-five was a good age. She'd thought thirty.

She was only thirty-four now, and she wasn't sure she ever wanted to have that life now. Men were dead weight. They required too much watering, and she didn't have the time or inclination. Out of the corner of her eye, she saw Dawson and Remy giving two men a hard time. Or maybe it was the other way around.

Wow. Remy had aged, but he was still as handsome as ever, and she wondered if he was still as kind.

"We love it." Paul nodded, glancing over his shoulder, waving to Dewey, the resident mangrove trimmer. "So, python hunting? Your dad would've loved to see you do that. One of his shining moments was the day you wrestled that gator without his help."

"I know. It's one of the reasons I'm doing it."

He nodded and shifted his gaze nervously while the two men Dawson and Remy dealt with raised their voices. "I'm sorry, but I'm going to say what everyone is thinking." Paul scratched the back of his head before readjusting his cap. "Your dad went missing out there, and you were with him."

"That's a kind way of putting that you and everyone else think I killed my dad."

He frowned. "Don't go putting words in my mouth."

"I don't have to. Is there anything else you need to remind me of?" she asked. She should have known that Paul would go down this twisty road eventually.

"Your father was my friend. Not a day goes by that I don't wonder what happened to him," Paul said.

"You mean, you wonder if I had something to do with it." Damn, she loved beating a dead horse.

"Little girl, you're testing my patience."

She squared her shoulders. God, she hated being called that, and everyone in this town older than fifty had called her that since she could remember. "I'm not a little girl anymore, and let's be honest, Paul. I know exactly what you and everyone else in this town thinks. You all have since the day Trip Williams brought me in for questioning."

"Don't go disparaging a good cop who isn't around to defend himself." Paul lowered his chin. "Trip was a decent man. He served this community well for over thirty years. He did what he could to find out what happened to your dad—as did his son."

"You can't be serious. Trevor's in jail."

The two men were not equal, and she had never accused Trip of anything other than doing his job, even if she hadn't liked how he'd handled things.

Paul let out a long breath. He glanced over his shoulder, lifting his hat off his head and raking his fingers through his thinning gray hair. "You don't know the whole story regarding what happened to Trevor or what he was really doing. No one does."

"I can't believe you're making excuses for Trevor. He

was stripped of his badge and sent to prison a little over a year ago. I heard they brought in an outsider to make sure there was no chance of corruption happening in this small town again." Having an outsider as chief of police gave her some confidence that the town's politics might have changed. However, it wouldn't change how anyone perceived her, and that was something she had accepted the second she'd agreed to take the assignment for *National Wildlife Magazine*.

She was just doing her job. At least, that's what she told herself. Perhaps if her boss knew her history, he might have seen things differently.

"I didn't come over here to argue with you," Paul said. "I wanted to say hello. It's been a long time. Stop by the restaurant. Gina would love to see you. Drinks are on me."

No point in continuing to be combative. She figured over the next ten days, there would be enough of that to go around. "I'll be sure to do that. Good luck out there."

"You, too."

She turned and made a beeline for the dock Baily had marked where her boat would be, and that's exactly where the rust bucket had been docked. She paused at the edge. Some guy in the distance told Dawson he was making a critical error. Interesting choice of words when a cop was slapping on the handcuffs. She'd be sure to find out what had happened there. It would give her an excuse to talk to Dawson again.

She rolled her eyes. Right. Because a sexy cop was exactly what she needed. *Not.*

She climbed aboard and pulled out her cell, tapping

on the challenge app. It had a map of the area, indicating all the ripe spots and marking places they shouldn't go, primarily because of the time it would take the boats to make it back before dark. It was easy to get lost in the swamplands of the Everglades.

The app also showed the locations of the few scout snakes in the area. She found it ironic that they used male pythons as "scouts."

But she supposed it made sense. They were looking for a female to mate with. Those snakes were off-limits. They were used to help hunters locate other snakes and also aid scientists in understanding the problem.

However, for her, today wasn't about finding a snake anyway. She'd do that tomorrow.

Quickly, she pulled out a towel, slacks, and a long-sleeved shirt. Wrapping herself in her towel, she wiggled out of her shorts and hiked up her pants. Next came the shirt. That was a little harder to do, but she managed.

She pulled out her camera. Clicking in place the smaller lens, she lifted the apparatus to her eye, focusing on the beautiful surroundings and not the people. She snapped a few shots, zooming in on the lush trees, a couple of ospreys, and the mouth of the river leading to the Everglades.

God, how she hated to admit she missed this place.

A small town nestled between the winding channels of the Everglades, the ocean, and the hustle and bustle of seaside towns filled with tourists. In some ways, it was like a forgotten city. A ghost town, only the ghosts were real live people.

She scanned toward all the people climbing aboard their airboats, reminding herself she had a story to write, and that meant she couldn't avoid snapping a few shots of the humans involved.

Benson filled her lens. He stood there at the end of the dock with his father. She stared at him through her camera. He'd aged some but otherwise looked exactly the same. He'd been a bit of an odd duck back in the day. Quiet. Kept to himself, except for his best friend, Trevor Williams. Now, that had been a strange pairing.

She set her camera aside and went about checking her gear. She had everything she needed to safely capture and humanely kill pythons. Her GPS was ready, though she knew these parts like the back of her hand. At least, she used to. She had water and snacks for the day.

Everyone who was participating had made their way to their boats. A man with a bullhorn stood on the end of the far dock.

"Good morning, everyone," he said. "My name is Keaton Cole, and I'm with Fish and Wildlife. In a roundabout way, I'll be your guide for the next ten days."

So, he was the guy Dawson had mentioned she should have a sit-down with. That meant he'd served in the military with him and Fletcher.

Which also meant he knew Ken.

She sighed.

Damn shame what had happened to Ken. He'd died almost three years ago. She'd read about it in the *Calusa Cove Gazette*. They'd done a full-page spread on him and his team, featuring Fletcher and how he'd gotten a medal. She was sure Fletcher hated both the article and the medal.

"You all should've gotten my contact information from Baily. We don't have any novices registered in this area, so we'll let you all go off. However, my team and I will be out there, checking in with everyone. You all know the rules. We expect you to follow them. If you don't, you'll be pulled from the challenge. Please remember why we're doing this. The sole purpose is to remove the pythons from this ecosystem, but we want to do it humanely and safely. We've already dealt with two people who thought they could skirt the rules. They weren't locals. Most of the rest of you are, so please make my team's job easy. Don't make me call the chief of police. You all know how he gets," he said with a grin. "Now, go out there and enjoy the hunt."

The sound of airboat engines firing up filled the air.

Silas and his crew were the first three boats out into the channel, followed by Paul and his son Benson, along with a few boats she didn't know and two more familiar locals.

Audra decided to hang back and let all of them race down the channel and into the Everglades in a mad rush. There was time and plenty of snakes to catch. She wasn't in this for the prize, though she did want to do her part. But again, today wasn't about that. Today was about the past.

Her heart hammered in the center of her chest.

Today, she would go to the spot where she last remembered seeing her father alive. The exact spot where he'd shown her the abandoned shack containing crates marked with unusual symbols. It had been so dark that night that even she had started questioning whether she'd really seen it. Hours later, she'd woken up on that boat—drifting in the swamp—cold, alone, and covered in blood.

She swallowed the bile that bubbled up in her throat as the last boats zoomed by.

"Excuse me." Keaton strolled down the dock. "Is everything okay?"

"Yes," she said. "Just thought I'd avoid the craziness of the rush."

"You must be Audra," Keaton said.

She cocked her head. "I guess I shouldn't be surprised the news of my name travels fast."

He chuckled. "I won't lie. Dawson texted me first, asking me to keep an eye out for you. Then Fletcher. But you were already on my radar."

"And why is that?" Her body tingled just hearing Dawson's name. She shoved that sensation down deep.

"Because you're the only boat flying solo, and I don't like that." He cocked his head. "Everyone else is in at least a team of two. I asked around to see if someone would buddy up and learned you refused. Now, may I ask why that is?"

"Sure." She reached over and untied the bow line while he released the stern. "It's simple. I don't play nice in the swamp."

"Fletcher warned me you were full of sarcasm." He waggled his finger. "I understand you're originally from this area, and Fletcher assures me you know these parts as well as he does—"

"Better."

"That's all fine and dandy, but wrangling these pythons alone is tricky business."

"I'm aware. I've done it before." She set the bow line aside and climbed on the captain's chair. "I'll be safe out there. Promise."

"Just use that radio of yours if you need help."

"Will do." She nodded. "Can I ask you a question?"

"Of course."

"Why did your buddy and Remy arrest two men a little while ago? What did they do?" She lifted her press badge. "And let me say I'm asking for an article I'm writing."

"You'll have to take that up with Dawson."

"Fair enough." She snagged her ear protection and wrapped them around her neck. "Any chance you'll let me interview you for my article? Dawson and Fletcher recommended I speak with you."

"I'd be happy to." He gave her boat a little shove with his foot.

"I'll be in touch." She fired up her engine. Time to visit the past.

# CHAPTER 3

Dawson opened the back door of his patrol car. "All right, gentleman, let's get you processed." He helped James Huber out of the vehicle first. Then came Eliot Commings. Both men were from Miami and were partners in a dynamite distribution company. Both men claimed they were moving product for a client who lived in the Tampa area.

What a ridiculous story. As if any sane human would believe it.

"This is bullshit," James said. "I showed you the purchase order to explain why we had the dynamite. It wouldn't have been safe to leave it in my truck. We had no intention of using it out there during the hunt."

"Are you kidding me?" Dawson sucked in a deep breath, choking on the humidity. "If I were you, I'd keep my mouth shut, remembering that everything you say can and will be used against you."

"What the hell does that mean?" Eliot asked.

Dawson wasn't about to waste his breath explaining

something *experts* should know. They had the necessary flameproof and moisture-proof tarpaulin protection in the truck. But why not make the delivery before the Python Challenge? And why was the amount so small? These questions had been asked, and the answers had sounded lame. The small construction company didn't need them just yet and it wasn't a big job.

Yeah, right.

"Listen, you're lucky I'm only charging you with a misdemeanor," Dawson said.

"What about our phone call?" Eliot said. "We know our rights."

Dawson opened the door to the Calusa Cove Police Department, located in the heart of Calusa Cove and only two miles from Mitchell's Marina. "Once we get the paperwork filed and get you fingerprinted, you can call whoever you want." He despised guys like these two. Men who thought they could skirt the rules—and the laws.

They didn't care about the Everglades. If they did, they wouldn't be dropping sticks of dynamite in it to catch damn snakes or possible gators for a fast buck and a picture to show off to their buddies.

Anna, his secretary, greeted them at the entrance. "Hey, Chief," she said with a smile. "I got the booking room all set up."

"Thanks." He held both men by the elbows. "The evidence is in my trunk. Mind collecting and processing it while I deal with these two?"

"You're the boss."

"Also, fax the arrest paperwork to the judge. Call him and get me the bond paperwork."

"Sure thing," Anna said.

He brought them past the front desk, which also housed a small kitchen area, and down the short corridor. The station wasn't very big. It had three offices. One for him. One for Remy, his second. And the third was shared by the two deputies.

The station had one interrogation room, which was barely used. Across from that was an open area referred to as the booking room. And finally, three holding cells. Those didn't get much use, either. They were occupied mainly by the drunk and disorderly and, usually, the same people.

Something like this was a rare occurrence for the quiet town, and it would become the chatter around every water cooler and, of course, Massey's Pub. The story would grow from a couple of bundles of dynamite to barrels because this town liked to weave a good yarn.

Dawson would have to sit back and let people talk. He'd correct where he could and laugh at the way some embellished, especially those who'd watched him and Remy slap the cuffs on.

The joys of small-town life.

And they were joys.

"Have a seat, Eliot." Dawson gave the man a little nudge toward one of the metal chairs in the hallway.

"How about you take these cuffs off," Eliot said.

Dawson ignored the man. However, he removed James's handcuffs and went about fingerprinting and taking the man's picture before putting the cuffs back on and repeating the process with Eliot. Once he was done with that, he allowed each of them to make their phone call.

He tucked them into the cell, which had been lonely the last four days since old man Jenkins had been on his best behavior. All that meant was he hadn't shot his mouth off and threatened to shoot Ed Cooney's roosters.

Talk about small-town problems. Only Dawson knew that, given the chance, Jenkins would absolutely blow the heads off those roosters.

"You can't keep us here," James said. "That's what my lawyer said. He's on his way here now."

"Good." Dawson rubbed his temple. "When he gets here, I'll go over the paperwork and release you to him, but you boys are facing possible jail time, so until your lawyer gets here, you're not going anywhere. Might as well get comfortable."

"This is an utter abuse of power," Eliot said. "We have a federal license to have dynamite. We'll have your badge for this."

Dawson wasn't going to get into a pissing contest with these assholes. He'd grown up with idiots like them—rich trust fund types who thought their shit didn't stink. They thought that money could solve their problems, and maybe, sometimes it did.

"Take it up with the judge." Dawson turned and marched himself down to the small kitchenette behind the main desk and made a cup of coffee. Flashes of his childhood bombarded his brain. He'd been dirt poor as a child. He'd gotten picked on at school because his clothes had come from a secondhand store—or worse, his mom had brought them home from the rich family she'd worked for as a maid.

They'd paid her crap money and treated her worse.

His dad had been their groundskeeper, and his nana their cook. Everyone in his family had to work, and they'd still barely made it.

When his parents had died, things had gone from bad to worse. His nana hadn't been very old, but she'd had health problems, and by the time Dawson was twelve, he'd handed all the money he'd earned from washing people's high-end cars to his nana to help keep the lights on. He'd kept that business until he'd joined the Navy, but he'd also worked two other jobs in the summer, and in the winter, he'd worked at the local grocery store and plowed driveways.

He'd been working his entire life. He wasn't bitter. Not at all. He was proud, and he knew his parents and Nana had been, too. He'd made something of himself. He'd done what everyone had told him was impossible. However, being around assholes like that brought him right back to his ten-year-old self and being beat up on the playground by Wendall with his stupid-looking fancy shoes.

"The evidence is all logged in," Anna said. "The judge sent over the bail bond paperwork. Easy-peasy."

He jumped. "Jesus, you scared me." He turned, raising the mug to his lips. He blew and took a long, slow sip, savoring the bitter flavor. Best freaking coffee in town. It was always the simple things that got Dawson. He didn't need much. A place to rest his head and hang his coat. He took being a minimalist a little too seriously, though he hadn't done that on purpose. It had just happened, and he was content. "You have to be the quietest person I've ever met."

"My husband says the same thing, except for when we're—"

"Too much information." He shook his head. "How is Mo? I haven't seen him around lately."

"He went to visit his mom." Anna snagged her chair and plopped down in it. "She's not liking the new nursing home. However, she doesn't know she's in a nursing home. Doesn't even know who Mo is anymore. She thinks he's some old friend of hers from high school."

"That's sad. I'm sorry."

She shrugged. "It's supposed to be the best nursing home on this coast, and it's killing us to pay for it. I just wish it was closer to Calusa Cove. It's only two hours away, but Mo hates going for just a few hours, and she had Covid last month, so he couldn't go at all."

"That's rough." Dawson often wished he had a parent to worry about. Losing them at such a young age had been hard. Sometimes, he could barely remember them. He often tried to conjure up their voices and failed. When his nana had died, he'd lost the last blood relative he had, and it often weighed heavily on his heart. "His mom is lucky to have you both."

"Yeah, Mo's a good egg," Anna said. But her forehead crinkled. Stress lined every inch of her face. There was more to that story than she let on, but it was obvious she didn't want to talk about it. He had to respect that.

"So, what's going to happen to those two idiots back there? This is about the most excitement we've had since Remy had to arrest his boss for smuggling drugs into Calusa Cove."

"That had to have been a shock for this town." That arrest hadn't ever settled right in Dawson's gut. Not because he didn't believe that Trevor was guilty, because the man was guilty as the day was long. He also knew that Remy was a good cop. Dawson knew Remy and the rest of his deputies had had nothing to do with it, which was why they were still with the department.

However, Dawson didn't believe that Trevor had acted alone. He wasn't the mastermind. He was the guy who'd turned a blind eye. He'd allowed it to happen, maybe took a cut, but he hadn't been the man in charge. However, no drugs had been found since. No chatter came from the DEA or any other law enforcement agency. And Dawson had been poking around. It was only a matter of time before someone tried it again.

"Was the town shocked? Yes and no," Anna said. "But, you and me, we've had that conversation before."

"Yeah, we have." Dawson nodded. "You mentioned more than once that Trevor had dabbled in coke when he was a kid. That his old man knew about it and hadn't busted him. Why had Trip done that? Everyone in this town loved Trip. Said he was a good cop. He was fair and reasonable but firm and didn't let anyone get away with too much. So why let his son become a cop if he had a drug problem?"

"No offense, but you don't have kids." She arched a

brow. "I'd do almost anything for mine, short of murder, and even then, I might consider it."

"Don't say stuff like that to me, and just because I don't have kids doesn't mean I don't understand the bond. But Trip had a duty to this community. Trevor shouldn't have been allowed to become a police officer in the first place if his dad knew he had—"

"I worked for both men," Anna said. "When Trevor went to the academy, he was clean. The only thing Trip was guilty of was not tossing the book at a seventeen-year-old child. Trip did, however, tell Trevor to either clean up his act or get out of town. Trevor left Calusa Cove for ten years."

"Didn't he leave about the same time as Paul Massey's kid did?"

She frowned. "Why is that important?"

"Other than those two were best friends—and they both went to Miami—I suppose it's not," Dawson said.

"Well, Benson worked in real estate. He's done pretty good for himself. Trevor took construction jobs and then a few security jobs. According to Trip, he cleaned himself up, so Trip welcomed him home."

"What about Ken and Benson?" Dawson asked.

She jerked her head and narrowed her stare. "There's nothing to tell there. I mean, Ken worked for Benson's old man for a short time, but that's it."

Dawson arched a brow. "You know Ken was one of my best friends. I know he and Benson had a fight. I just don't know what that fight was about." He'd learned when he first took this job that Anna was the eyes and ears of the station. She saw what came in and what went out. Remy had told him that her loyalty to Trip was strong. However, Remy also told him that in the last few months since they had moved her mother-in-law to a better facility, her work had taken a bit of a back seat.

Well, Dawson understood that. He wished he could have been a better grandson.

She shrugged. "I have no idea. Not sure anyone does. I didn't see it happen, but it could've had something to do with Audra. Unfortunately, if Ken was involved, it was always about that girl."

Dawson believed that statement, but only because Ken hadn't liked to talk about Audra or Calusa Cove. Time to move on. "I barely even know Paul's son. He slinks into town unnoticed half the time. Why is that?"

"He was always a quiet kid—and smart. It was strange that he and Trevor were as close as they were, considering Trevor was always getting into trouble. But even I thought Trevor had turned over a new leaf when he came back. When Trip died, Trevor won over the hearts of this town, much to Remy's dismay. Poor guy has been passed over now twice for chief. First time because of the family connection and the fact that Trevor was a damn good salesman. And the second time because we, as a collective, wanted an outsider."

"Fletcher's not really an outsider, and he's the one who recommended me for the job." Dawson decided to drop the Benson topic. No one in this town, not even Anna, seemed to believe that man could do wrong. Dawson would press later.

Anna laughed. "Fletcher might not have been a Goody Two-Shoes growing up, but he didn't skirt the big laws. The ones this town cares about. Anyone who came back with him was going to be the better choice, but now we're going down a different rabbit hole." She waved her hand toward the holding cells. "I want to know about those two back there."

"Not much to tell," Dawson said. "They've been charged. If I could've booked them with a felony and made it stick, I would have, but a good lawyer would plead it out anyway, making me look like a two-bit, small-town cop trying to make a name for himself. They have no priors. They've done the Python Challenge twice before. There's no reason to believe there was any intent other than to use the dynamite to stir up more snakes and maybe gators. The most they will get is a fine, probation instead of jail time, and community service. They might lose their license to distribute dynamite for a few years." Dawson shrugged. "But that's completely in the hands of the court system now."

"You enjoyed that arrest, didn't you?"

"You bet I did." He smiled. "Besides the insanity of blowing up dynamite to kill snakes and gators and what that would do to the ecosystem, they could've hurt someone. Plus, I don't like their shoes."

"Oh, I saw their fancy footwear." Anna chuckled. "They're all the rage these days. Hell, I bet some of those guys Trinity hangs out with are wearing them."

"Well, they won't be on my feet."

"Right, because all you wear are boots, sneakers, and flip-flops."

"Those are the only types of shoes that are even necessary in life." Dawson downed the last of his coffee, rinsed his cup out in the sink, and gathered up the courage for his next batch of questions. "What can you tell me about Audra McCain, her father Victor, and even Ken Mitchell?"

"I heard she was back in town." Anna turned, pulling a file off her desk. "I took the liberty of pulling Victor's case file, but before I get into what I know or don't know, wasn't Ken a buddy of yours? Wouldn't he have told you all about Audra and her dad?"

"Ken was one of my best friends." He folded his arms and sighed. "But Ken didn't discuss Calusa Cove, much less his high school sweetheart."

"I suppose that makes sense." She waved the paperwork in his direction. "What you have here are the official forms Trip filed."

"You make it sound like I should be looking somewhere else for information on what happened." He leaned across the space and took the folder.

"People have postulated for years as to what happened. The story has gotten bigger, and everyone likes to speculate about Audra wanting to be a Stigini."

"What is up with that Owl Witch crap?"

"It's one of the legends of the Everglades. But it gets all tangled up in the fact her mom was part Native American and her grandmother was a gypsy-hippie, who practiced some kind of ritualistic spiritual stuff that some believed was witchcraft. They had a deep belief in a connection to the earth, and some really believed they taught Audra how to be a Stigini. It's stupid. Add in the fight that Audra and her dad had the day he disappeared, and everyone decided it became physical, which never happened. Well, Audra didn't stand a chance in this town. There were even rumors that Audra was pregnant, and Ken and her father were making her have an abortion."

"That's ridiculous," Dawson said. "All Ken ever wanted was to be a father, and he was a great one. He and his wife had two kids. Cutest little buggers you ever saw."

Anna held up her hand. "I'm telling you what the town vibe was when Audra slinked out of here like a snake in the middle of the night."

"Okay." He waved the folder. "You worked here when Victor went missing, right?"

She nodded. "I'll never forget that morning," she said. "Silas found Audra floating about a mile from Mitchell's docks. She was blubbering something awful."

"You were there?"

"No," Anna said, "but Mo was. He was heading out to go fishing with some buddies. He said she was exhausted, dazed, and confused. She wasn't making much sense either. People misconstrued that she was speaking in tongues. Her clothes were covered in blood." Anna lowered her chin. "Both hers and Victor's blood. That's why everyone in this town believes he's dead, not missing."

"But this file was sent to the FBI's missing person division. Why?"

"No body. The evidence was circumstantial against Audra, and to be honest, Trip never believed she did it and wanted to drive that point home to everyone. He wanted to protect her. However, he wasn't sold it was an accident, and there was a lot of pressure on him from this town to arrest someone, which was odd because, in general, most thought Victor was a fly who needed swatting. Sending that file to the Feds was his way of shutting the town up and getting help, but it went nowhere. They shipped it right back to us," she said. "It added fuel to the fire when it came to Audra."

"Because the Feds believed she did it or because the town wanted blood?"

"The FBI didn't really give much of an opinion, but the town certainly has one. When you look at that file, it's hard not to think Audra either did it or knows something." Anna shrugged. "But again, there wasn't enough evidence for Trip to make an arrest, and one evening, Audra waltzed into this station and asked him what would happen if she left town."

"Jesus. What did he say?"

"He told her it would be a stupid idea. That it would make her look guilty as hell, but that he was filing it as an accident with a note that, technically, Victor was a missing person."

Dawson flipped open the file and lifted the top page. "This report is only a few pages long."

"I'm well aware since I printed it out for you." She laughed. "It has our one-page report, a forensic report with the blood analysis, a two-page report regarding Audra and her wounds, the damage assessment of the boat, and the final note about it being an accident."

Dawson rubbed his neck. "I'm really confused here. If Trip thought something nefarious happened out there, why the hell did he button this up, and who were his suspects?"

"Anyone and everyone in this town could've been a suspect. Even those who considered Victor a friend had a beef with the man, but nothing strong enough to scream murder. As to the second part of that question… well, Trip cared about Audra and wanted her to have peace in this town. The investigation might be bad police work, but this is a small town, and sometimes, we do things backward. Besides, Trip looked into it every chance he got," Anna said. "He thought Victor was off his rocker, and to be honest, Victor drove Trip crazy with his conspiracy theories, right down to the one where there were pirates in the swamp. But Trip was a good man. He went out there looking for them, and you know what?"

"He never found them."

"That's right." Anna nodded. "What you have to understand about Victor was the man was crazy. Harmless, but a loon. I always felt bad for Audra. I used to babysit her, especially after her mom died. That's when Victor really started to go off the rails. Audra was always more like her dad than her mom." Anna raised her hand. "I don't mean crazy, not like Victor, but that girl was full of piss and vinegar and always trying to prove herself. She wrestled gators and snakes. Did crazy shit. Anyway, once she ran off like she was guilty, Trip wanted to clear her name—in case she ever came back —and bless his soul, he tried."

"Dumb question here," Dawson said. "If he looked into all this, why didn't he keep a file on it somewhere?"

"Oh, he did. And not just about Victor's case, but about other issues this town faced." She leaned closer. "And people. Trip was weird like that. He preferred to keep a notebook full of personal sidenotes. Things that he couldn't put in an official file."

"Jesus. Where the fuck is it? I want to see that."

"No idea," Anna admitted. "When Trevor took office, it was after his father passed, and trust me, I looked for his father's personal files. Near the end, there was tension between Trip and his son. I don't think Trip would've wanted Trevor to have his notebook, but that's me being my normal suspicious self."

"Do you think his son would've destroyed it for some reason?" Dawson scanned the words on the page, which were few—just your standard cop write-up of events—and nothing jumped out at him.

"I wouldn't put anything past Trevor."

"Could Trevor have had anything to do with Victor going missing? Were they enemies? Have any run-ins?"

"Everyone had run-ins with Victor. He was a cross between Jenkins and Cooney, only Victor didn't wave weapons around. He didn't threaten to hurt anyone. But he would get in your face if he thought you were doing something wrong or if he believed you crossed him. Victor believed a lot of people in this town had done him wrong at one point or another. He was more talk than action and more concerned about his conspiracies than anything else. As far as Trevor goes, he wasn't a cop when Victor disappeared, but he didn't like the old man, and he didn't like Audra."

"Why not?"

"Because she stood up for herself. She might have been younger, but she showed him up more than once, and Trevor always believed a woman's place is behind her man, not out in the swamp."

"Sexist asshole," Dawson muttered. "I can't stand men like that."

"Anyway, Trevor absolutely believed Audra killed him. I once heard him discussing it with Trip, telling his dad he should arrest her and then find the evidence."

Dawson had more questions now than when he'd first learned of Victor and his sexy, redheaded daughter. There were so many questions that there was no way he could let this drop.

The front door flew open, and Paul Massey strolled in.

"Hello, Dawson." Paul planted his hands on his hips. He wore dirty jeans and a long-sleeved plaid shirt, and he smelled like the swamp. "You had to bring me in during the middle of the challenge."

"I didn't call you." He handed the file to Anna, strolled around her desk, and leaned against the counter. "But I'm guessing the two guys I arrested did?"

"You illegally detained two men who, as of a half hour ago, obtained my services," Paul said. "I want you to release them. Apologize. And drop all the charges." He lowered his chin. "Save us both a lot of paperwork. Otherwise, they're going to bring in some big fancy city law firm and chew you up and spit you out because they can."

"Nothing illegal about what I did, Paul, and you know it." Dawson turned, snagging the paperwork off

Anna's desk, who smiled wickedly. "I've charged your clients with a misdemeanor because they were loading the dynamite onto their boat—"

"You're seriously going to follow through with this bullshit?" Paul tapped his fingers on the counter.

"As I was saying, because your clients chose to move the dynamite from their vehicle to a boat they were about to use to hunt for pythons, a reasonable person would—"

"You're making a dangerous assumption." Paul lifted the paperwork. "This is a bullshit charge that will be tossed out as fast as a city slicker lawyer will have your badge. I don't think that's what you want."

Dawson hated it when he and Paul played this lawyer-cop dance. It had only happened twice before, but it was painful. He held out a file. "We've already spoken to the judge. Here's the bail bond. Let's just get this part over with."

Paul took the file Dawson offered and signed the paper. He plucked a cashier's check out of his pocket and pushed it across the counter.

Dawson found it interesting that he'd had it ready.

"Court date is in the paperwork," Dawson said. "Please make your clients show up."

"They won't be my clients when that happens," Paul said.

He handed Anna the paperwork to file. As soon as he got rid of the two assholes, he'd make a beeline for the Everglades. If he was lucky, he might be able to get out on one of the airboats before dark.

But not because he was interested in the redhead.

# CHAPTER 4

AUDRA SLOWED her boat down to an idle before cutting the engine. She'd taken her sweet time getting here, partly because she saw some great opportunities for pictures along the way, but also, she hadn't wanted anyone to see her take the turn through Snake River and Gator Junction. Of course, she ran the risk that people were back here snake hunting. This area would be ripe for the critters, but even the locals got skittish about the folklore after dark.

More than her father had disappeared in this stretch of the Everglades. It was a regular Everglade Triangle.

Her heart hammered in her chest as she glanced around. Not a single other hunter was in sight. It shouldn't surprise her.

Hector Mendoza had gone missing somewhere back here, and that man had been more of a gator whisperer than her father had been. He'd lived in the Everglades as a young man before he'd met his wife. There were a million stories about Hector. About his heritage. About why he'd chosen to live out here, but it had been Erica—his wife—who'd tamed the beast and brought him to civilization. No one ever knew the real story. Hector had never talked about his childhood or why he'd come to Calusa Cove, but something had happened, and Audra suspected it was traumatic. However, none of it mattered. According to her dad, Hector was a decent, hardworking man who respected the Everglades and loved his family.

Before that, there were stories about a man named Phil. Just Phil. A white guy with blond hair who'd caught massive rattlesnakes with his bare hands and had alligators for pets.

He'd come to the island with no name to release a few gators who had gotten too big and made the towns-people nervous.

He'd never returned.

That had happened when her father was a small child, and the story had grown over the years.

There were many others, but those were the two stories that stuck out.

The Everglades were deep. Lots of little nooks and crannies. Every hunter had a plan. The locals had already scouted the areas beforehand. People like Silas and Paul knew where to look for pythons, and they'd probably already caught one. She didn't need to concern herself with them outside of staying as far away from them as possible.

Tears welled in her eyes.

This was the last place she'd seen her father alive. The last place she'd heard his voice. According to him, he'd come out here a few days before that fateful night and had seen something he'd never seen before on the small land where the bow of her boat now pointed. Her father had told her a small shack had come into view through the lush trees. That night, he'd flashed a light, and she'd seen it, too. There had been crates with odd markings on the side near the small opening.

But then everything had gone black, and she couldn't remember anything until she'd woken up hours later covered in her father's blood. She rubbed her arms as if trying to remove the tacky fluid from her body.

Today, the brush seemed thicker in the sunlight than sixteen years ago. But she knew she had navigated to the exact location.

She pulled out her drone, hooked up her phone to the flying machine's controller, and prepared it for flight. She could maneuver her boat to the clearing and walk around, but checking out the area first was safer.

Once she had a layout of the land, then she'd hoof it.

"All right, Dad, let's see if what we saw that night is still back there."

Her father had had all sorts of weird ideas crammed into his brain. He hadn't trusted many people. All those stories about pirates using the Everglades—he'd believed them. He'd perpetuated the rumors. Told them around the campfire. Told her that Calusa Cove was just the kind of town and tiny port that was ripe for that kind of criminal activity because it wasn't a tourist spot. No one came here intentionally. Those who passed through were headed to somewhere else. They stopped for gas.

It was the kind of town where people stayed one night. If they happened to stay a second night, it was because they fell for its charm but still moved on quickly because there wasn't anything to hold their attention for more than a day.

For the last three weeks of her father's life, he'd believed something else was going on back in the Everglades. Something other than pirates from the high seas hiding for a night before moving on. Something bigger was happening, and before he brought it to Trip this time, he wanted proof.

Watching through the screen on her camera, she flew the drone low toward the island. She raised it higher over the trees as it went across the land, making sure to record. She didn't want to miss anything. She directed the drone to the right and deeper into the island.

She squinted, staring at the small screen, searching for signs of that old shack, looking for anything that would tell her that she—and her father—weren't crazy.

Nothing.

She pulled it back and to the left.

Ah-ha! A clearing. The shack had to be in that direction. It hadn't been too far from the waterline. Not too far out of sight. They'd seen it from their boat. It had been dark, and while she knew she'd seen something, her memory was fuzzy at best.

The trees ruffled, and a few birds took flight,

zooming overhead. The picture on her phone disappeared, and then her drone dropped from the sky.

"What the hell?"

She glanced between her cell and the area where her drone had been hovering. She'd checked the battery before she'd sent it off. It was fully charged. It shouldn't have died.

"Goddammit." The stupid thing was a couple of years old, but it had never failed her before. Setting the controller aside, she fired up the airboat, pushed the lever, and pointed the bow toward a spot between two trees. Just enough space to land her boat. She tied it off to a branch. She put on her heavy-duty pants and snake-proof boots, grabbed her hook, bag, and everything else she needed to deal with a python, including her air gun and screwdriver. She might as well bring in one and start the challenge off right.

That would've made her father proud.

But she also wanted to find her damn drone and figure out what had happened to it. Hopefully, it could be fixed by morning. Her funds were limited, and buying a new one wasn't in her budget.

Not to mention she'd have to drive to a more populated city at least an hour to the west. Calusa Cove didn't even have a Walmart. They were lucky to have a decent grocery store—if you could call Denny's Shopmart a market. But it had what you needed at decent prices. Most people made a run to the city once a month and stocked up. Of course, everyone had staples for when a hurricane barreled through.

She trekked through the thick brush, watching

where she stepped. All sorts of wildlife could come out of nowhere and do some serious damage to life and limb out here. People in this town might consider her a loon—like her dad—but she wasn't stupid. Nor did she want to die.

Nope.

Not by a snake or a gator.

She knew the dangers. She also knew where and how to spot them.

This was not her first rodeo, and she wasn't about to make it her last.

So far, no signs of the creatures, but they were here. This was their home, not hers, and she respected that. She continued inland, glancing at the compass on her cell—which had no reception. By her calculations, the drone had fallen ten degrees northwest of where she'd been on the water. She glanced over her shoulder. It was hard to gauge that exact location now, but she did know the drone had made it to the clearing, so that's where she needed to go.

She lifted her right foot and out of the corner of her left eye, she saw movement.

Pausing, she focused on the tall grass to her left. A freaking snake was only two feet away, and she guessed it to be about ten feet long.

Damn.

Well, last year, she'd wrangled an eight-footer.

She tucked her phone in her pocket, unclipped her air gun, and gripped her snake hook. She'd seen hunters catch these things with their bare hands. She'd done that a few times with a rattlesnake, but only because she'd had to. A python was a different story, and she wasn't about to do that. She was confident that she could handle this one with the proper tools and technique.

She sucked in a deep breath.

The python turned its head, stuck out its tongue a few times, and eyed her like she was dinner.

"Dad, I hope you're watching," she whispered as she inched closer, raising the hook.

The snake watched her every move. It slithered, coiling its body, preparing to defend itself.

She shifted her position so she could come around the other side of its head. She needed to get the hook in just the right spot. But every time she angled herself, the snake turned its head. As if it knew exactly what she was doing. If she didn't know better, she'd swear that snake smiled.

Her heartbeat pulsated in her throat, making it diffi-cult to swallow. She couldn't give this beast time to strike. If she did that, it would be wrapped around her body like a pretzel.

It was now or never.

As soon as she was close enough, she lunged forward. The snake lifted its head, with its mouth so wide she feared it could take off her arm in one bite. Only, pythons didn't eat their prey that way.

She shoved the hook around the nasty critter's neck, pushing it back down with as much force as she could. "Gotcha."

Immediately, the snake's body looped around the hook, its tail smacking her in the calf. She stumbled one small step backward, nearly losing the hold she had on its neck. She pressed harder, grunting.

Damn, that snake was strong. It constricted and did its best to shimmy its way out of her grip. Its tail slinked up the hook and smacked her midriff, nearly knocking her over. She adjusted her footing and applied more pressure, making sure the snake's neck and head couldn't move. If she let go, she was surely a goner.

She pulled out her air gun and aimed right for the sweet spot—between the python's eyes and jawbone. If she missed, well, she didn't want to think about that. She pulled the trigger.

The snake went limp.

But it wasn't dead. She had only seconds to destroy the snake's brain.

As quickly as possible, she removed her screwdriver, finding what was considered the access point to the cranial cavity, stabbing the tool deliberately in several directions. This was called pithing. It was gross, but necessary.

She sighed. "Well, that was a little anticlimactic." She stared at the snake. Pride swelled in her chest. Not just because of how much her father had loved the Everglades and wanted to preserve the wetlands. Growing up, this was the kind of life she'd wanted. Being out here had been a calling. A way of life. It had been in her blood, and she missed it.

She grabbed her bag and heaved the animal into it. The thing was heavier than it looked.

Scanning the tall grass, she made sure she wasn't stepping on another before heading in the direction where she thought her drone had landed. The sound of an airboat whizzing by in the open waters filled the air. Or maybe it was two, since it seemed as though one slowed down and an engine cut out. At least she wasn't completely alone, although that thought didn't necessarily make her feel any better because she was alone.

Trinity's words about not having friends in this town echoed in her ears.

Get the drone and get back on the boat.

She'd hunt more tomorrow. Or maybe not.

This was a dumb idea. She wasn't a teenager anymore and when she'd done the challenge last time, she'd done so with a partner. Yeah, this wasn't her brightest idea.

Then again, maybe she was just spooked being out here on this patch of land and searching for clues about a sixteen-year-old mystery.

Carefully, she stepped into the clearing. Ten paces away, her drone came into view. She dropped the sack with the dead snake and picked up her flying machine, examining it.

"No way." She held it up. "This can't be right. I didn't hear a gunshot." She pressed her finger to the hole. But sure enough, a bullet had damaged her drone, and she knew a bullet hole when she saw one.

*A silencer?*

"Mother trucker," she whispered. "Who the hell would do that? And why?" And now she was talking to herself.

Her father used to do that all the time. He'd pace and mumble.

However, the bigger issue was, she was standing on an island that was inhabited by snakes, gators, and possibly someone who wanted to shoot her.

Jesus, she needed to get back to her boat.

However, she couldn't just run back to it. That would kill her in a different way.

She picked up her snake and slowly headed back toward her airboat. She'd take two steps and look over her shoulder before taking another inch forward. If a python or alligator didn't get her, a human with a bullet would.

A part of her—the curious part—wanted to continue looking on this small patch of land for whoever had shot the drone—but that would be pure insanity. Sure, it could have been an accident.

Everyone out here had a gun—just in case.

No one was supposed to use them to kill a snake or a gator. That was illegal and considered inhumane. There were rules. But if it came down to a human life or a creature's life, humans won.

Yet it made no sense as to why her drone had been shot down. Many hunters had one. It was a great resource, and while prize money was awarded, the purpose was still to remove as many snakes as possible.

She should have never come back to Calusa Cove.

It took her twice as long to get back to the area where she'd parked the boat. Her heart dropped like a boulder to the bottom of her gut before lurching to the back of her throat. She stared with horror in her eyes as a masked silhouette boarded her vessel.

"Hey, you," she yelled. "Get the hell off my boat."

The man—or woman, because she couldn't actually tell—glanced up with a quick jerk of his or her arm. A metal object that was gripped in the person's hand glared in the sunlight.

With a flick of the wrist, her boat was floating in the murky water.

The silhouette hopped onto their small flat-bottom boat with a two-stroke engine. They pulled the cord and sputtered away.

As quickly as she could, she raced through the thick muck, praying she didn't step on an angry alligator or a spiteful snake. She tossed her belongings on the bow and climbed aboard. Her pulse pounding, it took a few moments for her to catch her breath.

With a shaky hand, she tried the engine.

Nothing.

She reached for the radio and pressed the button.

Nothing.

"Well, hell." She'd done a radio check before leaving the dock, and it had worked just fine.

She tried again. Still nothing.

Dead in the water.

She rifled through some of her belongings, lifting her camera bag. She gasped.

Tentatively, she raised a bundle of dynamite. "What the hell?"

She had expected a cold welcome from the townspeople of Calusa Cove, but this was something entirely different.

She snagged her cell and raised it toward the sky. There was no reception in this spot, and since the tide was coming in, the current was taking her in the wrong direction. Great. Reception wouldn't get better if she floated deeper into the Everglades. She checked the time. The sun would set in half an hour. Boats should be flying by, so she should be able to wave down someone. She hoped.

Only, she was a good forty-five minutes to an hour from the dock.

Yeah, good luck with that.

# CHAPTER 5

Dawson rolled to a stop in the parking lot of Mitchell's Marina. Benson Massey leaned against his SUV with his cell in his hands. He glanced up and waved Dawson over.

Wonderful.

"Chief Ridge, I need to speak with you for a moment," Benson said. "It's important."

"Sure thing." Dawson rolled up the window, slipped from the driver's seat, and strolled toward Benson. Dawson had only met the young man three or four times, even though he was aware he came to town relatively often to visit his parents.

Paul was quite proud of his son and talked about him constantly. But Paul spoke about both his children —and his grandchildren—every chance he got.

"What can I help you with?" Dawson noted the empty snake bag at Benson's feet.

"Would you mind taking a look at my tire?"

While Dawson didn't mind changing a flat for a kid or a little old lady or old man, he did take issue with helping out a strapping gentleman. "What seems to be the problem?"

"You tell me." He waved his hand over the rear passenger side.

Dawson knelt, running his hand over the rubber and fingering a slit in the tire. Not just any slit. Nope. It wasn't jagged. It hadn't been caused by a rock, a curb, or even a nail. No, Dawson suspected a nice sharp blade had done this damage. "I see your dilemma." He pulled out his cell, texting one of his deputies to request that he make his way to this location to take the report. If he didn't at least go through the motions of having it examined, Paul would be down his throat.

"I'm supposed to be back out there with my dad, but this is putting a damper on my day."

"My deputy is five minutes away. He'll take a report if that's what you want. He can even help you change the tire."

"That's all fine, but what about dealing with the bitch who did this?" Benson cocked a brow.

"Sounds like you're making an accusation."

"Damn right, I am." Benson nodded. "Audra McCain. She slashed my tire when she was a kid, so why would now be any different?"

"Did you see her lurking around your truck this morning?"

"No. But I'm sure she snuck back in after we all went out. That witch is sneaky like that."

"So, other than she did it once a long time ago, you have no real reason to believe this was her." Dawson glanced over his shoulder as his deputy pulled in. "Hang tight here. I'm going to head down to the docks. Everyone has to report in when they return. I'll find out if Audra has been back at all."

"That Audra is a slippery one," Benson said. "I'm sure she could've come in under the radar. She knows every nook and cranny of the Everglades—even ones no one else does."

While Dawson didn't doubt that Audra knew the area, there weren't many ways back out into open water, and they all snaked into one channel—the one that went right by Mitchell's.

He jogged down to the docks and found Fletcher sitting at the far one, chewing on a Twizzler. "Hey, man. How's it going?"

"Just dandy, you?"

"I've had better days," Dawson admitted. "I need a list of who's come in today."

"Benson, Ripley, Emmerson and his brother Rhett, and Jonas. That's it so far, but I suspect we'll see a few more come in shortly for dinner. Why?"

"Does everyone in this town believe Audra is a bad person?"

"Not everyone, but I'd say more than half, and almost everyone has trust issues with her because they don't understand her. She doesn't help herself by being so damn sarcastic and feeding into that shit."

"Just my luck," Dawson muttered as he stared at the

sky. "I need to ask you a question, and I need a straight answer."

Fletcher narrowed his stare. "Since when have I ever not been honest with you?"

"Since never, but things in this town sometimes are ass-backward, and I need to know what kind of relationship Ken had with Benson." Dawson arched a brow.

Fletcher rubbed the back of his neck. "Benson and I have never gotten along, so when he and Ken got a little buddy-buddy, I asked Ken why. He shrugged and said he was just being nice. But Ken also worked for Benson's dad, so it wasn't the strangest thing in the world. However, they had words before he decided to join me on my journey into the Navy."

"What was the fight about?" Dawson asked.

Fletcher rubbed his jaw. "I don't know. Benson probably said something about Audra. That's usually what happened."

"And you never asked Ken to elaborate?"

"No," Fletcher said. "Is there something I need to know about?"

"I'm not sure, but thanks for the intel," Dawson said. "I'll be heading out on the water in a bit. I'll be in touch later." He made a beeline for the parking lot. "All right, Benson. Audra hasn't reported to the docks since this morning." He raised his hand. "I'll have a chat with her." He scribbled the names that Fletcher gave him on a piece of paper and handed it to his deputy. "My man here will question those who have reported in. Also, if you can give us any other names of people who might not like you or have a bone to pick with you, that would be helpful."

"I gave you a name," Benson said. "Everyone else in this town loves me."

"I'll be in touch." Dawson turned and headed back to the docks. Specifically, the dock where he parked his airboat. He climbed aboard and did his best to leave the day's problems behind. He checked his watch. He still had another good hour and a half of daylight, and it was a nice afternoon for a boat ride in the Everglades.

He pushed off from the dock and headed down the channel.

Dawson's favorite part about Calusa Cove was being on the water, and he had a couple of options, making it even sweeter.

Boats were the only thing he was willing to spend money on, and currently, outside of the airboats for Everglades Overwatch, he owned two personal vessels. He had a nice Boston Whaler Outrage. It had cost him a pretty penny, but she was worth it. She gave him two options to enjoy the fresh salty air.

There was the ocean. He loved deep-sea fishing, scuba diving, and just the vastness of the open waters. His Whaler could handle open seas—if the chop wasn't over four to six feet. Maybe seven if the distance between the swells were six to eight seconds. Or more. Many times, he couldn't take his boat out in the ocean because of the weather. But no matter.

There was always option number two. Dawson liked options. Chokoloskee Bay was a beautiful bay nestled behind a bunch of barrier islands. The bay was suitable for fishing and floating, and on a clear day, there were some good scuba and snorkeling spots.

And, of course, he loved cruising through the channels of the Everglades on his airboat. He didn't have many days off between being the chief of police, helping to run Everglades Overwatch, and his latest purchase six months ago of Harvey's Cabins, but every free moment he got, he was on the water.

It was ironic since, as a child, he'd been utterly terrified of swimming, even in a pool. His nana had been shocked by his decision to join the Navy. Learning how to swim had been one of his biggest challenges in life.

His parents had died when a boat charter they had been on capsized during a squall that had come out of nowhere. His mom and nana had been scrimping and saving for that charter for years. They'd given it to his dad as an anniversary present. His parents had never gone on a honeymoon, and it was supposed to be their chance to have a romantic getaway. Dawson had nightmares about what his parents must have endured.

But now, being on the water made him feel as though he were closer to his mom and dad. It was as if he were honoring them and making them proud of what he'd accomplished with his life.

He pulled his sunglasses off his face and tucked them in his shirt pocket. He hadn't bothered to change out of his uniform, mainly because the day had gotten away, and he wanted to spend what little sunlight was left on anything other than dry land.

A few boats zoomed past, heading back toward the marina. He'd gotten reports of at least eight snakes being captured during the hunt. What an excellent start to the challenge.

An airboat slowed as it approached, pulling up beside his.

*Silas.*

Silas cut his engine.

Dawson checked the time, surprised he'd already been out on the water for over an hour. Time always flew in the Everglades.

"Got me one." Silas held up a bag. "Sucker's nine feet long. Saw one at least fifteen feet, but damn thing slithered into the water, and I couldn't catch him."

"That's too bad, but I'm sure you'll get many more. You're one of the best wranglers in these parts." Dawson didn't stroke that man's ego often, but today was about restoring the Everglades. Nothing more, nothing less. Dawson could handle giving the old man a pat on the back.

The sun dipped below the horizon, and it would soon be dark. Even with a clear night, the moon and stars wouldn't light up the Everglades. However, many hunters were known to come out here, and snakes tended to be active then, making it a little more exciting —and much more dangerous.

They couldn't stop people from staying out, but they tried.

"Are you heading in for the night?" Dawson dared to ask.

Silas laughed. "Yeah, right. I'm out here all the time at night. My partner's at the bend, waiting for me to bring him a sandwich and a beer," he said with a smile.

"We've asked everyone to come in after dark."

"You know that's not actually a rule. It's simply a guideline." Silas set the bag down. "It's not like I don't do this year-round." He jerked his thumb over his shoulder. "Everyone out there, except maybe two, are professionals. We know what we're doing. Just because this is only the second year this area has been open to the challenge doesn't mean shit. You're being overly cautious for no reason. Those snakes are destroying the Everglades."

"I get it, Silas. I do."

"No, you don't. You're from New York. You're a damn outsider in this town. You don't know shit." Silas sneered. "You shouldn't be wasting your time worrying about me or anyone else from this town." He lowered his chin. "What you should be concerned with is why Audra McCain decided to return to Calusa Cove after all these years."

One thing Dawson had learned over the years was that when an opportunity presented itself, he'd be a fool not to take it. This was one hell of an opportunity.

"Why should my hackles be up over Audra?" Dawson asked.

"Come on, don't play dumb with me. It's not a good look, not even on you."

"Rumors and folklore about Everglade Owl Witches don't give me a reason to believe anything," Dawson said.

"Well, that Stigini rumor bullshit is stupid. Audra isn't a swamp monster, but I went through the motions of giving her the benefit of the doubt, and how did she repay me? She snuck out in the middle of the night like a criminal."

*Motions.* That was an interesting word choice.

"You should be pulling that file," Silas said, waving his finger, "and using that badge of yours to finally give this town some peace over what happened." He leaned closer. "Or maybe she knew of something her dad had hidden out here. That man had all sorts of wild stories. Perhaps one was true, only he was the one doing the crime."

Now that was an interesting theory.

"Like what?"

"You're the cop. That's your job to figure it out, not mine."

Dawson wanted to remind Silas that he was the one who'd bragged about knowing every inch of the Everglades. Every nook and cranny. That he knew everything that went on in these parts. But Dawson had had enough of this conversation. It wouldn't get him anywhere. He knew what Silas thought; that meant that over fifty percent of this town believed the same thing.

Silas pushed the lever, engaged the engine, and took off.

Well, that was fun. Not.

Dawson reached for the radio. "*Chumrunner, Chumrunner, Chumrunner,* this is *Watchdog,* over."

"This is *Chumrunner,* go ahead," Keaton said.

"How many boats have made it back beside Silas and Chad?"

"Everyone except Audra," Keaton said. "But my little lecture about not going out at night isn't sticking. I've got five people scarfing down a quick meal, and they all plan on going on a night run. Looks like I get to work a little overtime."

"Not fun for you, but did you really expect people to come in and stay in before the sun set?" Dawson rubbed the back of his neck. "Anyone see Audra?"

"I can ask around, but Fletcher warned me she might stay out past dark. They all used to come out here at night as kids. It was their playground. His words, not mine."

"That doesn't make me feel any better," Dawson said. "She's the only solo boat, and I'm shocked you're not the least bit worried."

"I never said it didn't concern me, and honestly, I'm annoyed by it. Hayes is still out there, and I told him to look for her. However, the color of her hair also has my hackles up because of you."

"I'm not even going to comment." Dawson did understand his buddy's concern. His last girlfriend, Liz, had done a number on him—more so than any other redhead.

"Where are you?" Keaton asked.

"Near the loop. I'll head up toward the fork and see if she went that way."

"Negatory," Fletcher's voice boomed over the radio. "If Audra's still out there, my guess is she went west past the northwest bend and through Snake River to the island with no name."

"Why would you think that?" Dawson asked. Why would she venture that deep into the Everglades? Even the locals don't like to be caught out there when darkness overtook daylight.

"Because that's where she says she was right before her dad disappeared."

"It's not the easiest one to find." Dawson arched his back. The first few times he'd gone out that far in the Everglades, he'd gotten lost. Really lost. It had been embarrassing. At least he understood the night sky and had used it to navigate his way home. But the damn eyes in the water freaked him right out. Too many fucking gators.

He hated those creatures. Why anyone would want to wrestle one, he had no idea. Coming face-to-face with a few of them last year while dealing with pythons had been scarier than the first time he'd gone underwater. He'd nearly panicked, and he considered himself one of the calmest, laid-back men on the planet, next to Fletcher.

But he drew the line at alligators.

"And some wetlands look like islands near Snake River," he muttered. He'd made that mistake once or twice in the first few months he'd lived here. Sadly, the guys teased him, but he didn't give airboat tours as much as everyone else did. His job as chief required more daytime hours than everyone else. He often only did the occasional weekend tour, so his knowledge of the Everglades wasn't as extensive as the rest of his buddies.

And they loved to razz him about it.

"I told you, it's the island with no name," Fletcher said. "The one tucked back deep in the Everglades that almost no one goes to because it's a swampland. But it's simple to find. Head northwest. Take the Snake River around the second bend and loop through Gator Junction. There'll be a fork, so go west and just keep on going. The water will narrow. The trees will dance over your head like baby rattlesnakes. But then it'll open up, and the island will be on your starboard side. My guess is she'll be there."

"Your guess better be right, or when I get back, I'm going to kick your ass." Dawson hooked the mic in the cradle. Then he took out his phone, pulled up the map, and stared at it for a good second. He'd lose service shortly, but if he left the map open, he'd still be able to use it. He also had a chart in the glove compartment. He knew how to use that. Plus, he was getting better at understanding the twists and turns.

Still, the Everglades were scary as hell at night, especially this section. There was a reason most people didn't take Snake River at night.

And the eyes in the water were always watching.

He pushed the gas, turned on his spotlight, and headed west. As frightening as the landscape could be, it was also one of the most beautiful places in the world. He slapped his arm when a mosquito bit through his shirt. He headed up Snake River. It was only called that because it bent nine times. Gator Junction had gotten its name when one of the largest gators ever recorded in Florida's history had been found there. For whatever reason, they named the thing a "junction"—weird-ass name.

The waterway narrowed, and the trees covered the

sky. The sun had dipped completely behind the horizon, but her light wasn't totally gone. However, the thick branches of the trees made it feel like midnight. He checked the time. Nearly an hour had passed since he'd spoken to his buddy.

Thankfully, this part was short, and he eased into a wider body of water. He took the west fork and found the island.

No Audra.

Well, damn.

He continued when his light flashed across something—no, someone. He released the gas lever.

"Hey. Over here." Audra stood on the bow of her boat, waving her arms above her head. Her fiery hair was piled on top of her head in a sexy mess.

His fingers itched to wrap in the strands of that thick mane. Jesus, he had some serious issues.

He cut the engine and tossed her a line, helping her secure the boat so he could tow it back to the docks, which would be tricky through Snake River, but he'd manage. "What the hell happened?"

"Seems I've got a hole in the fuel pump." She tied the line to her bow.

"Not a good way to start the challenge."

"Nope, and someone cut it on purpose," she mumbled.

"Excuse me? How do you know that?"

"I saw them do it. They also must've messed with my radio as well as left me these." She handed him a small bundle of dynamite.

He stiffened. Well, that changed everything.

"You saw someone put this in your boat?" he asked.

"Well, no," she said. "But I saw someone in a mask on my boat while I was on the island with no name. They untied my vessel, and when I got to it, I had no radio, no way to start the engine, and I found that. So, I'd say someone wants me to go away. And what's interesting about this is my dad's boat had a fuel line issue when he went missing," she said. "Feels like a strange omen."

"Yeah, I read that." He nodded. "Trip put in his report that it most likely happened when you ran aground. However, my secretary believes it might not have been a malfunction."

"Because it wasn't—just like today." She took his hand and boarded his vessel. "And it's not the only mishap I had today."

He cocked his head.

"Someone shot down my drone."

"Excuse me? As in with a bullet and a gun?"

"No. With their finger and air." She raised her hand and pretended to shoot him. She blew on her index finger and shoved it in her pocket before winking.

He'd seen her sarcasm firsthand earlier. "I'll need to look at that drone when we get back to the docks. I'll text the mechanic we use for Everglades Overwatch to come to look at your boat tonight. I also need to take that dynamite and check it into evidence." This soured his mood even more. Things like fuel pumps failing on old airboats happened, but drones being shot from the sky didn't. And dynamite didn't magically appear—especially not right after he'd made an arrest.

"No, and not necessary, but thank you."

"Are you always this stubborn?" He shoved the spotlight in her hand and eased the airboat forward. It would be dark by the time they got back. His stomach growled. He hated going without a meal, and eating late only made his heartburn kick up. "I'm honestly not asking, and as the chief of police, I can't ignore a crime." He pointed to the explosives. "Especially when I might know where that came from."

"Seriously?"

He nodded. "I arrested two men earlier today who had it loaded on their boat."

"That can't be a coincidence."

"Probably not." He arched a brow. "All the more reason for you to stop arguing with me and let me do my job."

She kicked off her flip-flops and dared to put her pretty little feet on his console. "People in this town don't want me here, and I think this is my warning."

"All the more reason for me to investigate." He blinked, staring at her cute pink-painted toes. He groaned. That was unexpected but a total turn-on and the last thing he needed to focus on while he towed her boat back to Mitchell's Marina. He seriously had issues.

"Nothing for you to do." She sighed.

"I beg to differ because you just told an officer—"

"My God, you're uptight."

That he blamed on a lack of sex.

"I bet you're Fletch's work wife."

Dawson frowned. He hated that phrase. It wasn't just with Fletcher. All the guys considered him the work wife. Or the voice of reason. The one who raised his hand and reminded everyone of the dangers of whatever path they forged down. He'd been like that his entire life.

The buzzkill.

He was worse than Keaton.

Her eyebrows rose as she studied his expression. "Looks like I hit paydirt with that one."

"Fletcher wouldn't appreciate you calling me that or shortening his name." Dawson kept his gaze forward and not on the sexy lady sitting way too close for comfort, reminding him that the last time he'd shared a bed with someone of the opposite sex had been six months ago.

While the experience had been decent enough, the morning after hadn't gone well.

She'd been a blonde.

He thought he'd be safe. It turned out she was crazier than a one-eyed rattlesnake.

She wrinkled her nose. "What is up with that? I mean, I've only known Fletcher as Fletch. That's going to take some getting used to."

"I honestly don't know. I've only known him as Fletcher." Not true. However, not the point. "But ever since we came to Calusa Cove, he's been correcting everyone." Only Dawson knew why. While it might not make sense to most, it made perfect sense to Dawson, and he would respect his buddy's wishes. Still, he wasn't about to tell anyone why. The only people who knew were the team.

And Baily.

But it hadn't changed Baily's opinion—not yet,

anyway. And Dawson hoped it did for Fletcher's sake because that man was miserable.

"And you changed the direction of this conversation." He waggled his finger under her nose. "You'll let me look at the drone and your boat. You're going to give me a description of the boat and the person who boarded your vessel. You'll also give me the dynamite and let me do my job."

"Well, I'm not letting you do it at the docks, and I want some information in return." She folded her arms across her chest.

"What's that?"

"The name of the men you arrested."

"Eliot Commings and James Huber," he said.

"Wow. You gave that up real quick."

He shrugged. "It'll be public record, so not a big deal. Now, I need you to follow through with your end of this agreement."

She groaned. "It's not that simple. You don't know me or my relationship with this—"

"I know enough. I've read the file and gotten an earful from at least one townsperson." He turned, catching her gaze under the moonlight. "Come on. Besides, Fletcher's my best friend. I'm the town's chief of police. You didn't think I wouldn't know about one of the oldest cold cases in this town?"

"Well, I'm sure Ken gave you an earful of misguided and bullshit information, too," she said under her breath.

Now how the hell could he respond to that one without pissing off this chick even more. Guess it didn't matter. He might as well be honest. Hopefully, it wouldn't land him in the gator and snake-infested water. "While I served with Ken for thirteen years, I'm sorry, but he almost never talked about you."

She jerked her body so hard that she fell off the captain's chair, landing on the bottom of the boat with a *thud.*

"Crap," she mumbled.

"Are you okay?" He leaned over, stretching out his hand.

"I'm fine." She batted it away, hoisting herself back up on the bench. "Are you serious? Not even when they talked about their hometown? What about Fletcher?"

Well, this was turning out to be a dicey but interesting conversation. "Of course, your name was brought up, but it wasn't something Ken ever discussed, especially after he married. But they also didn't talk much about Calusa Cove. Fletcher and Baily were more off than on—more friends than a couple until Baily took over the marina, and then she was always fighting with Ken about what to do with it. Ken was married to Julie, and they wanted nothing to do with this town or the marina. Me, Keaton, and Hayes, we would walk away because it became this weird, awkward thing between those two." Dawson spoke so fast he could barely catch his breath. He'd asked Ken a couple of times about Audra, and once, he'd thought Ken would punch him in the throat.

"Wow. This conversation is making you really uncomfortable, isn't it?"

"Yup."

"Is it me, Ken, or—"

"All of it," Dawson admitted. "I thought I knew everything about Ken, but I'm learning I don't."

She patted his shoulder. "There are a lot of secrets in Calusa Cove. Everyone who has ever lived here has one, Fletcher included."

Yeah, but he knew Fletcher's.

"Okay, so what's yours?" he asked.

"I didn't kill my father." She arched a brow. "But I know he's dead."

Dawson narrowed his stare. "I might need you to say more because there was no body. He was never found. And according to Trip's file, you have no memory of what happened."

"I remembered something that I didn't remember sixteen years ago."

He pulled back on the steering lever, turning the boat toward the docks. Both Keaton and Fletcher stood at the end of the last one.

"And what was that?" Dawson asked.

She leaned forward. "Not here. I don't trust anyone in this town. I might not trust you," she whispered in his ear. "I have to check into my accommodations at Harvey's Cabins. Meet me there in an hour. I'll let you check out my drone and even let your guy check out my boat." She jumped to her feet, tossing her line to Fletcher, leaving a stunned Dawson to chew on her words for a few moments while his body tried to recover from the tickling of her hot breath.

* * *

Dawson pulled into Massey's Pub. The parking lot was packed, and he had to go all the way to the back to find a spot. He could have illegally parked. He was the police chief, after all.

But that would be an abuse of power, and he never did it—unless he had to.

While this technically fell under police business, he wasn't going to call attention to himself. Not tonight.

Remy pulled in next to him and stepped out of his vehicle. "You really want backup for this?"

"No, I want a witness," Dawson said.

"That's just plain weird. Mind if I ask why? You didn't give me too many details when you called me."

Dawson looped his fingers in his belt and strolled toward the entrance of the pub with his chest puffed out. He'd never quite taken to his uniform. It always felt like a power grab. A very different feel from his Navy whites or blues. Even when he'd been an MP in the military, wearing the uniform had never been about anything other than to protect and serve. It was all he knew. All he understood. "For now, just follow my lead."

"You got it, Chief."

"Good evening, Chief," the hostess said. "Remy." She nodded. "Would you boys like a table this evening? I've got one that opened up in the back."

"No, thanks," Dawson said. "We've got a little police business we need to take care of. We won't be but a few minutes."

"Oh no." The hostess covered her mouth. "You're not going to make a scene, are ya? Should I call Paul?"

"That won't be necessary," Dawson said. "I just need

to ask those two over there a few questions." He waggled his fingers and then zigzagged through the crowd, knowing full well that the hostess was already texting with the owner. It didn't matter. Dawson had a good feeling about how this was going to go down.

"Hello, James. Eliot." Dawson pushed his way through a couple of men he didn't know and didn't care to know, but he took full note of what they looked like and were wearing.

Remy had pulled out his notebook and pen.

God bless that man.

"Jesus Christ," Eliot said. "Small-town cops and their harassment. Should I call my lawyer?"

"Is Paul still representing you for what happened here?" Dawson asked, but he didn't really care about the answer. "If you call him, or any other lawyer, we'll have to take this down to the station. Do you really want to do that? Or do you want to answer my questions?"

"Fine. Fire away." James waved his hand dismissively.

"Where were you today during the Python Challenge?" Dawson asked.

"I spent most of it in the cabin at your establishment," Eliot said, "doing paperwork while James here met with a client down the road at Bowmen's Marina." He smiled as if he'd won the spelling bee.

Jerk.

"Does your client have a name? Mind if I have a little chat with him?" Dawson asked.

"I'm happy to give you his contact information, but sorry to say, he's already left town, heading over to St.

Augustine." Eliot shrugged, then raised his beer to his lips.

"You can give my colleague here that information." Dawson jerked his thumb over his shoulder. "Now, how about you tell me how some of your dynamite landed in Audra McCain's boat."

Eliot set his beer a little too aggressively on the table. He wiped his lips. "First, I don't know anyone by that name. Second, you have all my dynamite. If you don't, someone took it from your possession. Not mine."

Yeah, that's about how Dawson had thought that would go. If not that direction, then he figured Eliot and James would accuse Audra of stealing it. Either way, they would play dumb.

For now, Dawson wouldn't press that too hard.

"Do you two boys have any plans on leaving town?" Dawson asked.

"Are you suggesting we can't?" James asked.

"Nope." Dawson shook his head. "Not as long as you show up for your court date. But I'd still like to know as I have some concern about how this dynamite ended up on a participant's boat."

Both Eliot and James laughed.

"Seriously?" James shook his head. "I think it's obvious. Audra? Was that her name?"

As if he didn't actually know. But Dawson would let that one slide, too.

"She had to have stolen it," James said. "Fucking incompetent small-town cops. Have to do their jobs for them, too."

"We'll be in touch," Remy said with a stern voice that

Dawson didn't hear too often. He folded his notebook and shoved it in his pocket. "Watch how many you boys have of those tonight." He waved his hand over the pitcher of beer. "I'd hate to have to give you a DUI...on top of the charges my chief here has already arrested you for." Remy turned on his heel and took off toward the door—or more like marched.

Dawson was two steps behind him. He had to practically jog to keep up.

"Care to tell me what set you off back there?" he asked Remy once they were standing by his patrol car.

"Audra's a lot of things. She'll get in your face, especially when she believes she's right. She doesn't know how to back down from a fight, even when it's for her own damn good. But one thing I do know about that wild young lady is that she's always had an affection for this town. For the Everglades. For the history of it all. It's a deep connection that she got from her grandmother, who was a member of the same Seminole tribe my grandparents are from." Remy waved his hand over his head. "That red hair of hers makes her unique in our culture. Not a swamp monster. Not a witch. But someone grounded in earth and fire. A deep soulful connection that we revere."

"Was that something that Audra was taught as a child?"

Remy stared at the sky and sighed. "Her mother was raised in the white man's world. It wasn't until she became pregnant with Audra that she returned to her Native American roots. Her pregnancy was hard. Audra was born early, and Victor had already begun to spiral into his mental illness." Remy wiggled his finger. "And that's what everyone in this town needs to remember. But we're getting sidetracked." Remy rubbed his jaw. "Elana, Audra's mother, was sick for most of Audra's early childhood. She did her best to teach Audra our ways. Our connection to the Everglades. What others see as witchcraft, we see as a way to honor what the gods and spirits have given us. But people like Paul perpetuate the concept that Victor was a crackpot, and Audra was a chip off the old block." Remy laughed. "The older she got, the more she liked to use being called an Owl Witch to keep people away. But Audra would never steal dynamite. She would have no use for it. She knows how to use a gun. She's probably a better shot than me, but she'd rather snag a rattler with her bare hands than kill the critter."

"You sure took a long time to tell me that she respects the land more than the rest of us."

"I wanted you to understand there was a bigger reason as to why."

Dawson nodded. He'd been to Remy's house for dinner and had experienced some of his native culture. Dawson loved nature. Valued it. He wanted to make sure it was there for centuries to come. But it wasn't the same as Remy and his people's love or connection to the land.

"I want someone watching those two men. If not you or one of our deputies, I want someone from my team," Dawson said. "How do you feel about that, since bringing in anyone other than Fish and Wildlife goes against protocol?"

"Considering what happened to Audra out there today, I got no problem with it," Remy said.

"All right. I'll text everyone. Mind sitting here until they head back to my cabins?"

"Not at all. I'll enjoy pulling them over for a breathalyzer."

Dawson laughed. "Just make sure you have cause." He opened his car door. Time to deal with the redhead.

# CHAPTER 6

Audra slowed her SUV to a snail's pace as she drove down her old street. It wasn't on the way to Harvey's Cabins. No, it was two miles in the wrong direction, but she had to see it, even if nothing was there but a stupid vegetable stand.

Her childhood home—gone. Destroyed. Ken had told her that the Wheelers had leveled the old shack and used the property as a stand to sell all the things they grew on their land right next door. She knew when she'd sold them the house, they wouldn't keep it. Why would they? The place had been barely inhabitable. It probably should have been condemned years before. Something was always broken. There were leaky pipes, the kitchen sink constantly dripped, and the water wasn't drinkable.

*Victor, this is no place to raise a child. You need to consider Audra. She needs a proper home. Proper clothes. A proper upbringing. It doesn't take a lot of money, but you either need to do better or let someone else.*

Silas's words rattled in her mind. She'd been all of eight years old when she'd first heard him say them. The old pirate had come to pick on her dad, pushing him around to take what didn't belong to him.

After her mother had died, she'd honestly worried someone would take her away. That someone would call child protective services and accuse her father of being an incompetent parent.

She'd always believed that a knock on the door would come because of Silas.

But it had never happened.

Her father hadn't been a bad dad. He'd been loving and kind, always generous with his time. Food was always on the table, even if it was mostly mac and cheese, bologna sandwiches, or whatever fresh fish they caught. The only thing he'd been guilty of was a broken heart and having a mental illness.

She stared at the stand where the house used to be, and memories flooded her brain—both good and bad.

Christmas mornings had been a joyous time in her house. Presents hadn't been the focus, even though there was always a stocking and one or two gifts. Her parents had done their best with what little they'd had. But the big breakfast, followed by a day out in the Everglades, had made that day so special.

It was that tradition that had started the whispers about her family being swamp monsters.

Talk about crazy. All they'd done was honor their ancestors, following the traditions of her mother's Native American culture.

A car whizzed past. It was a big, shiny, fancy new SUV—an expensive kind.

She whipped a tear from her cheek. Ken had picked her up in a bright, fancy limo for prom. They'd shared it with Baily and Fletcher. What an epic night that had been.

How she'd wished her mom had been there to see her all dolled up in a dress. Her mother would have loved to see that. Audra had even worn high heels and makeup. She chuckled at the memory, but it was cut short as she remembered the day she'd watched her mom take her last breath.

She punched the gas and did a U-turn.

Too much pain. Too much sorrow. And this town brought it all back.

She passed the marina's entrance and drove through the center of town. Massey's Pub was lit up like the Fourth of July. Those hunters who hadn't gone back out into the Everglades were hanging out, bragging about the snakes they'd caught—or exaggerating about the size of the ones that had gotten away.

She squinted and eased her foot off the gas, staring at the two men Dawson had arrested for bring dynamite to the python hunt. "What the hell are those two still doing in town?" she whispered. "And with Benson." She really needed to stop talking to herself. But seriously, that was a weird trio. One that didn't make sense.

One of the city boys turned his head, and she swore he smiled at her, but that was impossible. She was across the street and hidden behind tinted windows.

She took the turn at the light. Harvey's Cabins was

the next left. Harvey always had an opening. The cabins weren't much to write home about. They were small one-room suites with a bed, a sofa, a TV, a table with two chairs, and a small kitchenette. They were clean-*ish*.

She knew this because, as a teenager, she had been the one cleaning the rooms, and sometimes, she'd worked behind the desk. Now, Harvey had stepped up his game and gone to self-check-ins after ten. Well, she was going to get there just before that, so it would be nice to see the old man. He had been mostly kind to her and her dad. She wouldn't call him a friend, but Harvey didn't bother much with gossip.

Of course, Lilly could still be working there, and that would be awkward, like most of their encounters.

Pulling into the parking lot, her jaw dropped. Damn, this place had changed. Most of the cabins looked as though they'd gotten a facelift or were getting one.

She parked in front of the trailer, snagged her small purse, and made a beeline for the door. It was still sticky as hell. But it was summer, and in Florida in August, you could fry an egg on the sidewalk.

The door opened, and Audra's heart dropped to her toes.

Lilly.

"Oh. Hello, Audra," Lilly said, waving an envelope. "I was just leaving this for you in the overnight box."

Audra checked her watch. Fifteen minutes before ten. Yeah, that sounded about right for Lilly, especially if Harvey wasn't around. In the past, she'd always come in late, left early, and made other people do the work she hadn't wanted to do.

"Since you're here, I'll just hand it to you." Lilly stretched out her hand. "There have been a few changes around this place and few new rules since Harvey passed."

"Harvey died?" Damn, that sucked. "What happened?"

"Heart attack. Just dropped dead about six months ago. His wife didn't want to deal with this place, so she sold it."

"To you?"

Lilly laughed. "No. My husband and I don't really have the funds or the time. Our new chief of police is the proud owner. I'm his manager—the eyes and ears of this place." Lilly pointed toward the street. "Here comes our chief now."

"And he puts up with you leaving early?" Audra wanted to ask who in their right mind would marry Lilly, but she decided to refrain.

"Wow, you haven't changed." Lilly folded her hands and tapped her toe on the wood porch.

Okay, so maybe that was a bitch move, but she and Lilly had never liked each other. Ever. Mostly because Lilly had had a thing for Ken. Lilly had been a grade ahead of Ken but the same age. She'd always run around bragging about how she'd skipped a grade and was planning on getting a scholarship to an Ivy League school so she could get the hell out of Calusa Cove.

Well, that had never happened, and she'd landed in community college forty minutes away. But Audra never knew what had happened after that because she'd left.

Dawson's patrol car rolled to a stop, and he slipped from the driver's side. God, that man was sexy, especially in his uniform. He had a five o'clock shadow that gave him this rugged look. He wasn't too tall, perhaps six foot one or two, and he was thick. Not so much that he looked like a bodybuilder, but enough bulk that no one would dare mess with him if they came across him in a dark alley.

"Lilly, what on earth are you still doing here? I told you it was fine to go home whenever you needed. That's what self-check-in is for," he said.

Lilly smiled.

Audra sighed. More like her hormones melted.

"Hondo's flight was delayed. He should be rolling in about twenty minutes from now," Lilly said.

"What about the kids?" Dawson leaned against the post.

"My mom took them out for burgers and putt-putt golf," Lilly said. "I did hire someone for the evening shift. He starts on Monday. So, I'll be going back to my regular hours."

"Good." Dawson nodded.

"Before I forget," Lilly said. "Those two guys in cabin three have not checked out."

"Yeah. I noticed that in the app." Dawson nodded. "Nothing we can do about it."

"Should I be worried?" Lilly asked.

"I don't think so, but I've got my guys keeping an eye on them. If you see anything that makes you uncomfortable, call me or one of my deputies."

"Will do. I better get going," Lilly said.

"Have a nice night." Dawson squeezed her shoulder.

"See you around." Lilly waved, then stole a glance at Audra. "Enjoy the cabin. We put you in number nine. It's completely renovated. You're going to love it."

"Thanks." Audra blinked a few times. "But wait a second," she said. "You and Hondo? Kids?" It wasn't that Audra couldn't see Hondo married with a couple of little ones running around. It was just that it was a struggle for Audra to believe that Hondo would marry anyone from Calusa Cove. He was one of those men who not only wanted out of this small town, but he had big plans. The kind of plans that didn't include someone like Lilly.

"Don't look so surprised." Lilly breezed past Audra, took the two steps off the porch, and turned. "Life around here might be mostly the same, but some of us change. If you need anything, I'll be here in the morning. Just stop by the office. I'm happy to help." With a strange spring in her step, Lilly strolled into the parking lot and got into a…minivan?

Damn.

"Grab your drone and follow me," Dawson said with a strained voice she hadn't heard before.

Not that she knew the man at all, but in the few hours she'd spent with him, he'd either been sarcastic—in a good way—or laid-back and calm.

This was not that.

"Where are we going?" she asked, trying not to give him the once-over, but that proved impossible. He filled out that uniform way too nicely.

"My place." He pointed to one of the cabins off to the

side. "It's been a long day. I need to change out of my uniform, and I want to examine that drone. So, let's get a move on."

"You're being aggressive."

"Sorry. I get ornery when I don't eat. I ordered takeout for both of us from Massey's. Burgers and onion rings. Should be here in twenty. Now, please." He waved his hand out in front.

"Onion rings?" She made her way back to her vehicle, popped the trunk, and pulled out the drone case.

"Yeah. Fletcher might've mentioned those were your favorite." Dawson chuckled. "I also got you extra pickles and made sure they put five times the amount of special sauce on the burger, which is just gross. You know that sauce is just ketchup, mayo, and hot sauce, right?"

"Yeah, but it's so flipping good." She flung the case over her shoulder. "You live in one of the cabins? What about Harvey's old house? Who bought that?"

"I did, and before you go asking what everyone else does, it's being renovated, and no, I'm not going to live in it. And I don't know what I'm going to do with it when it's done. Maybe I'll make it into a bed and breakfast or sell it. We'll see."

"What are you? Mr. Moneybags?" She followed behind him, watching his thigh—and ass muscles—flex with each step.

He chuckled. "No. But I have no family. No parents. No siblings. No wife or kids. When I first joined the Navy, I was in the Military Police, so I didn't have a lot of friends." He chuckled. "I lived on base, and for the first few years, in the barracks. When I moved off base before I became a SEAL, I lived with Keaton, Hayes, and Fletcher. The rent was dirt cheap."

"What about Ken?"

Dawson glanced over his shoulder. "He was married, and his wife was pregnant."

"Oh. Yeah." She'd never forget the day she'd learned that piece of news. He'd married a schoolteacher—a nice young girl from a good, normal family.

"Anyway, once we became SEALs, renting a big house seemed stupid. We were all deployed more than we were Stateside. So, back to the base we went. Well, all except Ken. The guys hated it. But I never minded. I don't need much—a bed to sleep in, a stove to cook my food on…."

"I get it. But that doesn't explain how you could afford to buy this place, the house, and start an airboat touring business." She stared at the front porch of the cabin, which used to be cabin number one, but now the sign that hung on one of the posts on the railing read: Watchdog.

That was cliché.

"I invested most of my paycheck." He shrugged. "And I took out a business loan. I happen to be good with numbers." He tapped his temple. "It's both a blessing and curse."

"Not sure how that could be a curse," she mumbled.

"I drive people nuts because, if the numbers don't line up, I have to know why." He tapped his fingers on the keypad of his cabin. "I'm always balancing the budget at the station and looking over the books with Everglades Overwatch, and while Lilly is amazing at keeping an eye on things for me here, she constantly tells me I'm micromanaging her when it comes to book-keeping."

"Not to be a gossip, but the Lilly I remember was a lazy worker, and all Harvey ever did was complain about her."

"I've never known her to be like that. She's a great manager. She does all the hiring but leaves the firing to me, which I get. I've only had to do it once." He pushed open the door and waved her in. "But she's told me what she used to be like, and Hondo has made many jokes about it."

"Still can't believe those two got married or that Hondo came back here after college. He had big plans. What on earth is he doing for a living?" She stepped into the cabin, and her breath caught in her lungs. This was not what she remembered. It still wasn't a five-star hotel, but it had all-new furniture that actually looked comfortable.

The sofa was leather—and appeared to be real, not that fake stuff. The table by the kitchenette sat four, not two. And the chairs were wooden, not metal.

The bed had a nice wooden headboard, and the pictures on the walls—well, she suspected these weren't hanging in other cabins because they were images of him and his team.

She set her bag on the coffee table and inched into the room. All the appliances were brand new. This guy must have spent a small fortune if he'd done this to the rest of the cabins.

"He works for a small private airline as a pilot out of

Naples. It's not a bad gig. He flies mostly rich corporate assholes. Occasionally, he gets government officials and a handful of movie stars and television personalities. Makes good money. I'm not sure why Lilly keeps working for me, but I'm damn grateful she does." He unclipped his weapon, discharged the chamber, and put it in a lockbox. "Give me five minutes to change." He opened a drawer and pulled out a shirt. Then he went to the closet and snagged a pair of jeans. "There's beer in the fridge if you'd like one. Or I've got liquor in the cabinet—no wine, if you're into that—but I can go back to the trailer. We keep small bottles of cheap stuff. I can get you some."

"Beer's fine."

He disappeared into the bathroom.

Damn, that man could talk when he got going.

She ran her fingers along the bed's footboard, ignoring the heat that filled her veins. Men generally didn't affect her on a primal level, but Dawson did a number on her mind, body, and everything in between.

She pressed her hand on the mattress. It wasn't too soft, but she wouldn't say it was hard. Actually, it was damn perfect. She hoped the bed in her cabin was just as nice. Making her way into the kitchen, she opened the fridge. "Jeez." It was fully stocked with fruits, veggies, eggs, fixings for a salad, and other healthy foods. She pulled out two longnecks, cracking them both open, before climbing up on one of the stools at the breakfast bar, which hadn't been a feature in the older version of this place.

She took a long swig of the cold brew. The bubbles

tickled her throat. Snagging her phone from her back pocket, she loaded the video from the drone. She'd watched it five times. Had she not been so nervous about being shot, she would have explored that island more because right before the damn thing got blown from the sky, the drone had caught a glimpse of something.

Only, she couldn't make out what it was—just that there were some wood scraps in the clearing. She tapped her notes app and found the one where she had the CliffsNotes version of all her thoughts regarding her father's disappearance—his death.

She rubbed her temple.

For years, all she remembered about that night was how her father had been adamant that the Everglades were being used to smuggle something in and out. That someone was back there moving either drugs or guns, or both, through Calusa Cove, and he was going to prove it. She'd seen the shack. The crates. And then the world went black.

That's what she thought she'd remembered.

But she'd also had this dream where she blinked open her eyes, and someone pushed her father overboard. That she screamed and reached over the side of the boat to save him, but it was too late.

Not only did his body disappear into the murky water, but someone tossed in gator chum. Bubbles appeared. Then tails kicked up.

And then a sharp pain filled her skull, and once again, the world went black.

However, that had been her nightmare. She'd had it

for six months nearly every night after her dad had disappeared. She'd wake up in a cold sweat. Eventually, it had gone away, and she'd done her best to forget.

And she'd never told anyone about the dream—except Ken and Trip.

Ken had told her it was a dream, that it wasn't real.

Trip had told her to keep those thoughts to herself because no one would believe her—they would twist it into thinking she was the one who'd pushed her father overboard.

That's what had happened anyway.

Her dad had considered alligators to be his friends. Most people believed him to be a gator whisperer. If he could have had one as an emotional support animal, he would have. He had been one of the few people who could get close to a big one. He could touch one, and it wouldn't do anything other than maybe scurry away. He had been the guy people called when gators got in their pools—or got too close for comfort. Hell, even animal control would call him for help.

So, to be taken out by one... That haunted her in so many ways.

However, when she'd seen that silhouette standing on her boat, that nightmare had snapped back into place. No blurry motion. No foggy imagery.

It was fucking real. As real as her red hair. Someone had pushed her father into the water, and she'd seen it with her own eyes.

*Knock. Knock.*

She jumped, falling off the stool. Luckily, she landed

on her feet. She strolled to the front of the cabin. She glanced out the curtain.

Delivery boy.

She opened the door.

"I've got an order for the chief," the young man said.

"What does he owe you?"

"Already paid," the kid said. "Tip taken care of, too." He handed her the bag. "Tell the chief I said thanks."

"Will do."

The smell of crunchy fried onion rings filled her nostrils. No one made better fried foods than Massey's. She should boycott the damn place, considering the way Paul had treated her earlier, but her stomach growled like a grizzly. However, there weren't many options in this town—a greasy spoon, a place down by the marina that did mostly fresh-caught fish and chips, and another restaurant heading out of town, but their food tasted like cardboard on a good day.

The door to the bathroom opened, and steam poured out, carrying with it the fresh scent of pine, musk, and...she wasn't sure. A spice of some kind. Whatever it was, it sent her hormones into overdrive.

Wonderful. She was attracted to the wrong kind of men. Even Ken, for as much as she'd believed she'd loved him—and he'd claimed to have loved her—had wanted her to change. He'd wanted her to be less her father's daughter and more like a normal girl.

Whatever that meant. And it wasn't ever going to happen.

Their breakup hadn't been just about what

happened that night. It was more complex than that, and their problems had started before her father disappeared.

"You took a shower?" She set the bag on the counter.

"Trust me, I needed it. Not only did I smell like swamp, but if I didn't, I would've been a bigger asshole than I have been." He pulled out two plates from the cupboard, a couple of napkins, and two knives.

What the hell did she need utensils for?

He sat down beside her at the breakfast counter and went about pulling out his burger. The weirdo cut it in half.

"What are you doing?" She stared at him.

"Eating." He lifted half his bacon cheeseburger, which didn't appear to have any secret sauce, only mustard, and took a bite. It wasn't even a big bite.

"That's a dumb way to enjoy a burger." She lifted hers and brought it to her mouth. A massive amount of sauce landed on her bare thigh. Before she could wipe it off with her finger, he snagged a napkin and cleaned it up. "Hey, that was wasteful." Not that she minded feeling his hands across her leg.

He laughed and continued to munch on his food like a dainty human.

Of course, her co-workers back at the magazine thought she was a slob, which was kind of true, at least when it came to food. "I once took an assignment up in Western, New York."

"Really?" He jerked his head. "What kind of wildlife were you focusing on there?"

"Birds. American bitterns, Northern harrier hawks, owls, mallards, and blue-winged teal. I also saw a couple of bald eagles in my travels. Got some great images of woodchucks, beavers, and muskrats. But that's not where I was going with this conversation." She waved an onion ring. "Rochester isn't known for much. Kodak, which is basically gone. Cold weather. Snow. And the grossest beer known to man."

"Genesee Cream Ale." He lifted his longneck. "Disgusting."

"Can't imagine why anyone would want to drink that pisswater. But the one thing that Rochester does well is the—"

"Garbage plate." He lowered his chin. "I'm from Rochester. I grew up on those things. It's kind of the best drunk food ever." He leaned closer. "Not that I got drunk underage or anything."

"Now, how can you enjoy a good garbage plate and not eat a cheeseburger with Massey's special sauce?" She waved her hand over his plate. "And you cut yours in half. What the heck is that all about?"

"I have severe heartburn." He plopped the last bite in his mouth. "If I don't slow down the way I eat, especially when I treat myself to fried foods and stuff that stirs up my GERD, I'll be up all night, in pain, cussing myself out."

"Is that why there's all that healthy shit in that fridge?"

He shrugged. "My nana was always worried if I didn't get killed by a bullet, my diet would get me. So, I promised her before she died that I'd do my best not to let either one happen."

She wiped her fingers on her napkin. "I have no idea what to think of you."

"Trust me, the feeling is mutual. Now, break out that drone. I want to look at it and any pictures or video you took."

She gave him a mock glare. "You're bossy, too."

"I've been told that before," he said, jumping from the stool, wagging his long finger under her nose. "I also need to ask you a question about Paul Massey's son."

"What about him?"

"For starters, why would he accuse you of slashing his tire today?"

She jerked her head back. "While I *might* have done that when I was ten, right after my mom died because he called my father a crazy lunatic, I certainly wouldn't do that today. Not even if he got in my face, but I can't explain why he'd say I did that. I haven't even seen him up close and personal to say hello. Only from a distance. And the last time we spoke to one another was about the time my dad disappeared."

"That's a lot for me to unpack," Dawson said. "Hard for me to believe you'd have the balls to slash a tire at ten."

"He said some pretty nasty things to my dad. It was cruel, and it happened right after my mom passed. Benson had no idea I was there, and I was too young and stupid, so I got caught," she said. "Trip read me the riot act, but what was he going to do? Throw the book at a kid who was barely in the double digits?"

"I suppose nothing," he said, helping her off the stool and guiding her across the room like a real gentleman.

She wasn't used to that kind of treatment. She opened the case and handed him the damaged drone. "See that?" She pointed.

"Yeah." He nodded. "Looks like a bullet hole to me." He narrowed his stare. "I want to bring this to the office in the morning and examine it more closely."

"I guess I'll let you do that," she said. "Here." She pulled up the video and shoved her cell in his face. She shouldn't trust him. He lived in Calusa Cove, and everyone who did was against her. Believed the worst—as proven by Benson's accusation. But everything about Dawson seemed different. He listened. He didn't shove her thoughts and opinions to the side. No. He treated her with respect.

Much like Trip had.

"Look at the last frame of the video. You can see wood scattered on the ground." She tapped at the screen.

He brought it closer. "I don't know. It's awfully fuzzy. Could be anything."

"Seriously, that's all you got?" Her pulse froze in her throat. "Look again."

"I am looking, and while it could be what you say, this video doesn't prove anything."

She should have known. "You're just like everyone else." She gathered her things, shoved them back in the case, and headed for the door. She didn't need his help. She didn't need anyone. She'd figure this out all on her own. She'd go back out there tomorrow…if she ever got her boat fixed.

And she'd go visit Trevor in prison.

She'd make him own what he'd done, and he'd rot there for the rest of his pathetic life.

# CHAPTER 7

"Put that down." Dawson grabbed the drone case from Audra's hand and tossed it to the sofa. He held her by the biceps.

Someone didn't want her out there. Whether it was because they didn't want her poking around that island or they didn't like her returning, he didn't know. But he was determined to find out. However, he couldn't do that if she was going to fight him every step of the way.

"Don't manhandle me." She shrugged her arms free. Her big teal-green eyes conveyed hurt, not anger, and he'd put that look there.

Why were redheads so damn feisty all the time?

"I'm not your problem. This isn't anything you need to concern yourself with." She bent over, reaching for the bag.

"Oh, for fuck's sake," he mumbled, stepping between her and the door. "I'm trying to help you. Just because I don't see what you do doesn't mean I don't believe you. Why can't you see that?"

"You belittled me, and you…you…" She blinked, staring at him with her mouth gaping open.

He raked his fingers through his damp hair. "I would never do that, and tomorrow, I'll go to that island and look around."

She narrowed her eyes as if she hadn't heard what he'd said. "I can handle that myself." She planted her hands on her hips and glared. Her green eyes shot daggers. If looks could kill, he'd been dead.

"Absolutely not."

"You can't tell me what to do."

She was worse than Lilly's four-year-old when he threw a temper tantrum. "If you go out there alone, I'm worried something bad will happen. Someone shot down your drone and screwed with your boat. Put dynamite on it, and we don't know the intent. None of those things were accidents. Don't be too stupid to live."

Her eyes grew wide. She gasped.

Damn. He'd really botched that one.

"You've got some nerve. How dare you say something like that to me." She raised her hand, finger pointed as if to poke him in the chest. "Wait. What?" She blinked a dozen times rapidly as if the last ten minutes had finally registered.

"Is it so hard to comprehend that I believe every word you're telling me?" He cocked a brow. "Now, why don't you calm down and I'll tell you what I plan on doing and what I need you to do, to keep you safe from whoever wants you to go away."

Her eyes turned to tiny little slits again.

Shit. He always managed to say the wrong thing.

"Who the hell do you think you are telling me to calm down? I don't need some two-bit small-town cop to protect me. You're a bully and a control freak."

He sighed. "Jesus, you're worse than Liz," he mumbled. "I didn't mean any of it that way. I'm really on your side. I swear."

"Who the hell is Liz?"

"My ex-girlfriend." He waved his hand over the top of her head. "Redhead, just like you, and thought I was a bastard and sexist pig."

"I think Liz and I could've been friends."

He bent over, grabbing his knees, and burst out laughing. Picturing the two of them even having a conversation was more than he could take. Talk about oil and water.

"I don't see what's so funny." She tossed the bag back on the sofa, turned, and snagged her beer, chugging the rest of it. She placed the bottle on the counter. Then, her lips curved into a smile.

At least now, he'd managed to amuse the woman. That was a start.

Leaning against the door, he cleared his throat. "Of all the women I dated in my life, Liz was the only one who wasn't outdoorsy. Nope. She was the designer handbag, fake nails, and weekly hair salon kind of girl. And those expensive shoes. I can't stand shoes like that. Between the red hair and those damn heels, I should've known."

"You have a thing against redheads?"

"Unfortunately, I have a thing *for* redheads. I just

don't like expensive shoes. Hell, I don't like anyone who wastes money on frivolous things." He waggled his finger. "You don't strike me as the kind of woman who would drop a grand on a handbag."

"I wouldn't spend that kind of money on anything other than a gun."

He chuckled. "That's why I was laughing. Liz would've hated you, and I'm sure the feeling would've been mutual. A daddy longlegs made her squeal like she was about to be eaten by a gator."

"That's kind of a mean thing to say about your ex."

"You should hear what she has to say about me." He chuckled. "Of course, I would've proven one or two of her points with how I fumbled through this conversation when all I'm trying to do is show you that I want to help figure this out."

"You're forgiven for your fumble," she said. "Outside of the hair, why did you date her if she wasn't your type?"

"I was trying something new since I have terrible luck with the ladies." That was an understatement.

"Maybe it's not the women that's the problem, but you?" She sipped. "Ever think about that?" She tilted her head and smiled as if she just won the grand prize.

"You're funny." He pushed from the door. "Get me another one, and let's sit down and talk calmly."

"Stop ordering me around, and I'll be more receptive. I mean, I don't dislike you or anything. As a matter of fact, I find you rather…interesting." She pulled another longneck from the fridge, pulled the top off it, and handed it to him. "But there is nothing worse than a man who barks orders like a buffoon."

"I apologize. It's been a long day." He chuckled. "And is being interesting a compliment?"

"From me, it is." She smiled. "Oh. Before we went off the rails, I wanted to tell you that I saw those two city boys you and Remy arrested at Massey's Pub tonight when I drove by. It looked like they were deep in conversation with Benson."

"With Benson? Seriously? I stopped at Massey's before I came home to chat with those two idiots, and I didn't see Benson." He took a seat on the sofa, lifted his legs, and stretched them out, resting his feet on the coffee table. "Those two are one of the reasons I'm in a foul mood. They're renting a cabin here, and I can't legally kick them out."

"That makes me nervous, considering what those two did."

"Me, too." He sighed, rounding his shoulders and contemplating why he not only trusted a woman he'd just met but why he'd break all the rules for another redhead. "Can you keep your distance from them?" He tossed back half his beer.

"I can promise I won't start anything since I don't know them, but I won't keep my mouth closed if they come at me."

"Fair enough." He patted his hand on the cushion. "Can you be quiet for ten minutes while I tell you what my plan is?"

"Yeah." She plopped down next to him. "But can I say

something first?" She tilted her head and battled her eyelashes.

This woman was going to be the death of him. "Sure."

"Since my return, I remember things."

"You mentioned that, and I want to get to that topic when I'm done."

"Okay, but I'm wondering if maybe Trevor Williams could've had something to do with my dad's death." She arched a brow.

"That thought has crossed my mind in the last couple of hours, but he wasn't a cop at the time of your dad's disappearance." He'd be a fool not to wonder that based on what he'd learned about Trevor's past—not to mention how Trevor had made it possible for the drugs to come right through Calusa Cove from Mexico. While the DEA had shut down that particular run, Trevor had only been able to give up one name, and by the time the DEA had gotten to that man, he was dead.

They knew the cartel was running the drugs into the country through other means. Trevor had told everyone that's all he'd known about. His role had been to turn a blind eye and let the ships and trucks pass right on through town—or run interference.

Dawson didn't buy it. Trevor knew more. Either he was afraid, or he had been promised something to keep his mouth shut.

Like protection in prison. Protection for his family.

Or both.

However, something had been going on in the Everglades long before that.

As well, Dawson had another dilemma he needed to deal with, and that was how much to tell Audra about his personal thoughts and how much digging he planned on doing.

"He left town shortly after my dad disappeared," she said. "Don't you find that suspicious?"

Good Lord. She was a rabid Chihuahua. "Maybe, but answer me this—when did Benson leave town?"

She narrowed her stare. "Maybe a year earlier. He got a job in Miami. I don't know what he was doing, but he didn't get into trouble like Trevor did. We should talk to Trevor."

"There is no *we*, and it's time for you to listen." He pinched the bridge of his nose. "Tomorrow, I'm going to let you use my personal airboat and drone."

"Gee, that's mighty big of you."

He turned and glared. The more she opened her mouth, the more he wanted to do one of two things—either lift her off the sofa and toss her out into the humid night or toss her on his bed and shut her up in other ways.

There was something very wrong with him. This combativeness between the two of them shouldn't be such a turn-on.

"I was being sarcastic. It comes with the hair." She raised her hand. "Go on."

"I have some police work I have to do in the morning, so I'm not thrilled about sending you out there alone, but Hayes is going to be right on your tail as much as he can be without it looking creepy."

"Sounds like fun, though I'd rather have you on my tail."

He closed his eyes and counted to ten before opening them again. If she made one more snide remark, he was going to hush her by sticking his tongue in her mouth.

Yeah, he had issues.

He cleared his throat. "You and I will have long-range walkie-talkies so we can communicate. You will go about python hunting like you want that damn prize money." He lowered his chin. "When I'm done with cop stuff, I'll have Fletcher or Keaton drop me off at that island, and I'll poke around. When I'm done, you'll pick me up, and we'll finish out the day hunting together. Any questions?"

"Won't people wonder about how you ended up on my boat or why you're there?"

"No, because it's my boat, and if anyone asks, it was always the plan. You can even mention it when you go out. I'll bring it up when I see people at the docks when I leave." He jerked his hand over his shoulder. "Five people from the challenge watched you walk into my cabin. They'll think my concern is about you being out there alone and the fact you're using my boat. It's a simple, easy plan."

"Are you kidding me? The last thing I need is people gossiping about me and the chief of police."

And that's all it took. He fisted her thick, lush hair into his hand and crash-landed his lips on her mouth. His tongue snagged hers, twisting and turning. Heat rolled across his skin like flames reaching out from a fire. He waited for the slap. Waited for her to push him away. Waited for that saucy mouth of hers to tear into him like a viper.

Instead, he got full participation. Her chest heaved up and down with every raspy breath, pressing into his body, reminding him of exactly how long it had been since he'd had sex.

Then she really did the unexpected. She tore off her shirt and straddled him, licking her plump, juicy lips.

He stared at her lacy black bra. She was full of surprises. "What are you doing?"

"Did you start something you had no intention of finishing?" She reached behind her back.

He swallowed. Hard. "No," he said, then managed a throaty groan. "But I honestly didn't expect you to go along with it. I mean, the gossip and all."

"Yeah, well, it's too late for that now, isn't it? Might as well give this town something else to talk about tomorrow morning at the docks." She unhooked her bra, letting the garment fall to his stomach.

"Small, but not itty-bitty." He gripped her thighs, stood, and strolled across the room toward the bed. He'd lived in Harvey's Cabins the entire time he'd been in Calusa Cove, and not once had he had a woman spend the night. Hell, he hadn't had sex with a woman who was from Calusa Cove. The one chick he'd been with had been from Naples. What a mistake that had been.

Audra wrapped her legs around his waist. "Oh my God. I can't believe you just said that."

"Perhaps you were right. It's not the ladies—it's me."

"Yeah. Because I have horrible taste in men, too."

"I can't be that bad." He laid her on the mattress and climbed on next to her, running his finger down the center of her chest. "You're half-naked in my bed." God, she was beautiful.

"Maybe I have low standards."

"I should be insulted."

"But you're not." She cupped his face. "Just like I wasn't when you made the dumbass comment about my breasts."

He cupped one, fanning his thumb across the taut nipple. "They're actually perfect." Leaning over, he took the other nipple into his mouth, ignoring the little voice in the back of his head reminding him that he was tangling himself up with another redhead.

A guttural moan escaped her sweet lips. She arched her back as she grappled with his shirt.

Even though he had no desire to stop what he was doing, he did want to remove some of his clothing. He raised his head, ripped off his shirt, and tossed it across the room.

Her hands splayed across his chest. "What happened?" She fingered one of his jagged scars before moving on to one where a bullet had torn into his body.

Lifting her hand, he kissed her palm. "War wounds."

"And this?" She kissed the burn marks.

"Nothing you want to hear about right now." He inched down the side of the bed, dotting kisses on her firm belly. This was not a woman he'd want to go head-to-head with. Her muscles were well-defined. She was strong. He fiddled with the button on her shorts, tugging them to her ankles and staring at her tiny, lacy thong.

Not what he'd imagined her wearing.

He'd pictured her more of a boy shorts kind of girl. Of course, he wasn't complaining. He rolled her panties over her hips, off her body, and flung them. All that remained was a little landing strip and a tattoo of an alligator. He chuckled, bending over to press his lips to the gator.

"You like that?"

"The gator? Or this?" He lifted her leg, resting it on his shoulder, and licked her, opening her and catching her hard clit, swirling his tongue over the hard nub until her hips jerked.

She clutched the comforter and groaned.

"Both are pretty damn sexy." He slipped his finger inside, stroking gently, while his other hand cupped her perfectly round breast, thumbing her tight nipple as it puckered under his touch. He loved the way her body responded. "Can't say I've seen a woman with a tattoo in that spot," he whispered, mesmerized by the woman before him. His gaze drifted over her body, soaking in every inch. Every crevice. Every freckle.

God, he loved freckles.

Her slightly darker skin was dotted with them everywhere, and he wanted to kiss each one.

"Do you always like to watch yourself work?" she cooed with a sexy voice that made his toes curl.

"What man doesn't?" He waggled his brows. "Especially when I can make you squirm and moan when I do this." He leaned over, bringing his lips to her body once again, sucking at first, then gently lapping, savoring every lick. She tasted like pineapples drizzled in coconut juice.

He'd died and gone to heaven.

"You're so...strange." She chuckled, squirming beneath his touch. The words seemed to blend in a weird sort of harmony with the silence that had taken over the room—only broken by their quiet whispers and the occasional moan. "In a good way."

"I'll take that as a compliment." He kissed his way up her body, giving each breast the attention it deserved, before gently nibbling on her lower lip and pulling her closer as he continued to explore her body. Every inch of her skin felt like a new territory, uncharted and alluring. Her reactions to his touch were intoxicating—enough to make him forget the world outside his cabin.

"Do I need to reach for protection?" he whispered, looking into her sexy green eyes while his fingers delved deeper, curling upward, causing her to moan and her hips to rise. There was an intensity in her gaze, a question buried beneath layers of confidence and carnal desire.

He wasn't sure what to make of that. She'd come here with a boatload of baggage and a massive chip on her shoulder. She trusted no one, including him, and he didn't blame her for that.

But he wasn't the enemy, and she was naked in his arms, moaning in perfect pleasure.

"I'm on the pill, and it's been a very long time." She responded breathlessly, her nails digging into the muscular expanse of his back. It was as if she were desperate, which wasn't her at all.

Not that he knew her, but he knew enough.

She tugged at his jeans. Her deft little fingers had them unbuttoned and unzipped before he could blink. She curled her fingers around his length, and he hissed. His breath caught in his throat. He couldn't expand his lungs. Nor could he release the air trapped inside.

As quickly as he could, he kicked himself out of his pants.

This was different than what he'd been used to in the last couple of years of his dating life. This wasn't a fling or a one-night stand. This was raw, unhinged—an exploration of desire and lust that had been buried deep within since they'd first met.

And then she did something entirely unexpected once again.

She pushed him onto his back and straddled him, her eyes glowing fiercely in the dim light of his cabin. Not in submission but in equal desire. He could see it— she wasn't just along for the ride; she wanted to feel just as much control as he did. It was intoxicating, addictive even.

"Jesus," he gasped as she pushed herself onto him, a wave of pleasure washing over him like wildfire. A low growl escaped his lips as he gripped her hips firmly and let her take control.

She rode him hard and fast, matching his every thrust with fierce intent that made his entire body tingle with pleasure. He lost himself in the rhythm of their bodies, the way her small breasts bounced with each movement, and the way her fiery hair cascaded over her shoulders. He bit down on his lip to suppress a groan as he felt himself nearing the edge. Squeezing his eyes closed, he did whatever he could to make this last.

For her.

"Look at me," she commanded, her voice straining with the kind of greed that drove a man wild. Her hands gripped his shoulders, nails digging into his skin as she rode him relentlessly.

He opened his eyes and met hers—looking into the depths of the thirst she held within. It was like diving into an ocean that was both wild and captivating at the same time. His heart pounded in his chest.

Together, they drowned out the last remaining echoes of their worries and fears, leaving only pure, unadulterated lust in its wake.

And when they finally found release, they didn't just climax. They exploded together. She screamed his name so loudly he was sure everyone renting a cabin heard it, while he clung to her fiercely as if his life depended on it. As if he were drowning in her.

Moments later, when they collapsed together on the bed, panting heavily and bathing in the afterglow, neither cared about reputation or rumors anymore—at least, he hoped she didn't.

They had wanted each other. Craved each other. Maybe even needed each other.

And they hadn't just given the town something to talk about—they'd given themselves a night they would remember for a lifetime.

He pulled the covers over their naked bodies and

held her close, tangling his hand in her fireball of thick hair.

She rested her head on her chest, her fingers dancing on his scars. Once again, she kissed the burn marks. A constant reminder of what had happened. Of life lost.

Of his many failures.

"Well, that was incredibly awesome and totally unexpected," she said.

He chuckled. "You took the words right out of my mouth."

She rested her chin on his shoulder. "So, are you going to tell me about these scars?"

He sucked in a deep breath and let it out slowly. "There are too many, and none of the stories are good." He kissed her forehead. "They don't make for good after-sex chatter."

"I think a therapist would have a field day with how we ended up in this bed."

"Probably right about that." One thing he knew for sure about him and women, he sucked at relationships. He could get a girl but couldn't keep one. It all came down to four things.

He was too bossy.

Too honest.

Cared more about his buddies.

And had war wounds that messed with his head.

Not necessarily in that order.

"Are you going to tell me?" she asked.

"You're like a dog with a bone."

"How about you tell me about one? Just one. Then

I'll tell you something about myself. Anything you want to know. I promise to be honest."

Sounded like a fair trade. "Okay. Which one do you want to know about?"

"The burns." She arched a brow.

"No," he said. "Any other but that one."

"Can I ask why?"

He shook his head. "Maybe another day." No way would he tell her about the day Ken had died, not after just having sex. A wave of guilt hit his heart like a bullet.

Ex-girlfriends had always been off-limits, and this was Ken's ex. Didn't matter that it had been sixteen years ago. Or that Ken was dead.

Because the latter was partly his fault.

"Okay." She tapped her finger on the bullet hole in the center of his chest—the one that had almost killed him. "How about this one?"

"Leave it to you to pick the two I hate talking about most." He sighed. "But I made you a deal, so this one it is." He rubbed the old wound. "It was six years ago. The guys and I were sent to an undisclosed area for an unsanctioned mission."

"What does that even mean?"

"Basically, when shit goes sideways, the government doesn't take responsibility; we're on our own."

"That sucks for you."

"It does." He nodded. "I was the team leader. I was responsible for the mission and for the men. We went in with our orders, but things got dicey real quick. I got new intel on the ground and had to make a split-second decision." Mindlessly, he continued to run his hand over the scar. He hadn't even felt the bullet tear through his body. "I acted on the information, shifting our plans but not our mission. I had the full support of my team, but in all fairness, they only had about four minutes to either agree or disagree. If we hadn't acted, we could've come home and faced disciplinary actions for failing to follow orders."

"That doesn't sound good."

"It's not, but it wouldn't have been the first time," he said. "Anyway. We executed the mission, only some of the intel was bogus. That was my bad. I put my men in danger."

"Who else got shot?"

"No one on my team," he said softly. "And as for the assets we were there to extract, my men did so. Unfortunately, because of my decision, twenty innocent civilians died that day. Fifteen men and women and five children." He closed his eyes and turned away. He couldn't believe he'd told that story. He hadn't spoken of it since it had happened. Since some stupid-ass Navy shrink had made him before he'd been approved to go back to active duty. The next couple of years had passed without incident. Well, not really, but at least he hadn't been responsible for any civilian deaths.

Sure, people had died, and he might have killed a few not-so-innocent enemies. But nothing to feel guilty about.

Until Ken.

Whether or not the rest of his team had wanted to retire from the Navy after that, Dawson was done.

So was Fletcher.

But Hayes and Keaton had been just as deeply affected. They'd all pushed aside their re-enlistment papers and walked.

A warm palm cupped his cheek, turning his head. He blinked.

"So, is that one of the reasons you became a cop instead of something else, like the rest of the guys on your team?"

"That's very Freudian of you."

"It's an honest question." She pursed her lips.

"I suppose that's what my psyche eval would say." He chuckled, giving her a quick kiss, trying desperately to lighten the mood, but it was impossible. The damage had been done. "I took one of those aptitude and personality tests my senior year in high school. The personality part ranked me the highest in protective instincts and loyalty. The aptitude part put me in a career as a cop or the military." He shrugged.

"Looks like you've stayed true to who you are."

"I followed my instincts." He rolled to his side and waggled his brows.

"You're cute." She smiled.

"Just what a man of my age wants to hear." He batted her freckled nose. "Your turn. Tell me something a lot of people don't know about you. Or maybe something that would shock me."

Her smile faded, and her eyes glazed over. "I'm scared. For the first time in a long while, I'm really afraid."

Well, now that damn near broke his heart. He wiped the single tear that dribbled down her cheek.

"Someone killed my dad. I know it. I remember blinking open my eyes that night after... after..." She hiccupped. "I don't know. Things went black. Then I saw my dad being pushed into the water. The alligators got him. I saw all the tails. Someone was chumming the waters. And then there was a sharp pain in my head again. I don't know why they left me out there. Maybe they thought I was dead. Or figured I'd die out there before dawn. I did lose some blood from a wound on my head. I was disoriented, dehydrated and—"

"Hey. Slow down. We don't have to talk about this right now."

"But do you believe me? That it wasn't a dream? That it was real? Please, you've got to believe me."

He kissed her. Softly. Tenderly. Lovingly. "Yes. I believe you. And I'm going to look into this. I've already pulled your dad's file. I'm going to talk to those who Trip interviewed. I'll reach out to any law enforcement he worked with. I'm not going to let it just sit there when something doesn't settle right in my gut."

She wrapped her arms around his body. "Thank you."

"Technically, I'm just doing my job."

"Giving me an orgasm has nothing to do with being the chief of police."

He chuckled. "You're giving me whiplash."

"Get used to it. I don't like being emotional."

"Anger and sarcasm are emotions, and you do those two just fine."

She pinched his nipple. Hard.

"Ouch. That hurt."

"Good. Because saying things like that won't get me out of my panties again."

"That would be a damn shame. I liked your itty-bitty thong." He burst out laughing.

"Dawson, that's really not that funny."

He cleared his throat. "I thought it was," he mumbled, letting out a long breath. Why did he have to have a type?

# CHAPTER 8

Audra tossed the snake bag into the boat's bow and climbed aboard. Three pythons. One five feet. One nine feet. And one twelve feet. Not too shabby for the second day. Actually, that was a fantastic day. She should be jumping up and down for joy. Many would come in without a single one in their bags. Catching snakes was not easy. It took patience. Skill.

And more importantly, luck. But she honestly had other things on her mind.

She glanced at her watch. Frustration needled her insides. It was almost two in the afternoon and still no word from Dawson. She pressed her fingers to her lips. Damn, that man could kiss.

She pushed the boat from Hog's Island. She'd purposely kept her distance from the island past Gator Junction and stayed closer to civilization. She would have been combing that place for the shack if she hadn't. But she'd made a promise to Dawson this morning over breakfast.

It was the least she could do after he'd not only made her pancakes but had given her two orgasms before she'd crawled out of bed. He certainly knew his way around a woman's body.

She let the boat float in the open water and stared at the blue sky. What the hell had she been thinking? Jumping into bed with Dawson wasn't the smartest thing she'd ever done. She needed his help. Nothing more, nothing less. Becoming involved would only bring trouble with a capital *T*. It could lead to more heartbreak, and Lord knew she'd had enough of that.

The death of her mother. Her father.

The breakup with Ken, though that had been for the best. No amount of love would've saved that relationship after her father had gone missing. Ken had never really understood her dad. He'd tolerated him. He'd pretended to accept his quirks.

But he hadn't understood that Audra would never have left Calusa Cove as long as her father still breathed.

When her dad had disappeared, Ken had expected her to follow him to the Navy. As in, the second she graduated from high school, she was supposed to be on a bus to wherever he ended up stationed. All in the name of taking care of her.

Audra didn't need anyone to be her savior.

What she'd desperately needed was someone to believe in her. To believe in what she'd seen, what she knew to be true, and that was her father hadn't been crazy—and neither was she.

She leaned back and let out a sigh.

Her life after Ken had been riddled with one ridiculous bad relationship after the other. If Dawson thought he had bad luck, well, he'd just met his match.

Her dating history read like a serial killer novel. Not that she dated killers—because she didn't. But they'd all turned out to be a little crazy. Of course, they'd blamed her for how badly things had ended up. And maybe they'd been right. She wasn't an easy person. And she didn't particularly like people.

One guy had described her as a constant ball of angst and anger.

Another one had told her she was emotionally detached—except for in bed. But the sex hadn't been that great, so she'd happily walked away.

Oh, who was she kidding? People strolled into her life—then ran away because she could be an utter bitch.

The sound of a boat fast approaching caught her attention.

Freaking Silas. He was like a bad rash that wouldn't go away. It was the second time she'd run into him today. At least she knew Hayes was somewhere close by.

Nice guy. Cute, too. Though not her type. Did she have a type?

Yeah. She did. Brooding, a little grumpy at times, with a wicked sense of humor and sexy as hell. Kind of like Dawson.

Silas slowed his boat down, but not quickly enough because he nudged hers. "Sorry about that, little girl." He smiled, adjusting his cap and peering inside. "Ah. Caught yourself a couple, did ya?"

"Why do you care?"

"Other than those things don't belong out here, I don't." He shrugged. "But then again, neither do you." He cocked his head. "Heard you moved in with the chief of police. Got him snowed now, don't ya?"

"I have no idea what you're talking about." She'd forgotten how quickly news traveled in this town. However, she hadn't moved in with Dawson. She'd agreed to stay with him, freeing up one of his cabins so he could rent it to someone who'd had the unfortunate mishap of having car trouble. It was some fancy foreign thing, and it would be a few days before it was fixed—even with Trinity's connection. Who was she to say no? So, she agreed to let Dawson move her into his place.

What difference did it make? She enjoyed his company. He was witty and good in bed. And he had agreed to help her.

"Right," Silas sneered. "Tell me, after all these years, why did you come back?"

"Does it matter?"

"Of course it does." Silas gripped the side of her boat as waves from another boat zipping by crashed into them.

It wasn't an airboat, but a small flat-bottom Whaler. She squinted, staring at the man behind the steering wheel. He wasn't a local. The boat wasn't a rental. She had to question why he was out in these waters. She also wondered if he was the same man who had boarded her boat yesterday, but she couldn't be sure.

"It's not that anyone has forgotten your dad—because we haven't. But we've accepted the mystery. It's become part of our history. Having you show your face stirs up all the unanswered questions—the legends, both real and made up." He arched a brow. "You frighten the town."

She swallowed the thick lump in her throat. "Why? Because my grandmother was Native American, gypsy, and a dash of Irish? And my dad was a hundred percent Irish, making me this weird mix of red hair with a mom who'd stapled herself in her Native American history? Her people saw me as something unique, something special. Everyone else here saw me as a swamp monster."

"What you fail to understand was that your behavior made everyone think of you as someone who practiced some weird kind of witchcraft." Silas waved his index and middle finger between his eyes and pointed toward hers, mimicking what she used to do to people when she'd come into town as a small child, barefoot, in ratty clothes with wild, uncombed red hair, and everyone would stare.

They all forgot her mother had been dying. That she'd sat at her bedside, holding her hand, and had eventually watched her take her last breath. Her father's mind had finally fractured between reality and fantasy. He'd known it and had done his best to keep one foot in the real world, but one couldn't control mental illness on their own.

"If your father had only allowed me to help—if you had allowed me to help," Silas said in the same kind voice he'd used when he'd found her floating in these same waters years ago. The same voice he'd used when he'd come by the house after her mother had died. It was as if the man cared.

But he didn't.

He sighed. "Go home, little girl," Silas said, "before something bad happens to you and your cop boyfriend can't help you."

"Are you threatening me?" She rested her hand on her air gun.

"Good God, no." He pursed his lips. "I've never been the enemy. But I'd feel terrible if a snake got you. Or a gator. Not to mention, everyone in this town believes you got away with murder." He leaned a little closer, gripping the side of her boat. "Did you do it, little girl? Did you murder your old man? Those questions have haunted me since you betrayed my trust and slinked out of this town like a coward."

"I'm not going to dignify that with an answer." She held his unnerving glare. "Now let go and leave me alone. There's room enough out here for both of us."

"Watch your back." He raised his hands. "And be careful who you take for a bed partner. He's not going to be able to help you if someone stabs you in the back." He arched a brow before engaging the gas and zooming off.

Jerk.

"Audra? Come in, Audra," the long-range walkie-talkie crackled.

Finally, she lifted the contraption. "Hey, Dawson."

"Hayes tells me it's been a fruitful day for you out there."

"Did he tell you that Silas just collided with my boat?"

"Well, no," Dawson said. "Are you okay?"

"Peachy. But Silas knows I'm staying in your cabin."

"Everyone knows you stayed there last night."

"No, I mean, like you moved my stuff in there today."

"Interesting. But I don't care," Dawson said. "Give me a second and let me radio Hayes. There was a problem a half hour ago, and he might still be dealing with that. I know he's not far from where you are. You're still in front of Hog's Island, right?"

"I am."

"All right. Don't move. I'll radio you back in a couple of minutes."

"Copy that." She rested the walkie-talkie in her lap. Part of her felt like a sitting duck. Hayes' job wasn't to watch her like a hawk. No. He was to ensure the safety of the hunters. While she'd only done two Python Challenges, she was well aware there were always a couple of guides—or Fish and Wildlife—out on the waters. She'd been surprised that Keaton and Fletcher also had at least two boats out. Then again, she figured that was because of her—and not because of her lack of experience—but also because of the bullshit that had happened yesterday and maybe because of the idiots Dawson had arrested.

Damn, she wished she knew what had happened with that.

"Audra, do you copy?" Dawson asked.

"Yeah, I'm here," she responded.

"Hayes is three bends over up the west second fork.

Someone had an incident with a python. I'm at the docks. I should be over to you in about a half hour, tops. Can you either hang in that area or head in my direction?"

"I'll put it in gear and start moving your way," she said.

"Just make sure you keep your eyes open."

"You sound like Silas," she mumbled into the walkie-talkie.

"Excuse me?" Dawson asked with a little bite to his words. "What exactly did he say to you?"

"I'll fill you in when I see you." She set the device on the dash. She shouldn't have gotten Dawson's hackles up more than they already were. Everyone had pretty much left her alone. No matter how much they didn't like her, no one was going to mess with the chief of police's personal boat.

At least, that's what she told herself.

A couple of eyes lifted from the water about ten feet from her boat. The creature moved slowly across the top.

"Wow. You're massive." She guessed the gator to be about fourteen feet. She wouldn't want to screw with that guy, no matter how beautiful he was.

A second later, two babies surfaced.

"Aw, aren't you cute?" But now, she definitely wanted to keep her distance. Mama alligators were worse than mama bears. That was until their babies got to a certain age, then they ate their young.

She shivered.

*Bang! Bang! Bang!*

She jumped, falling off the bench and landing on the bottom of the boat. At least she didn't land in the water. Her heart thumped in her chest like a jackhammer. Leaning over the side, she searched for the alligators, but they were long gone, lurking somewhere in the dark, murky waters of the Everglades.

Glancing toward the sky and scanning the area, she searched for the source of gunfire. The roar of an engine tickled her ears. An airboat came into view as it rounded the bend. It slowed as it approached.

Tim O'Toole stood behind the helm, waving his fist. "You are fucking crazy, woman. What the hell are you doing?"

A second boat maneuvered around Tim's, going a bit slower. It wasn't someone she recognized. Whoever it was, they pointed and hurled a couple of obscenities in her direction.

Her heartbeat pulsated in her throat like a python wrapping around its prey, constricting and slowly killing it.

"I don't know who you think you are, but you won't get away with this." Tim raced off.

She exhaled sharply, clutching her chest. Sixteen years ago, everyone in town who saw her coming would walk on the other side of the street. They'd point and whisper.

But this was crazy.

She tucked a few stray strands of hair behind her ears, adjusted her baseball cap, and eased the boat forward. She knew better than to be a sitting duck in open water.

* * *

*Bang! Bang! Bang!*

"Jesus, did you hear that?" Dawson's heart dropped to the pit of his stomach. They had been going slow, mainly because airboats made a significant amount of noise. But also because there was no reason for them to drive like maniacs when there were no known issues that needed tending to. They had no reason to draw attention to themselves.

Keaton eased up on the gas. "Sounds like it was north of us, but it's hard to tell out here."

"Don't slow down." Dawson glared. "Hayes is twenty minutes from Audra. Haul ass."

"On it." Keaton opened up the throttle.

Dawson reached for the walkie-talkies. "Audra, come in."

"Did you hear those?" Audra's voice crackled over the radio.

"I did," Dawson said. "Are you okay?"

"Just ducky," she said. "I'm headed toward the docks, but those gunshots weren't too far from me."

"We'll meet you halfway." Dawson adjusted his ear protection. He scanned the area as Keaton made a sharp turn around the second bend.

A man came flying around it at top speed, his arms frantically waving over his head. A smaller boat zipped right on past. It wasn't a local, and he shouldn't be driving like that either, but right now, Dawson had to deal with the man waving him down.

He pulled his ear protection off and tossed the set on the console. "That's Tim O'Toole."

Tim jumped to his feet. "Oh my God. That woman is crazy. She's a goddamn Stigini," he said. "And she's a cheater. A fucking cheater, I tell you." He pointed his finger. "Those two up ahead will agree with me. They saw it, too."

"Calm down, Tim." Dawson stood, leaning over the side of the boat, catching Tim's before the two collided. "What and who are you talking about?"

"Audra McCain, that's who." Tim stared at him with wide, angry eyes. "Didn't you hear those gunshots?"

"We heard them," Keaton said. "That's where we were racing off to, trying to figure out where they came from and why."

"Well, I can tell you. I saw the entire thing. The damn insane woman was on Hog's Island, shooting pythons. I watched her with my own eyes." Tim pointed to his face, wiggling his index and middle finger in front of his bugged-out eyes. "When she saw me, she tried to dump the snakes back in the water real slick and coy-like, but I saw it. I swear. So did the guys from Pimp Creek who just drove past. Then she waved her gun at me. I raced off as fast as I could." He glanced over his shoulder. "I'm shocked she didn't try to chase me down to stop me from reporting her. I would've taken a picture of her crime, but I was too afraid she was going to kill me or some-thing like she did her father. She had that wild look in those green snakelike eyes. You know her grandmother had eyes like that. She was half-gypsy, half-witch."

"That's a big accusation," Dawson said.

"Are you calling me a liar?" Tim huffed.

"I didn't say that." Dawson knew damn well the man was lying. Audra was a lot of things. Feisty. Fiery. Passionate. A little left of normal. But she'd never use her weapon to kill a python. It wasn't considered humane. Not that drilling a spike through their brain was nice, but it's how they were told it must be done.

He might have only known Audra for two days, but that was long enough for him to make that kind of judgment call. Besides, he'd spent part of the morning reading some of her articles and glancing at her pictures. Audra had a real love for the wilderness. She respected it. Valued it. Understood how ecosystems worked and why each species was important.

In their own environment.

"Of course, you're not going to listen. You're sleeping with her, practically living with her," Tim shouted.

Wonderful. "I'm going to pretend you didn't just say that," Dawson said. "Now, head back to the docks. Remy is there. He'll take your statement. Keaton and I will handle things from here."

"You better, or your days as chief of police will be numbered in this town." Tim pushed his boat off and punched the gas.

"Asshole," Dawson muttered, pulling out his cell. At least he had two bars of service. He tapped Remy's contact info. It rang once.

"What's up, Chief?"

"Tim O'Toole is heading your way. He's coming in hot," Dawson said.

"Does it have anything to do with the shots fired?"

"Yeah." Dawson sucked in a deep breath. "Try to keep his accusations quiet. You'll need to take his statement. Try to do it somewhere private. He mentioned there was someone else who saw Audra do something, and they flew by me—the team from Pimp Creek."

"I believe Benson knows that team. And Chief, if Tim's accusing Audra of something, he'll want everyone to hear it," Remy said. "They have history."

Jesus. Was there anyone in this town that woman didn't have some kind of beef with? "What kind of history?"

"It started back in middle school."

"You've got to be kidding me." Dawson shook his head. "I don't want to know. Just take his statement. Keep it professional. I'll be out of range for the next forty minutes. Text me when it's over, and if I need to know anything, don't use the radio. I don't want anyone hearing it." He ended the call and tucked his cell back in his pocket. "Does the entire town know she spent the night, and I moved her things into my cabin?"

"Pretty much." Keaton laughed.

"It's not funny."

"For the record, most of us have tried to squelch the whispers, including Baily, but all the hunters were chatting about it this morning."

"I don't need this shit." He pointed. "Just drive."

Keaton hit the gas, and the airboat glided across the water.

Dawson rubbed the back of his neck. His private life was just that—private. No one should be talking about it. But he didn't give a damn what anyone thought about him. That wasn't an issue. It was Audra he cared about. He was going to have to let Remy head up any real investigation—if it came down to that—because he couldn't deny the fact he'd slept with her, making it impossible for anyone to see him as impartial.

The next twelve minutes were the longest of his life.

"There she is," Keaton said.

Finally, Dawson's pulse settled. A little. But not much. Audra was going to go about as ballistic as the color of her hair when she found out what Tim was accusing her of. Dawson knew that for sure.

"Do me a favor and just drop me off. Then haul ass back to the docks. Get Fletcher and do your best to clear as many people away as you can. The last thing I want is a scene."

"Do you really think there will be one?"

"You know how Tim gets when he makes up his mind about something," Dawson said. "And I know how she gets."

"After one night, you know her that well?" Keaton arched a brow. "Or are all redheads the same?"

"Oh, she's something different altogether." Dawson squared his shoulders and made his way to the boat's bow. "Hey, Audra."

"Hey, yourself."

He jumped aboard his vessel, careful not to step on her snake bags, and waved to Keaton.

"Any idea what those gunshots were all about?" she asked. "Scared the crap out of me."

"Well, you're not going to like what Tim O'Toole had to say about them." He sat beside her on the captain's bench and kissed her cheek. "What did you do to him, starting back in middle school?"

She leaned away. "Who told you I did anything?"

"Answer my question. Please."

"Well, that depends on how you look at it." She pursed her lips. "The majority of people in this town will tell you that I sent him to the ER after punching him in the nose and kicking him in the balls."

Dawson cringed at the same time he shifted on the bench. "And your version?"

"He pulled down my tank top when I was in seventh grade and made a snide comment about how I didn't have zits on my tits." She held up her hand. "But that's not when I sent him to the ER. That's just what started my hatred for the guy."

"I can understand why you wouldn't like him. That's not nice, and in today's world, it's considered sexual assault."

"It was one of the most embarrassing moments of my young life," she said. "But like most things, I let it roll off my back. However, in ninth grade, he cornered me under the bleachers and tried to cop a little more than a feel. Sadly, he told everyone I went after him as payback for what happened two years prior, and that's what most believe."

"Jerk." He looped his arm around her shoulders. "I

hope he never tried anything like that again with you or anyone else."

She laughed. "Are you kidding me? The man's been terrified ever since. If he saw me walking down the halls at school, he'd turn and run. Of course, I gave him the good old Stigini stink eye." She sighed. "I kind of felt bad for the guy, though. He wasn't well-liked. Kids picked on him. Not just because he got beat up by little Audra McCain but because he was socially awkward. He tried to be cool and fit in with people like Fletcher and Ken, but he was a nerd. Not very athletic. At least not back then. I don't know how things are for him now." She held his gaze. "I never heard about him trying anything with any other girl. If I had, I would've done more than break his nose and made him sing like a girl."

"Well, things in this town are about the same for him," Dawson admitted. "I'm not sure his so-called friends actually like him, and he tries too damn hard. It's sad to watch." He handed her ear protection. "Let's get you back to the docks. I'll fill you in on what's happening when we get closer."

"Afraid I might lose my temper?"

"No. I know you will." He pressed his finger over her lips. "And I'm going to need you to remain calm."

Her brows drew close together. "Yeah, we both know that's damn near impossible."

"Promise me you'll try?"

"Will you make me French toast in the morning?"

"You bet." If he didn't have to arrest her and leave her in a holding cell overnight.

# CHAPTER 9

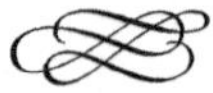

AUDRA BALLED her fists and rolled them across her thighs. She didn't need to hear what people were whispering to know that everyone in this town thought she was trash. Low-hanging fruit. A snake.

A murderer.

Hell, some people actually believed she was a swamp monster by night. She could almost tolerate that. Expected it.

But being accused of cheating during the Python Challenge grated on her last nerve. There was no reason for her to do that. The only thing she had to prove to anyone in this town was that she hadn't killed her father, and that was a battle she'd never win.

She eyed Baily as she strolled across the broken pavement with two beers in her hand. They hadn't spoken much, and it was a bit tense when they did.

"Thought you might like a cold one." Baily handed her a beverage.

"Thanks." Audra brought it to her lips while she

stared at Tim O'Toole and Dawson. They stood twenty paces away. Dawson had his arms folded across his chest. His stance was wide, and he didn't move a muscle, not even a nod or shake of his head.

Tim, on the other hand, practically danced. His arms flapped about like a bird unable to take flight. He'd always been an excitable character. A man in need of way too much attention.

"How are you holding up?" Baily asked.

That was a loaded question.

Dawson had told her to wait by the picnic tables while he reviewed Tim's statement. He'd told her not to speak to anyone. Lucky for her, no one wanted to chat, but she figured Baily would be the exception to the rule.

"Tim and Benson are bringing up those old stories about me being a Stigini. A fucking Owl Witch." Audra shook her head. "I'm sorry that my being here brought drama to your business."

"Tim's an idiot," Baily said, pointing to a souped-up Bronco. "He bought that truck over there last year, thinking it might impress me."

Audra gagged and coughed. "He's been hitting on you?"

Baily climbed up on the picnic table. "He hits on anyone who doesn't have a dick. Ever since he started working for Silas, he believes he's got game. Like he's some important man about town."

"I'm sure Fletcher put him in his place the second he returned."

"Oh, Fletcher had a lot to say about Tim trying to get into my pants. I considered going out with Tim just to piss off Fletcher." Baily sighed. "However, I have more self-respect than to go out with a joke like Tim. That guy probably has more porn loaded on his computer than every male in this town. I have to wonder if he's ever gotten laid without paying for it." She leaned closer. "He's been picked up twice for soliciting a hooker."

"Jesus, that's sad." Audra swigged her beer. "He tried to be so smooth and cool with me back in high school. Like he was sure I was into him. He said he knew all the signs, and I didn't need to pretend anymore."

"Right, because you didn't have a crush on my brother since the fourth grade, and everyone knew it." Baily jerked her head in Dawson's direction. "And now you've got the hots for the chief."

"And you're still in love with Fletch."

"It's Fletcher," Baily corrected with a laugh. "And even if I was, that ship sailed a long time ago."

"Why?"

"That's not a question I can answer in a couple of minutes." Baily's lips curved into a half smile. "I know tonight's not going to be a good night for you, but how about we have drinks tomorrow, and I'll tell you all about it."

"I'd love that." She reached out and squeezed Baily's hand. "But for the love of all things holy, why are we calling Fletcher by his full name? It's weird. It doesn't roll off my tongue naturally."

"While I believe he's been going by Fletcher for a long time, the fact that everyone in town is now calling him that is kind of my fault." She jumped to her feet, waving to *Princess Afloat* as it came down the channel. "Walk with me. I need to catch some lines for Trinity. She's coming in solo, and while she can handle that sucker all by herself, she's still a princess."

"We're going to chat about her, too," Audra mumbled.

Baily laughed. "She's changed. She's one of my better friends in this town. Actually, one of my only friends."

Audra stood and followed Baily toward one of the slips where the bigger cruisers were docked. "Next thing you're going to tell me is Lilly is your friend, too."

"She is." Baily nodded. "Both girls have changed. While Trinity is still a rich bitch who doesn't have to lift a finger if she doesn't want to, she's not a mean girl. And Lilly, well, ever since she hooked up with Hondo when he came home to take care of his dad, she's been a completely different person. She's a great mom, too, even if her kids are little pistols."

"They might be the only things that have changed in this town." Audra stepped out on the dock. "So, let's circle back to Fletcher."

"Long story short, it's all part of his plan to win me back. Or, at the very least, for me to forgive him," Baily said. "We weren't speaking much, but when Ken died, things just got worse. Not because I blame him for what happened, but because he and the team blame themselves."

"Do you know what happened?" Audra asked. "Dawson has like a billion scars on his body. He looks like he's been burned, tortured, shot, and spit through a woodchuck."

"So, the rumors about you and him are true."

"Not commenting."

"You don't have to. Not with that grin." Baily winked. "As next of kin, I was given the official story from the Navy. Unfortunately for me, Fletcher showed up here, bawling like a baby, and gave me a few details I wish I didn't know."

"And that's why you blame him?"

"Logically, I know that what happened to Ken could've happened to anyone on that team. They were SEALs, and SEALs die in combat," Baily said. "The blame aspect isn't so much about what happened on the mission. It followed years of arguments. You and I both know that Ken and I weren't as close as this town would like to remember. We had our problems, especially about what to do with the marina if and when our dad died, and dad was drinking himself into an early grave faster than Superman. Because of that, Ken always wanted out of Calusa Cove and thought I should leave, too." Baily shrugged. "This was home for me, and having my brother and boyfriend take off fucked with my head."

"You knew Fletcher was never going to stay. There was nothing left for him in this town—not when his mom left, and his dad's business folded." Audra lowered her chin.

"He had me. The Navy wasn't supposed to be a career but an education. When I saw that wasn't going to happen, or that he wasn't going to come home, I couldn't do it anymore. I wouldn't hold on to a man who loved the Navy more than he loved me."

"I get it. I do." Audra nodded. "But what does this have to do with calling him Fletcher?"

"When he and the boys moved back and made it clear they were going to make this their home, that they were going to help me save this marina since I was on the brink of having to shut it down, it made me nuts. Fletcher was the last person I wanted to be indebted to, but he's relentless. He's always coming around, wanting to make things right—to do what Ken never would. And Fletcher wants a second chance. I told him I'd consider going out on a date with him when he grew the fuck up. He thought going by his given name was a good start, and he acts all serious around me. It's weird."

*Princess Afloat* turned and backed into the slip.

Baily caught the bowline and Audra the stern. They tied the pretty cabin cruiser to the dock in silence.

Trinity hopped off the boat with her pretty heels dangling from her fingertips. "Good evening, ladies," she said. "What's the good gossip? Besides Audra and the sexy chief."

"Do you want to get shoved in the water?" Audra took a step forward. "Because I don't mind a repeat of the second grade."

Trinity tilted her head, lowered her chin, and smiled. "Just so you know, and everyone will back me up, I've told all those chattering about it to shut up, it's not their business, and that they have no idea what they're talking about."

"Then why bring it up?" Audra narrowed her eyes. "You shoved it in my face like you're enjoying it."

"You still have a chip on your shoulder." Trinity

sighed, shaking her head. "I was getting coffee this morning with my friend Mallary. I saw you and Dawson. I'm certainly not judging. Lord knows that man is wound tight in a weird, sarcastic kind of way." Trinity looped her arm around Audra. "Anyone up for a drink tonight?"

"Can't," Baily said. "But we're doing something tomorrow night. You should join."

Audra glanced over her shoulder and glared. She wanted to spend time with Baily—alone. Having Trinity tag along was like forcing her to enter the Miss Everglades Pageant.

"I'll be there. Text me the deets. Maybe we should invite the boys. You know...Audra's new man, Fletcher... And now that I'm single again, perhaps I should give Keaton Cole a little second glance." Trinity gave Audra a good hip check before sitting on the bench at the end of the dock. "*If* we can get through a conversation without yelling at each other."

"Is he still giving you shit about searching for Jared's boat?" Baily laughed.

"He believes I'm being reckless." Trinity rolled her eyes. Not much had changed, except she was nicer. Kinder. Maybe a little softer. "I won't be taking out the boat tomorrow. She's getting cleaned."

"Good to know." Baily nodded.

Audra glanced toward the parking lot. She couldn't see Dawson anywhere. That wasn't a good sign. He would have her hide for disappearing. Now, that was an odd sensation. Being concerned about others wasn't her strong suit. "I better get going."

"I'm looking forward to girls' night tomorrow." Trinity waved.

Audra inched closer to the parking lot, searching for Dawson, but all she found was Paul and Tim, huddled not far from the picnic tables she'd been sitting on a few minutes ago.

That was strange. She would have expected Silas to be standing there with Tim, but whatever.

She sucked in a deep breath and made her feet move. She had to walk past Tim and Paul to get to her car or Dawson's patrol vehicle. To get anywhere.

"Don't say anything," Baily whispered. "No matter what they toss at you, just keep walking."

"Right. Because that's real easy for me." Audra's heart stuck in her throat like a massive frog.

"Hey, Baily," some male voice called. "I need help with the pumps."

"Dammit. I've got to go. That's my dockhand. My credit card reader's been acting squirrely lately, and I can't afford to have these clowns drive down to the next marina to fill up because I can't handle it." Baily squeezed her biceps. "Seriously, don't engage. Those two aren't worth your breath."

Folding her arms across her chest, she kept her head down, focusing on putting one foot in front of the other. Back in the day, she would never dream of making her way anywhere without her head held high. She'd always given as good as she'd gotten. Oftentimes, she'd tossed the first insult. That attitude had given her a nasty reputation.

She didn't care.

It honestly kept the riffraff away. If she started it, she didn't have to finish it.

But today, with all the questions and memories swirling in her brain, she didn't want to test fate.

"You've got some fucking nerve," Tim sneered. "You really are a swamp monster."

She swallowed the bile that smacked the back of her throat and kept walking. It took all her energy to let this slide. Tim was a wannabe. He didn't have any friends in this town any more than she did. But at least people had respected her talents. He had none.

He was an insecure dick who'd tried to buy his way into popularity. Even his own family tended to brush him under the rug, pretending they didn't come from the same stock. It was probably why he worked for Silas and not the family crabbing business.

"Hey, I'm talking to you," Tim called. "Don't fucking ignore me."

"Considering the situation, I think it's best," she said, not glancing over her shoulder. For the seventeen years she'd lived in Calusa Cove, she'd never backed away from a war of words.

Except maybe when she'd snuck away in the middle of the night. This felt very much like that, and she resented it.

The uneven pavement vibrated under her feet.

Quickly, she shifted, turning and holding her ground. She raised her hand. "Tim, this isn't the time or place." She continued to stumble backward toward the entrance of the marina. The sooner she found Dawson, the faster she'd be safe from opening her big fat mouth. "I'm not going to discuss this matter with you."

"You're a crazy person." He now stood only six feet away. He planted his hands on his hips. "A witch, just like your grandma. I heard she spoke in weird languages and was nuttier than your old man."

She glanced around. Silas and his crew had gathered on the other side of the parking lot. Silas actually inched forward, but she didn't know if it was to protect her or Tim.

Out of the corner of her eye, she saw Dawson come into view as well as Hayes. Dawson marched in her direction like he was a man on a mission.

*Just back up. No need to engage.*

Tim closed the gap. "You're a liar—a cheat. I saw you use your weapon to kill those pythons," he said loud enough for everyone to hear. Slowly, he took four more steps. She could see the wildness of his eyes.

He believed his own bullshit.

Wonderful.

"That's enough, Tim," Dawson said, wedging himself between her and Tim. "It's time to calm down."

"Calm down?" Tim shifted his gaze, glaring at Dawson. "I'll calm down when you arrest this woman— this *Stigini*." As if that word could cause her harm.

"Tim," Dawson said in his strange, firm, but soft voice, "I need you to back away." He tapped his badge. "We've got both statements and—"

"And what are you going to do about it? Take her side because you're fuck—"

"I would not finish that statement if I were you."

Dawson rested his hand on his weapon. "Now, walk away."

Tim didn't listen. Instead, he leaned closer. "She's a fucking murderer. Everyone knows she killed her father in cold blood and dumped his body in the Everglades like gator—"

"You shut the fuck up." She lunged forward, cocking her first, ready to land it right between that asshole's eyes.

"Oh, no, you don't," Dawson's voice boomed in her ears. A strong arm came around her midsection and lifted her feet right off the ground less than a foot away from Tim.

She kicked and tried to wiggle herself free. "Let me go, Dawson."

"Yeah, put her down. Let's see what she's made of," Tim said.

"I'll fucking tear you limb from—"

"Be quiet, Audra." Dawson covered her mouth. "You don't want to do this," he whispered. "He'll press charges."

She gripped his wrist, digging her nails into his skin, kicking, wiggling, and doing her best to break free. "*Put. Me. Down,*" she demanded. No way would she take this from Tim O'Toole.

"Are you going to behave?" Dawson's breath tickled her skin.

She turned her head and glared. Why did she have to behave when Tim was the one being a total dick?

"I told you she was dangerous." Tim waved his hand

wildly in her direction. "I didn't do anything, and she came at me, ready to hit me. She's a lunatic."

"Are you kidding? You got in my personal space. You called me names," she said, kicking her feet, struggling once again to break free. "I was defending myself."

"She's right, Tim," Dawson said. "If I hadn't stopped her from hitting you, I'd be hard-pressed to ignore the fact that you were being aggressive and accusatory. I was worried you might attack her."

"I was a little worried he might do that, too," Silas piped in out of nowhere.

That was strange, but she wasn't about to question someone coming to her defense, even if it was Silas.

"That's bullshit," Tim said. "I don't know why Silas is taking her side, but everyone knows why you are. I hope she's worth it."

"You better shut up," Audra said. "Once Dawson puts me down, I'm going to—"

"Be quiet." As if she were a sack of potatoes, he tossed her over his shoulder. "Tim, if I were you, I'd go home. I don't appreciate you antagonizing anyone, including me, and that's exactly what you did. Unless you'd like to join us at the station."

"No. I'm fine," Tim said.

Audra sighed. She let go of all the fight she had left inside. This was a battle she could not win.

"That's what I figured," Dawson said. "Let me do my job. Now get in your car and leave."

"Does your job include kicking her out of the challenge and arresting her for not only using her weapon when it wasn't necessary but threatening me?" Tim asked.

Audra couldn't see anything other than Dawson's ass. It was a nice ass, but she'd rather have a bird's eye view of what was happening with Tim right now, yet it wasn't worth the argument.

"Leave the detective work to me," Dawson said. His voice was tight and filled with frustration.

"I'll have your badge if she's back out here tomorrow," Tim muttered.

"Good luck with that." Dawson turned and strode across the parking lot. His thick muscles flexed under his uniform. He set her on her feet and opened the back door of his patrol car.

"Oh no. I'm not getting in that thing."

"Get in the vehicle." He pointed.

"Make me." She folded her arms and cocked her head.

He pressed his hand on the top of her head. "Do not make me get out the cuffs." He leaned in. "Because this is not how I envisioned using them on you." He arched a brow.

"You're arresting me?" She blinked. Why did every man she ever went to bed with betray her?

"No," he said. "But I am taking you down to the station to do a gunpowder residue test."

"I can't believe you're going to believe that dick over me." She narrowed her stare. "I didn't fire my weapon. Those other idiots that flew by didn't stop and give a statement. They disappeared, so no witness."

"I know that. Now get in." He gave her a little shove,

reached across her body, and buckled her in the back seat.

"You're an asshole."

"I've been called worse." He sighed before slamming the door and slipping behind the steering wheel. He revved the engine and pulled out of the parking lot.

"I left my long-sleeve salty shirt on your boat," she mumbled. "It's my favorite."

"I'll circle back and get it for you when we're done," he said. "For the record, I know you didn't shoot anything. This is a fucking formality. I need to do it so I can get this entire town off my ass and let Remy close the complaint against you—proving Tim wrong and a liar." He glanced in the rearview mirror. "You're too busy letting your emotions get the better of you to listen or even think logically about the situation."

"Oh, really? How would you feel if someone accused you of the things Tim did?"

"I'd be pissed," Dawson said. "But I'd like to believe that if I was sleeping with the police chief, I'd be smart enough to let him work for me instead of making his job that much harder." He rolled to a stop at a light. "Do you think it was fun for me to toss you over my shoulder and manhandle you into this vehicle?"

"Yes," she said, holding his smoldering gaze.

He cracked a smile. "Okay, maybe a little." He blew out a puff of air. "But when are you going to trust that I'm on your side?" The patrol car inched through the green light and turned into the station's parking lot.

She contemplated her answer while he shut off the engine and opened the back passenger door.

In true cop form, he took her by the elbow and led her toward the front door, which only added to her annoyance. However, that was tempered when she realized Tim had followed them to the station and was parked across the street.

*Fucker.*

"Hey, Chief." Remy stood in the main room of the station. He waved a file. "I took the statement of that other witness."

"I thought they never stopped at the marina?" Audra glanced between the two men. Remy had been a cop when she'd been a kid. He was a good man. The kind of man who was impartial. He did his job and treated the people of this town with kindness and respect, and that included her and her dad. "What the hell did they say?"

"Relax, Audra." Remy handed Dawson the file. "They didn't. This is someone else, and it doesn't jibe with what Tim reported."

"Oh," she said. "Still doesn't make me feel better."

"You've always jumped to conclusions, and it's never done you any favors," Remy said. "What do you want me to do, Chief?"

"For starters, since Tim followed us here, you can tell him I'd like to have a chat. Bring him inside and to your office. I don't want these two crossing paths." He jerked his thumb over his shoulder. "You'll do the residue test. I don't want anyone coming at me, saying I'm tampering with evidence or playing favorites with my girlfriend."

*Girlfriend?*

*What the hell?*

"Got it, Chief." Remy smiled and strolled down the hallway.

She followed Dawson into his office. "I'm sorry," she managed. "I don't mean to cause you all this grief."

"It's okay." Dawson tossed the file on his desk, waved his hand over one of the chairs, and then took a seat in the big leather one. He let out a very long breath.

"Aren't you going to look at that?" she asked.

"I already know what's inside. It doesn't prove you didn't fire your weapon, but it gives us something else to look at. Or should I say, someone else."

"Are you going to tell me who?"

"I'm sorry, I can't. Not right this second anyway."

"I see," she said. "You're mad."

"I'm frustrated." He leaned back and clasped his hands behind his head. "I asked you not to talk to anyone. I have no problem with you chatting with Baily or Trinity, but I don't give a shit what Tim or Paul said to ruffle your feathers. You were going to haul off and hit him. Had I not stopped you, we both know Tim would've filed charges because he can, and I would've had to follow through." He tapped his badge. "It's my job to serve this community, even jerkoffs like Tim O'Toole."

"At least we agree that man is useless."

Dawson leaned forward, resting his arms on the desk. "I'm begging you to make my life easier from here on out."

She sighed, slumping in her chair. "All I want to do is figure out what happened to my dad. I've put off doing this for way too long. But it's hard when everyone in

Calusa Cove treats me like I'm the one who killed him or like I'm some kind of witch."

"Yeah, well, don't come gunning for me, but you're making yourself an easy target." He lowered his chin. "I need you to rely on me. You need to trust that I know what I'm doing. Responding to everyone who gets in your face about what they might think of you only adds fuel to the fire and creates this narrative, making idiots like Tim do stupid shit," Dawson said, then cleared his throat. "Moving on to something more important, I spoke with a detective from State today. A Detective Lester. He worked with Trip on your dad's case but also helped put Trevor away."

She sat up a little taller. "And?"

"It didn't go very far, but he directed me to the FBI, who then directed me to the local DEA office."

"That sounds like a circle jerk if I ever heard one."

Dawson chuckled. "The bottom line is I have some new paperwork to comb through first thing tomorrow morning. My goal is to see what kind of dots I can connect between what Trevor was doing and what your father thought was going on."

"Yeah, but we don't know much about what my dad—"

"But I learned a little more." Dawson waggled his finger. "Your father loved his conspiracy theories. He loved stories about pirates, right?"

"He told them all the time. Old tales about how pirates in the seventeenth and eighteenth hundreds would use the Everglades to hide when they were pursued. They would build old shacks to hide their treasures because no one would dare go back there. There's even an old sunken ship out in the island barriers to prove he's not crazy about that." She smiled. She used to love to listen to her dad get all riled up around the campfire while she roasted marshmallows. "And then there was the Ghost Ship of the Everglades."

"That one is my favorite. Keeps some people from going out there at night." Dawson nodded. "But it turns out, Agent Ballard of the FBI and Agent Pope with the DEA think there might be some merit to some of your dad's ramblings."

She bolted out of her seat. "Are you serious? Why haven't I been notified? Why hasn't anyone done anything about this before?"

Dawson chuckled.

"This isn't funny." She stood over his chair with her hands on her hips and glared.

"No. It's not, but your reaction is." Slowly, he rose. "The DEA is constantly dealing with drugs coming in from all directions. Mexico, South America, to name two places." He ran his hands up and down her arms. "Right now, Agent Pope is dealing with the Mendoza Cartel."

"Hector Mendoza," Audra whispered. "There's an old story my dad used to talk about—"

"I know the tale." Dawson nodded. "I've asked the DEA to see if there is a connection between Hector and the cartel. That will take time. Pope has asked me to be on the lookout for anything suspicious, but so far, I haven't seen anything. I've worked with the Coast Guard and the FBI in case the drugs have made it inland. It's an ongoing battle. And then there are gun runners—which the Mendoza Cartel is also rumored to be part of. It appears that what Trevor was doing was small potatoes. Yet the DEA saw—and I agree—it was a tiny portion of a bigger operation in the transport of drugs and maybe other things. Only Trevor wasn't—still isn't—talking."

Audra opened her mouth, but Dawson silenced her with his finger.

God, she hated that, but she'd let it go for now.

Of course, she didn't care for being manhandled either, but when Dawson had flung her over his shoulder, it had felt more akin to caring than being treated like a second-class citizen.

"I believe Trevor was a peon," Dawson continued, "and the more I think about it, he's got a lot to protect— an ex-wife and a kid. That's something. But my point is, I've always wondered if someone else in or near this town controlled things—is still controlling things."

"All the more reason we need to get out to the island with no name."

Dawson cupped her cheeks and kissed her softly. "Hayes already checked it out. There's nothing out there but old driftwood—old remnants of a cabin." He arched a brow. "If something's going on in our part of the Everglades, it's on a different island. There are eight days left of this challenge. I suspect whoever is keeping that shack is incredibly nervous with all of us out there, stomping around, looking for snakes, and potentially stumbling upon whatever they're hiding out there. It's time to use that to our advantage."

"Do you believe the gunshots and the possible drug running are connected?"

"I generally don't believe in coincidences," Dawson said, pointing to the file on his desk. "But based on what's in there, and how some feel about you in this town, it's hard not to wonder if it all doesn't circle back to the day your dad died."

She jerked her head back. "So, maybe we should focus on those who spoke out the loudest about hating me."

"For sixteen years, this town has whispered your name and what happened around campfires like a scary story. You're folklore. A ghost. Silas liked to bring up your name every now and then. So did Paul." Dawson tucked her hair behind her ears. He stared deeply into her eyes. "A lot of people mentioned the girl with the fiery hair and soul connected to the swamp. That doesn't mean they killed your dad, but you're back, and they're reminded that a man disappeared, and everyone believes you hold the key."

"Why don't you just come out and say it." She leaned back on his desk. "Everyone's afraid I'm going to kill someone else."

"When they don't have a reason why you did in your dad, it makes it much scarier, so yeah, they worry you'll go off on someone else because you lose your temper like that's the normal thing to do—even when someone's being nice."

"Well, it's kind of normal for me," she said. "Because nice always came with a price. So, I never trusted it. If someone smiled at me or gave me a compliment, I'd narrow my eyes, stick my tongue out, and say something crazy."

"Jesus, no wonder—"

"Hey, Chief," Remy called. "I've got some bad news."

Dawson pinched the bridge of his nose. "What?"

"When I went outside, Tim was gone. No sign of him anywhere."

"Wonderful," Dawson said under his breath. "Do the residue test on Audra. I'll take her home when you're done. Then, you can find Tim and question him about the contradictions of our other eyewitness. If he gives you a hard time, call me."

"What aren't you telling me?" Audra glared, folding her arms.

"You're going to have to trust me." Dawson side-stepped her and strolled out of his office.

Trusting anyone was like asking her to Wine Wednesday with the girls in the office. It had happened once. She hated every second of it and learned that most people didn't like her, and the feeling was mutual.

# CHAPTER 10

DAWSON KICKED A PEBBLE. "I can't believe Tim's dead. Killed on my watch and right under my flipping nose," he mumbled. His first murder since becoming chief of police of Calusa Cove, and it was possible he'd have to recuse himself from the entire process, all because his girlfriend and the victim had exchanged words. That fact was only made worse by images sent by Tim's cousin that put Audra at the crime scene.

Utter crap, and now Dawson had to deal with the fallout—but he couldn't even do that while standing in the thick of things. No, he had to take a backseat, and that just pissed him off.

Not that he was happy someone had been killed, but still. He wanted to be the one to link the pieces together. It wasn't about being a hero. That had never been his reason for joining the Navy, being an MP, or being a SEAL. Or for becoming a cop.

It had always been about helping people. Taking care

of his community. Doing for others what they had done for him when he'd had no one.

"What did that rock ever do to you?" Hayes came up behind him and squeezed his shoulder. As a first responder and firefighter, Dawson was grateful that Hayes had been on duty last night and this morning. It made his life a little easier.

"Nothing. Just frustrated."

"I don't blame you. Anything new?" Hayes asked.

Dawson shook his head. "My team's still down there on Tim's boat with State. I'm keeping my distance while they gather evidence. I don't want to be accused of tainting that process. So far, Remy's been a little too tight-lipped for my liking."

"I'm sure he's doing exactly what we would in this situation." Hayes nodded. "Fletcher and Keaton are five minutes out. Are you sure you don't want one of them at Harvey's Cabins?"

"Each one of my deputies is willing to tail those two city assholes while off duty. Plus, Hondo's got two weeks off charter. Outside of helping my general contractor, he's totally bored." Dawson's lips twisted. "He doesn't mind hanging out with his wife while his kids drive his mother-in-law nuts. Besides, everything that's happening is making him twitchy. He would prefer being where his bride is, and I don't blame him."

Dawson leaned against the post near the docks. He stared at the State CSI unit as they continued to take pictures of the crime scene. If he could afford to give Lilly time off work at the cabins, he would. But he needed someone there during the day. "Both Eliot and

James have confirmed that the dynamite belonged to them. They said it was in the crates when I loaded it into my police vehicle. I call bullshit on that because I have a log of it, and Anna is anal-retentive when it comes to evidence. I also counted the sticks myself before she brought them inside. So, I know they're lying. It's proving it that's going to be difficult."

"Well, after this call, I'm done for the day," Hayes said. "I can take over at the cabins if you want."

"I've got something else in mind for you," Dawson said. "But I told Lilly that if she was uncomfortable working because of the situation with Audra, she could ask the other staff. She told me to shove it."

"Sounds like Lilly," Hayes said with a slight grin.

Dawson eyed his team as they moved about the docks, careful not to disrupt anything. Dawson was proud of his team.

Remy was an excellent cop, and while they'd had a rough start of it when Dawson had first taken the job, the last five months had been smooth sailing. He trusted that Remy would not only crack the case, but he would keep him informed, feeding him intel and allowing him to wet his whistle, so to speak—without compromising the case.

Hayes pulled an envelope from his back pocket. "Anna wanted me to give this to you."

Dawson took the envelope and ripped it open as if he were a kid on Christmas morning. He unfolded the piece of paper and stared at the words on the page. "Jesus," he muttered.

"What is it?"

"Remember those old wood pieces I had you take from the island with no name?"

Hayes nodded.

"I sent them over to the FBI and the DEA on a whim. Well, Agent Ballard with the FBI just got back to me. He can't be sure, but it looks like it could be remnants of crates used to transport cocaine."

"When Trevor Williams was chief of police?" Hayes asked.

"No." Dawson shook his head. "This was from about seventeen years ago. He remembers the cartel markings. They would use out-of-the-way towns like Calusa Cove, where they'd find small fishing charters, touring boats, even personal yachts that wouldn't draw attention, to bring them into places like the Everglades to hide product until they could move it."

"Do you think Trip could've been doing the same thing his son did?"

"Anything is possible, but my gut says no," Dawson said. "I requested to see Trevor in prison. He refused to see me. I think he's scared."

"Makes sense," Hayes said. "Did you interview Silas yesterday?"

"I'm supposed to meet with him this morning." Dawson checked his watch. "Here at the docks in about an hour." He ran his fingers through his hair and let out a long breath. "I'm baffled by his statement. Silas is a lot of things, and he's a royal pain in my ass on most days. But in the nine months I've been chief of police in this town, he's never once come to me with a situation that was false. He's always been honest about things."

"He has insinuated that Audra might've killed her dad."

Dawson pinched the bridge of his nose. "He questioned why she left the way she did. When Remy asked him about that yesterday, he said, what else could he believe based on her actions? He told him he didn't want to believe it, but there wasn't another logical explanation. He swore it pained him to even think it, and that if I could come up with a better explanation—one that worked—he'd listen."

"Do you think he's redirecting? Or trying to get you to look elsewhere?" Hayes cocked his head.

"It's possible. Silas can be a slick bastard when he wants to be, but why would he turn on Paul Massey and accuse him of firing those shots—even if they were at nothing? They're about as close as two men can be. That one doesn't make sense, and to make matters worse, we couldn't locate Paul last night to come in and take the damn test. I couldn't find his son either, and that bothers me for different reasons."

"I've seen him more than once with those city boys, but I'm sure he'll show up here this morning, and you'll get your chance," Hayes said. "Whatever happened with Benson's tire?"

"Nothing." Dawson shrugged. "He decided to let it go. He figures we can't prove anything, and he's right, but I've heard he's been telling those who will listen he still believes it was Audra. That he thinks I've got shit for brains and that this town would love to see me get canned."

"We both know that's bullshit. In the meantime, what do you want me to do?"

"Let's get into that when Keaton and Fletcher get here," Dawson said. "I called Baily and asked if she could go over and have breakfast with Audra. We're not letting any boats out of here until we clear the crime scene. No point in Baily opening the marina until that happens, but I promised her I'd give her a heads-up when I think we're about done."

"How did Audra take the news?"

Dawson stuck his index finger in his ear. "Let's just say that woman cusses more than a drunken sailor. She takes everything so personally."

"Can you blame her in this instance?"

"Can't say that I do, but she gets so fired up. She has two speeds. Out of control and barely in control." Dawson sighed. "However, I find it very suspect that we couldn't find Tim last night. My deputies searched for him for hours into the night before giving up. Then we get a call from his cousin at five that he found Tim dead in his boat after waking up to a series of texts that he was in fear for his life. He told him that he thought Audra was stalking him and that if anything happened to him, Audra was behind it."

"Don't forget the picture Tim sent to Dennis of Audra's car parked at the marina," Hayes said. "And of Audra sneaking around Tim's house."

"We both know Audra's car was left here last night." Dawson glared. "That other image is grainy as fuck. Hasn't been authenticated, and I know exactly where Audra was all night." He lowered his chin. "No one in this town wants to fuck with me or my integrity, and Audra didn't leave my bed. She uses sex to deal with her problems, and I swear she—"

"I don't need the details, and there's no need to get defensive with me." Hayes jerked his chin toward the road. "What are you going to do about the press? Or about the gossip?"

"Remy will handle the press after we've had a chance to chat about the details of the case." Dawson raked his fingers through his hair. "I'm not going to address the gossip. If I do, they'll hang me. If I don't feed the beast, they can only speculate. If it gets really out of hand, I'll make some calculated corrections."

"Are you sure that's a good idea? I get why you're tiptoeing around this, but if you let things fester, it'll only get worse."

"Yeah, but if I bullet point the rumors, I look like I'm hiding something—or I'm ashamed of my actions. Which I'm not. I'm still the chief of police. I'm allowed to have a personal life. Technically, I don't have to take a step back. I just can't interview Audra since I'm her alibi." Only this time, a gunpowder residue test wasn't going to save her from further speculation since it appeared Tim had been killed by a hunting knife. It shouldn't be too hard to rule out any knife that Audra had in her possession.

But an autopsy still needed to be performed. Prints needed to be run. Images needed to be run through all the tests.

There was at least two days' worth of crime lab work before he and Remy could make deductive decisions. In the meantime, it was all about keeping the town calm.

And Audra out of trouble.

"Then why are you handing this case over to Remy?"

"Optics." Dawson chuckled. "You know I rented cabin one yesterday."

Hayes pounded his chest. "She's basically living with you."

"Staying with me would be a better descriptor." Dawson cocked his head.

"You don't need the money. Why rent it so quickly?" Hayes asked.

"I felt bad for a city slicker driving a Range Rover that broke down. He needed a place to stay until the auto shop could get his part. Trinity called her dad, but he can't get the part for a few days."

"That has my hackles up. Doesn't it make you suspicious?" Hayes asked.

"I know where you're going with this, and I've already run the plate on his vehicle," Dawson said with a chuckle. "His name is Decker Brown. He's a land developer. There's no reason to be suspicious about him. He has no ties to this town and no connection to Audra, Tim, or anyone else, but just to be safe, I had Agent Ballard do a deeper dive."

"Still, he's not the kind of person we want staying in our sleepy little town and getting ideas," Hayes said. "People are always trying to change the landscape of places like this."

"Except, with the Everglades being our backyard—literally—it's impossible. You can't build condos. There are no beaches here in Calusa Cove. Nothing to bring in tourists. Anyone trying to develop here would lose their shirt. I'm not worried about Decker Brown spending a couple of nights in my cabins. Poor guy probably can't wait to get out of here, anyway." Dawson pointed to the police barricade. "Who the hell is that?" A tall woman—mid-thirties—wearing a standard issue dark suit flashed a badge. She'd pulled her long hair back into a ponytail at the nape of her neck and pushed her sunglasses on top of her head.

Hayes turned. "I have no idea. Never seen her before."

"Looks like a Fed," Dawson mumbled as he watched her flash something to one of his deputies on her way toward him. "Wonderful. Just what I need."

"Excuse me." The woman stuffed her hands in her pockets.

Dawson glanced at his buddy, who was practically salivating.

Jesus.

"Can I help you?" Dawson asked.

"I'm sorry to bother you," the lady said. "My name is Special Agent Chloe Frasier. Are you Chief Dawson Ridge?"

"I am," Dawson started. "But we didn't call for the FBI."

"I don't believe I'm here for whatever you've got going on—unless you've found one of these people." She held up her phone, showing off an image. Two women. One man. All in their late teens or early twenties. "Two of them I'm not sure you would have. But that young girl right there." She tapped the screen. "She was last seen about an hour north of here."

"Mind if I take a closer look?" Dawson asked.

"Please." She pushed her phone forward. "And your firefighter friend, too."

"How long have these people been missing?" Hayes asked.

"This girl, only forty-eight hours. That's why I'm scrambling, chasing every lead. But the other two? Well, that one has been missing for a year. The other, one for six months," Chloe said. "Unfortunately, they all fit the victimology of a killer I've been chasing for the last two years."

"Jesus," Dawson muttered. His day couldn't get any worse. "I can't say I've seen her or the other two. But if you send the information to my office, we'll keep a lookout."

"I'd appreciate that." She tucked her phone in her back pocket. "Anything I can help you with here?"

"Not right now," Dawson said. "I've been speaking with an Agent Ballard about a cold case. I'm not sure if it's related, but he's been my point of contact."

"Ballard's a good man," Agent Frasier said. "We work out of the same office—different divisions—but we've worked on a few things together over the years. Be sure to call us if you need anything at all. We're both always happy to help the locals."

"I will. Thanks."

Chloe handed him a business card. She smiled, but not at Dawson, only at Hayes.

Interesting.

And Hayes stared at her ass as she walked away.

Dawson nudged his shoulder. "You can put your eyes back in their sockets."

"Dude, I'm trying." Hayes pounded his chest with his fist. He coughed. "I've never seen a woman fill out a standard issue black boring suit like that before."

Dawson laughed. "I can't tell if you're trying to make me feel better or if you're really contemplating hitting on that Fed."

"Oh, that's about the only thought on my mind right now." It was rare that Hayes made any comments about women. His love life had always been insanely private, like all the guys. But Hayes more so than the rest. He'd had a couple of girlfriends over the years, but no one had broken his heart—to Dawson's knowledge. As far as he knew, Hayes just didn't want to settle down and get married.

Maybe it was because he was one of twelve kids or had a twin who had died when he'd been very young. Or maybe it was his religious upbringing. Who knew? Hayes didn't talk about it much other than a shrug of his shoulder and to laugh it off, stating that Cupid hadn't caught him—yet.

"Here comes the rest of the team," Dawson said.

They each might represent a different facet of Calusa Cove, but these men were still his team. His family. They were all he had left in this world, and he couldn't imagine his life without them in it.

"We stopped by Harvey's Cabins," Keaton said as he marched across the pavement. "It's mostly quiet. I did have to chase off one reporter lurking in the bushes."

"Someone told the media about this murder before we even got here," Dawson said. "I suspect a local tipped them off based on the spin." He took the mug of coffee that Fletcher offered and made his way to the picnic table. "You told me her return would cause a ruckus, but damn, this has gotten out of hand." He sipped the hot, bitter brew. "A lot of people in this town don't like Tim. While no female has ever come to me saying he crossed the line, I've seen a few fend off his advances at Massey's." Dawson held up his finger. "However, I learned that he did assault Audra in high school. I don't give a shit that she handled it herself, but it should've been reported. Am I dealing with something more sinister?" He stared at Fletcher.

"Not that I'm aware of, and he was hitting on Baily when we first got back. Nothing bad. Just asked her out and didn't easily take no for an answer until I told him to back off," Fletcher said. "Why are you asking me this now?"

Dawson sighed. "Because I need to find myself a suspect—other than Audra—the local witch. Or swamp monster, depending on who you're talking to."

"I see." Fletcher leaned against the tree on the other side of the picnic table. "Normally, it wouldn't be too hard to find a dozen or so people in this town who didn't like Tim—and with good reason. But unfortunately, with Audra back in town, everyone dislikes her—and is afraid of her. Who has more of a reason to want her gone? All her life, if someone said something negative about her or her family, she played into the rumors.

Before she became a teenager, she ran around this town barefoot, with ratty hair and torn clothes. She looked like a wild child, and her only friends were me, Ken, and Baily. When she hit fourteen, she at least started looking like a human, but it was too late. She was the local Stigini, and all the kids were told to stay away from her."

"Well, those kids are now adults, and my gut tells me someone is framing her for Tim's murder," Dawson said. From the second Audra had stepped foot in Calusa Cove, weird shit kept happening to the point none of it could be a coincidence.

Messing with her drone and her boat was one thing. The dynamite added a different element, but it all came down to wanting her gone.

Accusing her of killing snakes with a gun—well, as inhumane as that was, those damn snakes were a menace. Dawson and the gang might let something like that slide under certain circumstances.

But murder?

There was more to this story. Tim was either collateral damage—and that just sucked—or he had betrayed someone. Dawson didn't know the players. However, he did have a theory as to why.

Drugs. Weapons. Or both.

Dawson pulled out his cell phone and tapped his notes app. "I'm sending you all my notes, with some files I shouldn't. But I need eyes and your honest opinion," he said, "because I think this all goes back to when Victor disappeared." He sent his buddies the files. "I also need to do a sweep of the swamp. The darkest, most out-of-the-way places in the Everglades near us. Anywhere someone could hide—"

"Hey, Chief," Remy called. "We need you down here, pronto."

"Coming." Dawson stood and glanced around the group. "Do you all hear what I'm saying?"

"You honestly think there was truth to what Victor was rambling about all those years ago?" Fletcher arched a brow.

"Considering the former chief of police is in prison for running drugs through this town, yeah, I do. Also, I think we owe it to Audra to find out one way or another." Dawson turned and jogged down toward the dock. "What's up, Remy?"

"You're not going to like this."

Dawson followed Remy toward the waterfront. He could feel the daggers of everyone standing behind the crime scene tape. If he wasn't mistaken, a few locals mumbled for him to go home, to crawl back under the rock from which he'd come. He didn't dare glance over his shoulder. It had taken him months to gain the trust of the majority of the town. Sure, people like Paul and Dewey would never trust him. They constantly questioned his loyalty. If you weren't born in Calusa Cove, you didn't belong. If you left Calusa Cove, you weren't welcome back.

The medical examiner and his team lifted the body onto the gurney and wheeled it past. The CSI unit had placed numbered placards beside different objects, and they continued to snap pictures.

"When the ME moved the body, we found something interesting," Remy said.

"And what's that?" Dawson pinched the bridge of his nose as he stood on the dock by Tim's airboat. He scanned the spot where the body had been found, and his heart dropped to the pit of his stomach.

Remy didn't say a word. He didn't have to. They both knew they were looking at Audra's shirt.

"Seems strange that a killer would tuck that under a body," Remy whispered.

Dawson rubbed the back of his neck. "I'm pretty sure that's Audra's, and she left it on my boat last night."

"We can easily confirm that." Remy nodded.

"Only problem is, I already looked for it when I came here and couldn't find it."

"Well, shit," Remy mumbled.

"What about the security cameras?" Dawson pointed to the one by the dock and the second one near the front of the marina. "I get someone shot them, but we might be able to pull something before that happened."

"Baily just got back to me with the code to her computer." Remy waved his cell. "Why don't we go into the marina and check it out."

"Let's do it." Dawson spun on his heel and marched off the dock.

"Chief Ridge," some reporter he didn't know called out.

"Hey, Dawson. What can you tell us…" another one he did know rambled.

"Yo, Dawson. You're sleeping with a murderer. How does it feel?" a familiar voice vibrated in his brain.

Dawson paused, clenching his fists.

"Do what you'd expect *her* to do," Remy said quietly. "Let it go and keep on walking."

"Yeah. Yeah." Dawson wiggled his fingers and picked up the pace. He stood by the front door of the marina and waited for Remy to open the door with the keycode he'd gotten from Baily. His pulse pounded between his temples. For most of his life, he'd been calm, cool, and collected. The only time he'd panicked or struggled had been when he was learning how to swim. He'd taken a crash course six weeks before he'd left for the Navy. His will had been powered by imagining if he'd arrived there and couldn't even manage to tread water.

But he'd survived. He figured if he could overcome that fear, he could do anything.

Now he wondered if this damn town was going to kill him.

"Baily said the cameras are glitchy. That they don't always work, but she doesn't have the money to update them," Remy said as he made his way behind the counter. He flipped open the laptop and tapped away on the keyboard.

Of course, Baily hadn't updated them. Damn, the girl was lucky she kept this place afloat, and she wouldn't let them help. She'd almost refused to let them run their airboat tour company at her docks, which had brought her a decent penny just in boat slip rentals. However, she'd quickly changed her mind because it was either close and lose her shirt or take them up on their offer.

However, she was still drowning in debt. It drove

Fletcher crazy that she wouldn't let him and the rest of the guys do more.

"All right. Here we go," Remy said.

Dawson leaned over his deputy's shoulder. The image was beyond grainy. The frame came in and out as if the internet turned on and off. "There." Dawson tapped the screen. His heart bounced in his chest. "Freeze the image and blow it up."

"Sure thing."

Dawson squinted. "Whoever that is, it's not Audra. No way could she fit that mane of hers under a baseball cap. She has to pull it through the hole in the back, and there's no hair floating down the center of that person's back." He tapped the top of the screen. "Timestamp is four twenty-eight in the morning. Roll tape."

The video moved along for another forty-three seconds before the person lifted a gun. A flash filled the screen and then went blank.

"Well, I guess we know what happened to that camera," Remy said.

"Rewind it. This time, focus on the boat. Let's see if we can see any markings on it."

Remy glanced over his shoulder. "It's dark and grainy. Why don't we let the CSI team do it?"

"Because once you hand it off, it goes to State, and while I trust them—"

"It'll be logged into our system," Remy said. "We'll have access to it, and I think Detective Lester had a hard on for you."

"Not the point. Just do it." Dawson sucked in a deep

breath and let it out slowly. "I want to see it one more time. Humor me, man."

"All right, but that's not even an airboat. It's a flat-bottom—"

"Boston Whaler, and it's too fuzzy to make out any numbers if the damn thing even has any," Dawson said. "Who do we know that owns one of those?" He cocked a brow. "Silas. Tim. Paul. Dewey. Andrew. Morgan. Even Trinity owns one." Dawson smacked his fist on the counter. "Hell, Baily has three of them for rent out of these docks."

"And don't forget Paul's son owns one," Remy said. "He keeps his boat down the street at the big marina because he's an asshole."

"Wonderful," Dawson muttered.

"We have the other camera footage to look at," Remy said calmly as he tapped on the keyboard, pulling up the second camera.

For the next five minutes, they watched the wind rustle a few leaves across the ground before the camera went dead, catching nothing.

"Damn," Dawson muttered. That video had told him absolutely nothing. The only thing he knew for sure was someone didn't just want Audra to leave town.

They wanted her gone in a more permanent way, and they were willing to frame her for murder to do it.

# CHAPTER 11

Dawson leaned against the hood of his patrol car and rubbed his temple. He'd gotten all of a few hours of sleep before the call had come in. He was running on fumes.

"Thanks for meeting with me," Silas said, startling Dawson.

He jerked, smacking his elbow on the window. "I don't like games, and I hate secrets even more." He sighed. "Why are you being so cagey about the statement you made?"

Silas plucked the toothpick from his mouth and narrowed his stare. "Nothing cagey about me reporting what I saw."

"You've asked us to keep it quiet. Not discuss it with anyone, especially Paul. Why?" Dawson had planned on keeping everything about this case buttoned up tight now that it had turned into murder. He needed to keep things from the public eye. Speculation would happen no matter what he did, but he had to protect not only the townspeople—but Audra.

She was taking a beating in the court of public opinion, and Dawson took that personally.

"For all we know, Paul was signaling to his son." Silas folded his arms across his chest and leaned against the driver's side of the car. "Or even Dewey. They might not be registered as a team, but they worked in tandem last year, and we all know how Dewey gets when he sees a breakdown in the density of the mangrove. He wants to protect it. At first, I didn't want to make a big deal about things because Paul could've been trying to get someone's attention. He's pulled shit like that before."

"You're backpedaling." Dawson arched a brow. "And making excuses."

"I gave them the benefit of the doubt until Tim accused Audra and Paul and lied to my face. He had no idea I was standing in a river of grass, so he didn't see me." Silas nodded, waving his finger toward the waterfront. "Ever since those damn pythons were introduced to the Everglades, I've been hunting those slippery bastards. I don't need no stinking challenge to go out there and do it. I don't do it for a stupid prize or the notoriety but because the Everglades is my backyard. I want to protect the beauty of this place and the ecosystem. That little girl knows exactly what I'm talking about. Her father was the same way, and he raised her to respect this land." Silas lowered his chin. "Paul's my friend. Has been for years, and he and I have always believed the same thing when it comes to this shit. He's out there hunting pythons not because he gives a shit about this stupid challenge but because we do this year-round. So why did he lie? Why did he fire those rounds and let Tim accuse her? What's their end game?" Silas shoved his toothpick back in his mouth and twirled it around. "Other than she makes us all nervous."

"You all have an opinion about Audra and what happened the night her father died. None of you have any hard facts about that, yet you're willing to toss her under the bus."

"Come on, Dawson. That's different. Hugely different. Paul knows she didn't shoot anything, and he stood there like a damn moron and didn't call Tim out on his bullshit. Why?" Silas plucked his toothpick out again and waved it around. "Even I wouldn't do that, and I've admitted to doing some shady shit over the course of my life."

"Let me ask you this—and I'd like an honest answer." Dawson pushed away from the vehicle and glanced around. The crime scene had been cleared, and the hunters had begun to prepare the boats for a long day of python catching. "You didn't believe she killed her dad at first. Why not, and what changed?" Dawson lowered his chin. "And be a little more specific than you have been."

"Nothing's changed," Silas said. "It's all pretty simple, and the truth is, I don't know for certain she did kill him, at least, not in cold blood. The fight she had with her dad the day before he went missing was verbally vicious. No one who heard it could deny part of that little girl meant those words. Her mother was the glue that held that family together, and without her, Victor continued to lose his grip on reality."

"You really think she went out there and took an opportunity to get rid of the town crazy?"

Silas let out a long breath. "No. Maybe. I don't know. It's possible that weird shit went down, and she made up a story to protect her own ass. Or it was an accident, and she honestly doesn't remember. But the fact that Trip continued to investigate it—and no matter what that file says, I know he did—tells me he believed it was no accident. Add her slinking away in the middle of the night like a criminal?" Silas shrugged. "What's a man to think? Especially after I was the only one—outside of Trip—who believed her. She might as well have slapped me across the face."

"And based on the encounters that Audra has told me the two of you have had since her return, you've essentially accused her of killing her dad, and you've threatened her."

"That's what she said?" Silas sighed. "I told her she should leave because something bad could happen if she didn't. I didn't say I was the bad."

"Doesn't matter, Silas. It's how you said the words and the tone you used." Dawson cocked a brow. "You did the same thing everyone accuses her of doing and accused her old man of doing."

"Look. As crazy as Victor was, I considered him a friend. If she had anything to do with what happened, I want to know why. That little girl has always been a tad terrified of me, so I thought I could scare it out of her back then."

"What about today?"

"Old habits die hard," Silas said. "But none of this is what I wanted to talk to you about."

Dawson knew when to stop beating a dead horse. "All right. I'm listening."

"Now that Tim's been murdered, there's a lot of chatter about how Audra came at him last night with her fists ready to fly. She would've clocked him good had you not tossed her over your shoulder."

"Tell me something I don't know," Dawson muttered.

"Yeah, well, it was amusing to watch." Silas chuckled before clearing his throat. "But all that talk has taken a weird turn, and honestly, I don't like it."

"Outside of everyone thinking she killed Tim?" Dawson couldn't imagine anything more absurd.

"Oh, yeah." Silas nodded like an old man bobblehead. He waved his toothpick like it were a sword. "While waiting to get to my boat this morning, Paul, Benson, and Dewey discussed how they keep seeing Audra going to strange, out-of-the-way places, like the island with no name. Her going there's not a big deal, and I'd honestly expect her to go there, but Reaper Island? That's a bit out of the way. While I'm sure snakes are back there, there are so many other places to go looking than making the trek all the way up there. It's too close to one of the other challenges, and we don't cross streams, if you know what I mean. But they believe she's hidden something there. They also talked about how she must've been doing something illegal back in the day and that her dad must have caught wind of it. Them saying that is strange all by itself, but they weren't trying to be quiet about it. It's spreading through town like wildfire."

"Now that's interesting, considering you mentioned that it was possible Victor could've been doing something nefarious out there." Not that Dawson cared about other people's opinions, but Silas had gone out of his way to call this meeting. Besides, it was a new and interesting twist that the town was taking, and he wanted to know why.

The why was always important.

"I like to talk smack," Silas said. "Sometimes seeing people's responses to the shit that comes out of my mouth gets me the answers I need."

"Well, then tell me your thoughts. If Audra could've been hiding something sixteen years ago, why did she wait so long to come back and get it?"

"If that little girl was doing anything against the law, Victor wouldn't have taken her out there with him to find out what it was. But outside of having a mouth like a truck driver and an attitude the size of Texas, Audra wasn't a bad kid. Actually, I always found her to be amusing. I enjoyed her energy. Worse thing she ever did was take matters into her own hands when someone wronged her instead of taking it to her old man or the law." Silas stepped from the vehicle. "I know I've been hard on her since she returned."

Dawson snorted. "You flat-out accused her of killing her dad."

"No. I implied it. Two different things." Silas shrugged. "I struggle to believe she doesn't know something about that night. Whether it was through those nightmares of hers she refused to tell me about or something else." He waggled his finger. "But she didn't fire her weapon, and I don't believe for one minute she killed Tim or slashed Benson's tire. She's not ten anymore." Silas sucked in a breath and let it out slowly.

"Well, you're about the only one in town who believes that," Dawson said. "Want to tell me why?"

"While I know she's got reason to hate Tim, she's got no reason to come back here and kill the man. That said, no one in this town, myself included, has made her return easy." Silas scratched the side of his face. "You need to know that everyone is going to come gunning for her, hard. Harder than before. That means they're coming for your badge, and while I haven't always been your biggest fan, you've proven to me that you have Calusa Cove's best interests at heart."

"Are you feeling okay, Silas?" Dawson reached out and placed the back of his hand on Silas' forehead. "Have a fever or something?"

"Fuck off." Silas slapped Dawson's arm away. "My point is, she's going to need a protector now more than ever." He pointed toward Paul, Benson, and Dewey. "They might have tolerated her presence yesterday. They won't do it now."

"And you will?" Dawson asked. "Tim worked for you, not Paul, though you're all good friends. Either you're turning on your pals, or you're setting me up."

"I'm not doing either." Silas ran his hand over his beard. "I was going to fire Tim when this was over."

"Nothing like burying the lead." Dawson planted his hands on his hips. "Why?"

"He was stealing from me." Silas cocked his head. "No, I wasn't going to turn him in. Just wanted to humiliate the little bastard. And no, I didn't kill him."

Dawson raised his hands. "I didn't say you did, but since we're on the subject, where were you last night?"

"I was python hunting until midnight, and then I went home. You can check with my wife." Silas moved the toothpick from one side to the other. "But seriously, any real suspects?"

"I'm not having that conversation with you."

"Well, I need to get going. We're going to have a moment of silence down at the docks. If you need me, you know how to get ahold of me."

Dawson rubbed his jaw. Next year, he would for sure take this week off work. He turned and headed toward his patrol car when his cell phone went off. He reached into his pocket and stared at the caller ID flashing on the screen.

*Florida Federal Prison.*

He jogged to his vehicle and tapped the green button as he slipped behind the steering wheel. "This is Chief Dawson Ridge."

"Hi. This is Warden Marsden. I have here in my office, Trevor Williams. He'd like to speak with you unofficially. Are you willing?"

"That's an interesting request."

"It's for his safety. He needs to know that this conversation never happened."

"Agreed." Dawson rubbed his jaw.

"Hello?" a male voice echoed over the speaker. "Thank you for taking the call and agreeing to my terms. I need you to first listen and, second, never reach out to me again—unless you button things up, and then I'll be at your beck and call."

Dawson frowned. "That's a bit cagey."

"Look. If word gets out that I've said anything to you, I'll die. My family will die. I'm taking a big risk even doing this. But I've heard some things have happened in Calusa Cove. If you think something is happening, it's happening. Just probably not the way you believe. I didn't do the things I was accused of. At least not like I was charged. I took the fall because I valued my life and was promised protection."

"Are you saying you didn't run drugs through Calusa Cove?"

"I wasn't the one doing it, but I did turn a blind eye. I did allow it to happen. I am guilty of that. I could give you a million reasons why I did it. Blackmail. Money. Power. They all played a role."

"Are you calling to give me names?"

"I'm sorry. I can't do that."

Dawson pinched the bridge of his nose. "Then why the hell did you call?"

Trevor sighed. "If you can get me and my family into the witness protection program, I'll flip. I'll testify. I'll give you everything I've got. And trust me when I say it's a lot."

"What's the difference between flipping now or later?"

"Because if I'm the one who gives them up, they

won't kill me, they'll kill my family, and they won't die quick. It'll be slow and painful," Trevor said with a slight tremor in his voice. "Do we have a deal?"

"First, I'm not the one who can make that deal, and you know that," Dawson said. "Second, in order for me to help get you that deal, I need a hell of a lot more information…like for starters…I need know exactly who you were helping? Give me names and I'll go to my contacts with the FBI and the DEA."

"I give you that now, my family is as good as dead." Trevor let out a hefty sigh. "Why the hell do you think I've been so quiet this past year. I don't know who I can trust."

"What makes you think you can trust me?"

"Because your friends with Fletcher," Trevor said. "He's about as straight as they come. I know that from Ken."

Dawson sucked in a deep breath. "How does Ken factor into all this?"

"He doesn't," Trevor said with a sharp tone. "Start with the cartel that was known to run drugs when my old man was chief. Talk to Anna. She knows those names. Get someone to agree to help me, and I'll give you everything you need."

"It's a tall order and I can't promise anything, but I'll make some phone calls," Dawson said. He had nothing to lose.

"Thanks. And good luck." The line went dead.

Now that was interesting.

# CHAPTER 12

AAUDRA STARED AT THE DOCKS. The morning had ticked by at a snail's pace as she waited to hear from Dawson. Minutes turned into hours, and it was well past the lunch. She'd given up all hope of going back out into the Everglades for another day of python hunting. A slight breeze rippled across the water. A few hunters milled about, staring—more like glaring. A searing pain tore at her heart. This town was her home. Her soul. All she'd ever wanted was to belong. To fit in. To be anything other than a swamp monster.

"You probably shouldn't have told me about your conversation with Trevor," she said softly.

"Nope. But I did." Dawson lifted her chin. "Am I going to regret doing that?"

"I can keep a secret." She nodded. "It just seems weird he'd do that."

"It is. But there was no reason for me not to agree to it. I don't believe in coincidences and too many strange things have happened. I've got to connect the pieces and if Trevor has intel that will help me, I need to find a way to get him talking. Trading it for his protection is something we do all the time, if it puts bigger fish away."

"I struggle to believe Trevor isn't one of the big fish, but maybe he did turn over a new leaf. Anything's possible." She sighed.

"Are you going to be okay?" Dawson asked softly. His long fingers rested on her shoulders, squeezing gently.

Shoving all the painful emotions and memories back into the dark corner of her mind, she pulled open her car door and tossed her bag across the seat. "I'm just driving back to the cabins. I'll be fine."

Dawson took her by the forearms. "I'll follow you just to be safe."

She sighed again, realizing that's exactly what she wanted. Needed. For the first time in her adult life, she allowed another human to worm his way into her bloodstream. It felt warm and comfortable. No. It was more than that. She craved it. Desired it. Even demanded it. "You don't have to do that."

"Yeah, actually, I do." He took her chin with his thumb and forefinger. "I'd never forgive myself if anything happened to you." He leaned in and tenderly brushed his lips over hers in a sweet kiss.

If knees could buckle, hers did. She gripped his shoulders, wrapping her tongue around his, swirling and sucking it into her mouth in a desperate attempt to feel everything he had to give.

She shuddered, remembering where she stood. "People are staring," she whispered.

"And you think I care?"

"You should," she managed. "Everyone thinks I—"

He hushed her with another passionate kiss—one that matched the last one and then some.

Heat rose to her cheeks.

He pulled back, and his lips curved seductively upward. "You're cute when you blush."

"And you're a pain in the ass." She eased behind the steering wheel, glancing around the parking lot. Baily stepped from the marina shop. She smiled and waved. At least there was one other person who didn't look at Audra as if she were a scum-sucking bottom-feeder. "You know I'll have to go back out there tomorrow. I do have an article to write."

"If all goes well, I can go with you."

"You're not my babysitter."

He chuckled. "Perhaps not, but I don't want you out there alone. Not with what people are thinking and saying." He batted her nose. "And it is my job to protect the citizens of this town."

"Well, I don't live here."

"That's a technicality." He reached across her and tugged at the seat belt. "Don't make me chase you down the street. I won't hesitate to turn on my lights and pull you over."

Her lips twitched. "You'd like that, wouldn't you?"

"Only if I get to break out the handcuffs and get to use them…in bed."

She laughed. "Oh my God. You're insufferable."

"I've been called worse." He closed the door and strutted across the parking lot with that sexy swagger.

Audra sucked in a deep breath. She'd expected to be treated like an outsider when she returned.

But she'd never anticipated Dawson. He was something else.

She put her vehicle in gear and pulled out of the parking lot, Dawson right on her ass.

A weird rattling noise vibrated from somewhere inside her car. Shit. Her car was older, but it had served her well. The last thing she needed was for it to have issues in this small town. The local body shop was owned by Mark Lamin and his old man. Mark was a nice enough guy, but he'd been friends with Ken.

Not someone she wanted to spend any time with.

Or ask for help.

Maybe Dawson knew something about cars. Worst case, she could always ask Trinity. Her dad owned a bunch of dealerships.

Or Hondo. Yeah, Hondo had been a bit of a grease monkey back in the day. She'd stop in at the office and have a little chat with Lilly when she got back to the cabins.

*Rattle. Rattle. Rattle.*

What a weird noise. It didn't sound mechanical. No. It was more like something was falling apart.

She glanced in her rearview mirror.

Dawson was still literally right behind her. He gave her a little finger wave. The man was too damned adorable. If she were anyone else, she might consider staying in this stupid town a little longer just for him. But she couldn't. Wouldn't. And not only because of what Calusa Cove represented, but because no one wanted her here.

Baily and Trinity were nice enough. Welcoming enough. But even their kindness had a timetable on it, and it would end the second the Python Challenge was over.

She turned into Harvey's Cabins and rolled to a stop in one of the designated spots near Dawson's unit. She collected her purse and made her way to the rear of her vehicle, popping the trunk.

"Let me get that for you." Dawson jumped in front of her. "That's a lot of equipment." He lifted the hatch.

*Rattle. Rattle. Rattle.*

"Do you hear that?" She reached into the trunk to grab the smaller bag. "I heard it the whole way home."

*Rattle. Rattle. Rattle.*

It got louder. And louder.

She handed Dawson the bag and went for the larger camera case when two beady little eyes locked with hers. A long, forked tongue darted out of the snake's mouth as it coiled in the corner, its rattle raised high, singing its warning.

"Don't move," Dawson whispered, his hand on his weapon, slowly releasing it from its holster. "We need to shut your trunk."

"I'll reach for it," she said so softly. She hoped he heard her because the only sound that rang in her ears was a combination of the beating of her heart and the singing of the rattle. It was as if the two were in perfect harmony.

It wasn't a pretty sound.

She held her breath as she slowly reached for the trunk hatch.

The snake inched back, coiling tighter. Its eyes narrowed and then widened. Its tongue waggled as if it were tasting her smell.

And then, in a split second, it lunged forward with a hungry mouth… poison dripping from its fangs.

With her left hand, she reached for the beast's head, and with her right, she pushed Dawson. "Don't shoot it," she managed with a ragged breath as her fingers curled around the snake's neck. She squeezed. Tight.

The rattlesnake's tail flipped and flopped, smacking her hip. Her elbow. Even her cheek, as if to slap her for daring to destroy its ability to bite.

"Jesus Christ." Dawson adjusted his weapon and shook his body. "I can't believe you just did that."

"Could you please get me one of those python bags to put this snake in? Last I checked, it's still illegal to kill these things in the state of Florida."

Dawson snagged a bag and held it open. She eased the nasty three-foot thing into the bag. The damn thing went wild.

"It's not illegal if your life is in danger, and I'd say our lives were in question," Dawson said, setting the bag down. He pulled out his cell phone and tapped on the screen. "I can get Keaton here within the next fifteen minutes." He raked his hands through his hair. "Are you okay?"

"Peachy." She shivered. "That thing was roaming free while I was driving."

"Damn lucky it didn't bite you on the way home." He took her by the hand as he spoke into the phone. "Keaton, I need you at the Harvey Cabins ASAP to take care of a snake. No, not a python. A rattler." His gaze met Audra's. "We found it in Audra's car. I'll also need you to check for any other stowaways." He paused to listen. "No idea how it got there." Again, he listened. "See you in fifteen." Dawson ended the call, dropped his cell phone into his pocket, and reached out to tuck a strand of fiery red hair behind Audra's ear. "I can't believe you snagged that rattler the way you did." His lips pressed into a thin line. "Putting on my cop hat for a second, I have to wonder if—"

"Someone put that bastard in there on purpose." She inched closer, peering inside the window, looking for more. "It makes sense. Whoever killed Tim would've seen my car there. They put my gun under his body. It's just another way to get rid of me. But why?"

"That's the million-dollar question." He palmed her cheek. "My conversation with Silas had me thinking something new."

Her brow dipped. "I don't trust that man."

"I think he might be more on your side than either of us thought, but we'll table that for now." He bent over, lifted the snake bag, and set it on the side of the porch. Then he lifted her camera bag. "When I was in the Navy, specifically as a SEAL, one of the tactics we used on missions was redirection."

"In theory, I'm aware of what that means." With her

insides shaking like the buttons on that snake, she followed him inside the cabin.

"Calusa Cove is focused on you and what you're doing. Everything that's happening has you at the center and me chasing my tail." He set her bag on the counter. "I honestly believe James and Eliot meant to put that dynamite on your boat."

"And blow me up," she muttered.

"No. I think they wanted to report it missing, have me find it, and arrest you. The question is, why? Right now, the only connection to the town they seem to have is Benson."

"That means they're connected to Paul."

"That could be true." Dawson leaned against the counter. "When that plan failed, they came at you on the water. We don't know who that masked man was who untied your boat and cut the fuel line, but they didn't want you finding remnants on that island, like old wood that belonged to crates used to hide cocaine."

"What are you talking about?" Audra stared at Dawson. She blinked. "What crates? What cocaine? Am I going to want to throttle you?"

"Probably," he said, grimacing.

She made her way to the liquor cabinet and pulled down a bottle of tequila, pouring herself a nice glass on the rocks. She didn't bother offering one to Dawson, knowing he was still on duty for a few more hours. She plopped herself on the sofa and sipped her beverage. "I'm listening."

"I sent the wood you saw on the island with no name to the Feds and the DEA. It came back that it's possible the paint markings are from an incredibly old case. A seventeen-year-old case," Dawson leaned against the counter with an arched brow.

Her hand paused with the glass halfway to her mouth. "You've got to be kidding me."

"I wish I were." He shook his head. "Your dad wasn't crazy at all."

"No, he wasn't. But he did suffer from a mental illness. No denying that. And he mixed shit up all the time." She set the glass on the end table, guilt gnawing at her gut. "He knew something was going on back there in the swamp." She'd gone along with him that night, not because she'd believed him, but because he was her father, and she'd felt bad about their earlier argument.

"Well, he was right, and something tells me it never stopped," Dawson said, glancing at his cell. "It might have paused. Or even slowed down. But someone—and my guess, a local—is still running drugs through Calusa Cove, and I'm going to put a stop to it."

She smiled. "Is it weird that I'm turned on by how you said that?"

"No." He laughed. "Felt kind of sexy rolling off my tongue." He sauntered across the room and hoisted her off the sofa, crushing her against his chest. "Keaton just rolled into the parking lot. I need to chat with him, and I have to go back to work. I want you to stay in this cabin. You can visit with Lilly. Or have Trinity or Baily over. But I don't want you leaving. Can you do that for me? Please?"

She brushed a strand of his hair off his forehead. "I kind of love it when you beg."

He cocked his head, tilting her chin with his thumb and forefinger. "Promise me."

Audra cocked an eyebrow. "Can I at least sit on the front porch?"

"Yes. As long as you don't get pissed off that I'll be having someone drive by every so often."

"I can live with that."

"Good." He brushed his lips across her mouth. "Call or text if you need me." And with that, Dawson was out the door, leaving her with her thoughts.

Which weren't good.

Someone wanted her gone.

And not just out of town anymore. That snake wasn't a message. It could have been a nail in her coffin.

* * *

AUDRA SAT on the front porch of Dawson's cabin with Trinity and Baily. She stared out at the evening sky. "Do either of you need another drink? Maybe a snack?"

"I'm good. Really. But thank you," Trinity said.

"Me, too." Baily raised her glass. "Is there anything we can do for you?"

The day had ticked by like a slow-motion movie. After Dawson had left, satisfied there were no more snakes in her car—or in the cabin—to finish his work for the day, Audrea had looked through the images on her camera.

She'd taken some great shots.

But she'd been hoping to see something that would shed some light on what her father had seen out there that night sixteen years ago. Or maybe something that would tell her who was trying to kill her.

But nothing jumped out at her except a few images that showed a flat-bottom boat in the background and a man driving it. It could have been the same one used by the guy who'd boarded her boat that first day. But it was off in the distance, and she couldn't make out anything. However, she sent it off to Dawson. Maybe he could have the CSI team enhance it.

He thanked her for texting it and then sent her an inappropriate sexual message, asking for a picture of her gator tattoo that showed more than the ink—something to get him through the rest of his day.

Dawson was quite the unexpected surprise, and she found herself diving into the deep end. As much as she'd always dreamed about making Calusa Cove her home again, it was a fantasy. She'd always be a Stigini in most people's minds, and she was too old to keep playing the part.

She needed to put him out of her thoughts and, especially, out of her heart. But when she did that, everything else came crashing into her soul like a runaway freight train. It barreled into her body, and she got tangled up in all the pieces of her past and present.

She'd tried reading and watching television, but nothing had held her attention.

So, she'd taken a bath.

All that had done was unleash the waterworks.

She hated crying. It was the worst thing in the world. Unfortunately, she hadn't been able to stop the tears until she'd cried them all out. Thankfully, that had been a few hours earlier, and she'd managed to pull herself together before Baily and Trinity had shown up.

She smiled at the girls, glad for the company. "Honestly, there's not much you could do for me unless you can make the town suddenly see me as a human." Audra sighed. "I have half a mind to do what I did sixteen years ago and leave."

"Trust me. That's not going to accomplish anything." Baily glared. "Except maybe piss me off."

"I know." Audra nodded. "It's just so hard. No one wants me here."

Trinity leaned forward and grabbed her hand. "I want you to stay."

"I do, too." Baily nodded. "And what about Dawson? He's basically moved you into his cabin."

"And you're all he talks about," Trinity added.

"Yeah, because he's knee-deep in strangeness and a murder case," Audra muttered, waving her finger over her head. "All because of me."

"We don't know that for a fact," Baily said, but her lackluster tone wasn't all that convincing.

"Even if I did commit to following through with the Python Challenge, I'd only be here for another week. Regardless of what's happening between me and Dawson, I'd still be leaving."

"You don't have to," Baily said. "This is your home."

"Yeah." Trinity downed the rest of her beverage. "Take it from a girl who's struggled to fit in my entire life. All you need is a couple of good girlfriends to get you through. You've got that in us." She stood. "I hate to do this, but I have to go. Mallary has been texting."

"How is that poor girl?" Baily asked.

"Not well." Trinity ran her fingers through her hair. "The entire town has turned on her family, and her stepmother blames her for everything. Her father's business is failing, and Mallary's desperate to get her deep dive scuba certification so she can come out with me." She sucked in a deep breath and huffed it out. "She's making me crazy. I go out as often as I can, but I can't find that boat."

"Are you talking about the one everyone believes went down a year ago with the Jewels from *Flying Victoria*?" Audra asked.

"Jared—Mallary's little brother—was the captain of that small vessel. It was a crazy night. I was out there. Two storms collided right on top of me. A few miles out, I could see a small fishing boat heading right into the storm. I couldn't leave them out there in good faith, so I tried to find them. To help them. But they were lost at sea," Trinity said with tears welling in her eyes. "But then, there's Keaton. If he sees me loading *Princess Afloat* with scuba equipment, he's lecturing me on safety. He's been doing that ever since that night. Heck, his lectures started before then, but that's when it got real bad."

"I heard he can be worse than Dawson, and trust me, that man can be uptight." Audra's laugh quickly caught in her throat. "I hope your friend finds the answers she's looking for."

"Thanks." Trinity nodded.

"I'll walk with you to the parking lot," Baily said as she rose and embraced Audra. "Do not engage with anyone."

"I hear you." Audra eased back into the chair and watched her friends stroll across the gravel to their vehicles. She waved one last time. Having those two in her corner made all the difference in the world.

Out of the corner of her eye, she saw Benson strutting along the path with the two men who'd been arrested the first day she'd arrived—the two men who had brought the dynamite. A tinge of fear prickled the back of her neck. The timing of their arrival couldn't have been worse. It made her wonder if it had been planned. As if they had been watching and waiting for the right moment to make their move.

She shivered. She should go inside and lock the door, but she was like a deer in headlights.

"I hear you're some kind of Owl Witch," Eliot said. He shook his head, laughing. "Too bad because you're damned hot."

"Yeah, I'd tap that," James said.

*Don't engage.*

She stared into her drink, swirling it. A million retorts raced through her brain. One of them included speaking in tongues. Not that she knew any, but faking them had always worked when she'd been a kid.

"Let her be," Benson said. "Old wives' tales, and trust me, she's not worth the energy."

Benson had been mostly a squeaky-clean kid with a holier-than-thou attitude. He'd gotten good grades, and most of the adults around here had liked him. He hadn't been a brownnoser. He hadn't been a loud kid and had kind of flown under the radar, working for his dad.

Her heart lurched to the back of her throat.

Ken had worked for Paul at his lawyer's office and loved it at first. Well, he'd loved the money. He'd even talked about becoming an attorney, and Audra had dreamed of him staying in Calusa Cove.

The job hadn't lasted long because Ken had gotten into a big fight with Benson. After that, he'd joined the Navy with Fletcher.

The trio paused in front of Dawson's cabin.

She swallowed hard. She wanted to confront them, but she'd promised Dawson. While she'd never been very good at keeping her word, Dawson was, and she felt as though she owed it to him to keep her big fat mouth shut.

"I'll catch up," Benson said as he waved his hand, encouraging Frick and Frack to continue down the path.

The other two men turned their heads. One smiled —well, more like curved his lips into a sinister sneer. The other waved and snickered.

Assholes.

Her pulse lurched to her throat and got stuck there. She froze, holding her breath, hoping Benson would keep walking. He marched himself right up the porch steps as if they were old friends.

"I heard you had a little bit of excitement today," Benson said with a grin plastered on his face. "Showing off your snake-taming skills again, were you?" He made a *tsk-tsk* noise, shaking his head. "Only feeding the rumors about your swamp monster life."

She brought her index and middle finger toward her face, narrowed her eyes, and waved her hand between herself and Benson. "Better watch out, or I'll cast an evil spell on you." She lifted her cocktail and sipped. It was only her second one of the day, and she wanted to down it but decided that wasn't a good idea.

"You're one lucky young lady." Benson leaned against the railing. "That snake could've bitten you right in the face. It would've sucked if he'd taken out one of your eyes or attacked you while you were driving and caused an accident."

"What do you want?" She swirled her glass, staring at the melting ice cubes.

"I came to say hello. To check on you. It's been a long time," Benson said, leaning a little closer. "I'm shocked to see you *slither* back to these parts."

"Interesting word choice." She glanced up, meeting his gaze head-on. "And I'm here for the same reason you are."

He tossed his head back and laughed. Hard. "Right. Because you have family or anyone here who cares about you." He rested his hand on his knee. His face turned serious. "You were always a misfit in this town. You thought you belonged, but you never did fit in. Not even Ken wanted you. Hell, I remember one time he came back here with his wife. He was so proud of her and never even thought twice about you."

"You don't know anything about Ken." She gripped her glass so tightly that she worried she might break it, but even she could admit that Ken had wanted—*needed* —her to be different. He'd begged her to comb her hair and wear shoes, even if they were only flip-flops. He'd even bought her nice clothes. It wasn't until she'd left town that she'd realized Ken had cared more about appearances than he had about her, but she wasn't about to admit that to Benson. "And you don't know anything about our relationship. So, why don't you go back to your bottom-dwelling friends?" She leaned forward. "You know, the ones who put dynamite on my vessel." She arched an eyebrow. "I bet one of them shot down my drone, crawled onto my boat, sliced a hole in the gas line, and—"

"You really do have quite the vivid imagination." Benson chuckled. "Or perhaps you're losing your mind just like your daddy."

She recoiled, sloshing a bit of her drink over the rim of her glass.

"And Dawson's a small-minded cop whose days are numbered." Benson inched so close she smelled the beer on his breath. "Go back to whatever rock you crawled out from under. If you don't, someone will find the evidence they need that proves you killed your father and Tim. A cop other than Dawson will be tossing your pretty little ass in the slammer. Mark my words."

She drew in a deep breath and leveled a hard stare at Benson. "Is that a threat?"

Benson shook his head. "Just stating facts." He stood and descended the porch step. Then he turned on his heel, stuffed his hands in his pockets, and strolled down the path like he didn't have a care in the world.

She stood, marched herself inside, and slammed the door.

Tears filled her eyes.

Deep in her heart, Calusa Cove—The Everglades—

felt like home. When she wandered through town in the dark of night, it brought her a sense of calm. A sense of happiness. Even when she had to suffer the whispers and stares from the townspeople who thought the worst of her, this place still brought her joy.

Her heart was connected to it as if it pumped the blood through her veins. However, the secrets surrounding her father's death had clogged it, making it impossible for her to stay.

The front door rattled, making her jump. Her damn nerves were fried.

"Lucy, you got some 'splainin' to do," Dawson said in some stupid accent as he stepped through the door. He closed it, unclipped his gun, removed the magazine of bullets, and placed it in the lockbox like he had the night before.

"You're not funny." She let out a big puff of air. She'd spent her entire life acting as though she wasn't afraid of anything—or anyone.

But the truth was—she was terrified of her own shadow. A murderer was loose and might make her his next target.

"And it's not like I meant to open my mouth with Benson," she said, "but he pushed my buttons."

"Not sure what you're talking about, but I'll take your word for it because he's a jerk." He leaned in and brushed his lips over hers as if they were a couple. "Sorry, I'm late." He held up a bag. "I brought home a couple of salads. My heartburn couldn't handle more fried foods. I didn't want to cook, and I figured neither did you."

They'd known each other going on four days. She shouldn't be staying in his home, but where else would she stay? With Trinity? Baily? No. That meant he'd put someone like Remy or, worse, one of his buddies on them as a bodyguard. She wouldn't do that to her friends.

He set the food on the counter and pulled her close.

When she tried to squirm away, he held her tighter. "Sweetheart, don't let him get to you. He's not worth it." He palmed her cheek. "Want to talk about it?"

"Not really."

"Okay," he said softly. "Just remember I'm a safe space to land."

She'd never met anyone like Dawson before. At least not someone who treated her as if she were a normal human with real feelings. "I'm tired." She swiped at her face, unable to hide the emotion. "I didn't kill my dad. I didn't come back here to cause trouble, and that rattlesnake wasn't a message or a warning. Someone wants me dead. I might as well do what I do best and disappear."

Dawson took a step back and raked his fingers through his hair. "I can't let you do that. Before you start arguing with me, it's not because I think you're guilty of anything or that I'm worried about what this town will believe if you do."

"Then why?"

He pulled out his cell phone. "Hayes may have found something today." He held up an image. "Can't tell much from this snapshot, but he believes there's something on Coonts Island. Something that wasn't there a few months ago, and we've all been back there."

"Way up Loon River? That's a hike from here and hard to navigate during low tide, even hard for some airboats." She took his phone and zoomed in on what appeared to be a roof hidden in the trees. "Not to mention some locals won't go back there because that's where the ghost of Edgar Watson settled."

"Our airboats can navigate Loon River during low tide, no problem." Dawson nodded. "But I figure if we leave at high tide, which is at five in the morning, we could be back over by Hog Island by seven. We'll just say we got an early start." Dawson didn't acknowledge Captain Watson or the many stories that surrounded him.

Missing boats. Planes that had disappeared.

The Ghost Ship of the Everglades had been haunting South Florida for as long as anyone could remember, and if a human dared to go back to Captain Watson's home—especially at night—beware. Of course, it was just a story, and how could a pirate ship not only make it back this far but be kept hidden for hundreds of years?

However, locals respected the area because too many strange things happened there.

Of course, half the town believed she was a swamp monster—an Owl Witch. So, there was that.

"You seriously want to go there before sunrise?" she asked. "Hasn't anyone told you about Edgar Watson?"

"I know all about him and every single story behind his pirate ship." Dawson arched a brow. "I also know your dad told those ghost tales every chance he got. Please tell me you don't believe them."

"It's not that I think they're real, but I feel the same way about that section of the Everglades as I do about the Bermuda Triangle. Not sure it's real, but I don't particularly want to fly over it or float into it."

"I'm a retired Navy SEAL. I've been through the Bermuda Triangle more than once. I've spent much of my career at sea. I know all about legends and pirates. I'm not afraid, and I need to investigate this. You're welcome to come with me. Your choice."

She glanced between him and the cell phone. Her hands trembled. A tear dribbled down her cheek. "You'd do that for me?"

"How many times do I have to tell you that I'm on your side? That I believe everything you're telling me?" He tossed the cell phone on the counter. Cupping her face, he kissed her softly. "Everyone in this town is acting crazy. I'm suspicious of most people right now. But not you. You're the one person who hasn't given me any real reason to doubt you."

She flung herself at him, wrapping her arms and legs around his strong body, crash-landing her lips on his mouth. If honesty, loyalty, and kindness had a taste, then that's what Dawson tasted like.

His steadying hands wrapped around her waist, their bodies blending into each other. She could feel his heartbeat in sync with hers, rapid yet soothing. Dawson carried her back to the bed. His hands massaged her muscles, kneading into her flesh as if she were clay and he was molding her into a fine piece of sculpture.

There was a quiet understanding as they shared another soft kiss, the worries of the world momentarily stilled by their shared emotions. He brushed a loose strand of hair away from her face. "You're not alone," he whispered. "I'm right here, and I'm not going anywhere."

She'd been alone for so long that she'd forgotten what it was like to rely on another human.

Her memories of her mother had only been of when she'd been sick. But her mother had loved her. She'd championed her daughter. Audra cherished those moments. Her father had been fractured, and her mother's death had only made him worse. Ken had brought Audra some normalcy, but in the end, he'd betrayed her trust.

Dawson was different. He didn't pretend to be her knight in shining armor. He knew he was just a man, but he was a man who hadn't judged her. He believed her.

That was something.

She fumbled desperately with the buttons on his shirt as if it were the first time she'd ever undressed a man.

But Dawson gently captured her trembling hands and smiled softly, stealing her breath with a glance. "Slow down," he whispered, his voice rich with affection. "We've got time."

She looked at him as a myriad of emotions stared back at her in his amber eyes. Her fingers relaxed under his touch as he deftly unbuttoned his shirt, his every move unhurried and deliberate. Every second was an eternity as she watched the cotton slide off his broad shoulders to reveal his torso.

He was magnificent; tanned skin stretched taut over rippling muscles, adorned with only a light dusting of dark hair. He was like a painting—a masterpiece carved by a master craftsman, and she was the artist given the honor to etch every inch of him into her memory canvas.

He took her hands, kissing each knuckle tenderly while maintaining eye contact. Leading her hands to his chest, he let her trace the outline of his muscles—and scars—each contact sending electric sparks through her body.

Her breath hitched as she pulled herself closer, the heat radiating off him making her feel intoxicated. She buried her face into his neck, inhaling deeply—the scent of sea spray mixed with an undertone of fresh pine stirred something primal within her.

His strong arms cradled her slender body against his chest. Their bodies intertwined like puzzle pieces, fitting together perfectly.

A sense of serenity washed over her as she surrendered to their shared passion. They drew strength from each other amid a whirlwind of chaos looming outside their safe haven.

"Dawson," she whispered, her voice barely audible against his skin. "This feels—unreal."

He tucked her head under his chin, his hand splaying against her back as he held her in a protective embrace. "It's us... it's real," he stated, his affirmation carrying a weight that grounded her to the reality of their situation.

She clung to him, absorbing the rhythmic thud of his heart, allowing it to serve as a lighthouse in the storm of emotions she was experiencing. The shared solitude and intimacy brought an unspoken promise—an assurance that no matter how much the world outside their bubble raged, here, within these walls with him, she was safe.

His long fingers traced patterns along her spine, soothing her nerves, each stroke like a light balm over open wounds. Although the night was cold outside their sanctuary, the heat radiating from his body provided warmth that a thousand fires couldn't.

She looked at him beneath her lashes, tracing his features with her gaze. His sharp jawline softened as he stared back at her with an intensity that made her feel seen—truly seen—for perhaps the first time in ages.

He cradled her face with one hand, delicately tracing the slope of her nose as if he were a sculptor molding wet clay. Their lips met in a sweet exchange—a slow dance without urgency. It was purely them: raw and unhurried.

There was no need for spoken words between them; their bodies spoke volumes—an intimate language only they understood.

Slowly, they succumbed to the rhythm set by their beating hearts—the crescendo of emotions pouring out from each other's souls through silent whispers and punctuating sighs. As moonlight cast an ethereal glow around them, their shared solitude felt like home—a place of refuge where they could bare their vulnerabilities without fear.

And there, against Dawson's chest, under the moonlight, she realized something profound. She was no longer alone; her heart had found a companion in Dawson. And with that realization came a peaceful sigh as she surrendered herself to him. No matter what chaos lay ahead, she knew they'd face it together.

# CHAPTER 13

AFTER DAWSON'S parents had died, he'd become afraid of almost everything. A thud in the dark night would send him into a panic. Hell, a stroll down the street in broad daylight could make his heart race like he'd been running all day. It was as if the boogeyman were chasing him. Had it not been for the love and strength of his nana, he never would have had the courage to face his fears.

To forge the path that led him to the Navy.

He'd traveled a difficult road. One riddled with obstacles that took conviction to overcome. His battles were internal, and most never even saw them—but he felt them to his core.

The hum of the airboat vibrated through the ear protection. The warm air blew across his face like the first rush of a tropical storm. A flash of lightning in the distance—way out over the ocean—filled the sky. It was like the tentacles of an octopus reaching down and snagging its supper. That storm would dance over the sea, moving slowly toward shore until it dumped its destruction on Calusa Cove. A small vessel warning had already been issued and would be in place for the remainder of the day. The sea would be no place for the faint of heart for the next twenty-four hours, with waves between ten to fourteen feet and only two seconds apart.

The python hunters would have their own challenges with wind ripping across the Everglades. While protected by islands that created a barrier between land and ocean, it would still cause them issues.

Not to mention the torrential downpour that was expected to begin in a few hours and last well into the evening. Between high winds, the rain, and poor visibility, those hunting for snakes should've stayed at home. The smart ones did.

He glanced at his watch. They had left fifteen minutes before their scheduled departure. He shouldn't have been surprised when he swung his legs to the side of the bed before his alarm went off that she, too, was already awake.

Audra was perfect.

Everything about her was everything that excited him about a woman, right down to her fiery personality. That included her stubbornness. He loved a lady who dug her heels in when she knew what she wanted. That meant she had conviction. He admired that. Respected it. He didn't want a partner who would roll over and do whatever he expected.

He'd thought Liz was that woman until she'd gone and done the one thing Dawson couldn't stand.

She'd lied. Worse than lied. She'd betrayed his trust. His love. And, in turn, had crushed his soul.

He slowed the boat as they approached Loon River. Legend had it that those who dared to follow the river at night met with Edgar Watson's men—or worse, the Skunk Ape—and they either died or came back a changed person. Crazy as a loon.

Everyone in Calusa Cove perpetuated this silly ghost story. It was literally the first thing Dawson had been told the second he'd rolled into town a couple of months before the rest of his team. When he and the boys had started up their Everglades Overwatch tour boat business, they'd been told not to go back there—or give tours in the area, but not because of the tides and the fact they could get stuck—another tall tale because most airboats could handle a tide that low.

But because of Captain Edgar Watson.

The ten-year-old kid inside him had been utterly terrified.

The Navy SEAL thought it was the dumbest thing he'd ever heard.

The chief of police making the port turn into Loon River wasn't sure of anything.

He took off his ear protection and set them on the center console. He looped his arm around Audra. "It could be a nasty ride back between the wind and rain." He pointed to another flash of lightning that blew up the sky over the ocean. In the distance, it was a beautiful sight. He loved to watch storms roll across the sea—as long as they stayed miles offshore.

"Did you know you can get back here on foot from the island with no name?" she asked.

"Yeah, but only at low tide, and it's a three-mile walk. I wouldn't want to do that between the snakes, gators, Skunk Ape, and I've also heard about the Stigini or the Owl Witches." He grinned.

Audra chuckled. "Some people in this town still believe I'm a Stigini or somehow related to them." She turned, catching his gaze. "That I practice some old form of witchcraft, which allows me to turn myself into an owl."

"I've heard a lot of weird shit in this town, but that's one of the stranger ones." He eased the boat up to Coonts Island. "Makes them look like the nutty ones, not you."

"It's not that they actually believe I can turn into an owl." Audra laughed. "It's that they believe when I was a little girl, I'd come back here and practice witchcraft with the Stigini. That's why I was always barefoot, with ratty clothes, and my hair was always a mess. They never considered that for six years my mother was dying. That after one full round of chemo and radiation, she was done. She didn't want to do it again and tried a holistic approach, but it failed, and my father, while a loving man, struggled to care for both me and my mom, all while trying to run a business and keep the bills paid. It didn't help that his brain wasn't firing on all cylinders."

Dawson didn't know what was worse. To lose your parents suddenly or to watch them slowly die. He palmed her cheek. "I'm so sorry."

She leaned into his hand, curling her fingers around his wrist. "I honestly had a happy childhood with my parents. I knew I was different—that they were different—and I didn't care. My folks wrapped me in a big blanket of love. But it couldn't protect me from the cruelties of the world. Not after my mother died. Once she was gone, it was as if the bubble burst, and the bad parts of this town wormed their way in." She stared into the distance. "What sucks is that Calusa Cove is one of the most beautiful places I've ever been."

Dawson's chest tightened as he ran his thumb across her cheek. "We can't change the past, but we can change our relationship with it."

"Can I ask you a question about Ken?" she asked.

"I suppose."

"How did he die?"

Dawson stared at her for a moment and contemplated his answer. Telling her the truth meant he'd have to disclose Top Secret information about a mission. And worse, he'd have to admit his failure. The latter he'd come to terms with. The former, well, what difference did it make now? He trusted Audra like he trusted his brothers-in-arms. "The official story is we took on enemy fire during a mission that went sideways. He was injured, as we all were, and died because of a gunshot wound to his chest."

"And the reality?"

"Ken was the first of us not to re-enlist. That was supposed to be his last mission. He had forty-two days left. The problem was the minute I got those orders, I knew we were screwed. I knew we'd be making some hard decisions on the ground and doing it blind." He held up his hand when she opened her mouth. He couldn't be sure of her question, but no matter, he wasn't answering anything. If he was telling this story, he was doing it his way. "We learned our target had not only moved positions but had gained gunpower. We decided—based on intel—to come in from a different direction. We did question that information, but we only had a small window of time. It was ultimately my call. Fletcher plays it like he pushed me since he was my communications officer. But at the end of the day, I sent Ken out as point man. Eight minutes later, we were all captured."

"Oh no," she whispered.

Mindlessly, he rubbed the scars created by electric currents bolting through his muscles. "For three days, we were all tortured."

"The burns," she said. "That's how Ken died?"

"No." Dawson squeezed his eyes closed. "They couldn't break us, so they tried a new tactic. They took Fletcher and Ken in another room, and they... they..." He blinked. Could he even say it?

"What did they do?"

Dawson sucked in a deep breath and swiped at his cheeks, his fingers wet with tears he hadn't been aware he'd shed. "They slit Ken's throat in front of Fletcher."

Audra gasped and clapped a hand over her mouth. Her teal eyes grew wide with a combination of fear, anguish, and rage.

Dawson wrapped his arms around her and hugged her tight to his chest, stroking her long, lush hair.

She wept softly.

"I'm sorry I couldn't save him. That I didn't make a different—"

"No. You don't have anything to apologize for." She jerked from his embrace and glared. "You did what you were trained to do, and don't you dare go and tell me any one of those men would've made a different decision because we both know they all would've made the same one. Hindsight is perfect vision."

Running his finger across her cheek, he gazed into her eyes, searching for a reason not to allow his heart to beat with hers, but he couldn't find a single one. "It's hard when Baily and Julie often look at us like we might as well have taken that blade to—"

She touched a finger to his lips. "I don't know Ken's wife, so I won't say a word about her. But Baily doesn't blame you for Ken's death. She might say she does, but she blames Fletcher for taking him from Calusa Cove. For giving him something other than the marina, and then there's the fact she still loves him, even if she won't admit it."

"He's been madly in love with her for as long as I've known him. We followed him back here, partly to honor Ken and keep him alive in our hearts, but also because Fletcher's a miserable man without Baily. We can only hope she comes to her senses soon."

Audra laughed. "She's almost as stubborn as I am."

"No one is as stubborn as you." He kissed her sweet lips and then pulled away.

"That's true." She bit down on her fingernail, something he'd never seen her do before. Ever. She always screamed confidence, even when it came out in anger.

"What's wrong?"

"Nothing's wrong, but I feel like there's something I should've told you about Ken. Or something I've been wondering about Ken."

"To be honest, we've all been wondering a lot about Ken, and it's not good." Dawson gripped the steering wheel with both hands, bracing himself for whatever betrayal was coming his way. "I'm listening."

"Ken worked for Paul for about a year right before he decided to join the Navy," she said softly.

"I know." Dawson nodded, releasing the tension in his hands but not his heart. He hated secrets. Had she held back important information? Was that going to be her betrayal?

God, he hoped not. He prayed this was the thing that had haunted Ken, and she was just now seeing it.

"I have no idea what happened. I just know that he and Benson got into a fight—a public fight. Ken lost his shit and punched Benson. Ken never went back to work, and we stopped eating at Massey's. He wouldn't talk to me about it. He swore it had nothing to do with me, which I didn't believe, but now, I'm not so sure. Maybe he was telling the truth, and it had to do with something entirely different because that's when Ken decided college would never happen. Not that he had the money, but he had the opportunity—through Paul. Instead, he joined the Navy."

Dawson let out a long sigh of relief, grateful there was

no deep hidden secret. He adored Audra more than he wanted to admit, but there it was, and he could no longer deny it. He turned. "That's not quite the way Ken told that story, and Fletcher tried pushing him a couple of times to tell him what really happened—why the sudden switch—because Fletcher said it happened literally overnight. He even tried to get Baily involved." Dawson glanced toward the stars as if they might have some answers. "Only, that caused more issues between those two. Hayes, Keaton, and I would walk away, and we all stopped asking."

"Maybe Ken knew something. I just don't understand why he wouldn't say anything to someone."

"That's the million-dollar question." The boat tapped land, and Dawson nudged it forward a little.

Audra hopped to her feet.

He watched in awe as she jumped off the boat. Not that he expected her to wait for him to give her a hand. She wasn't the kind of woman who waited around for someone to help. If she could do something, she did it. If she didn't know if she could, she tried it, and if she failed, she learned from it and forged on.

Just the kind of woman he'd always wanted. And that was dangerous.

That kind of woman always ended up breaking his heart, and he worried that when this was over, he'd be watching her walk right out of his life.

# CHAPTER 14

Audra adjusted her headlamp, taking each step carefully. Pythons, water moccasins, rattlesnakes, and gators were all one misstep away from her demise. As a small child, her grandfather and his brothers would bring her back to this sacred land. They would participate in spiritual rituals. Remy told her the old-timers no longer came to this place but went up around LuLu River and on to Beaver Island, where it was less likely they would encounter a critter that would kill you before you could defend yourself.

Dawson paused. "Do you see that up ahead?" He pointed through the bright light. His hand cast a shadow across the lush green of the Everglades.

Audra squinted.

A grassy hut? Maybe. Yes. Like the newfangled tiki bars that were lined up and down the Intracoastal Waterway.

"Watch your step." Dawson held her elbow, guiding her through the watery mush of Coonts Island.

If she were any other woman—and this were any other town other than Calusa Cove—she might consider staying more than the ten days. She'd grown bored of her job. It had served its purpose. It had given her a chance to run. To hide. To lose herself in the wilds of beautiful, faraway places.

But she'd been all over the globe. Seen so many different places. Different cultures. Nothing had brought her peace.

She tilted her head and gasped. "That's a cabin."

"Not sure I'd call it that, but yeah, it has a roof and walls," he whispered, crouching down, dimming her light, then his.

*We are not Owl Witches. We do not turn into monsters in the dark of night and torment humans. Nor are we gypsies. You, my child, are just a little girl. To the Native American people, you are special because you have fire hair, white skin, and freckles, yet you are still one of them. They do not fear you. They worship you. The wanderers—or the gypsies—well, they see you as a unique child. One with the heart of a gypsy and the soul of someone connected to the elements. Do not ever let the people of Calusa Cove take that away from you. Don't ever change. Be free. Be you. Be as wild as your heart sings. You were born to be connected to the waters of the Everglades. To the land the Cove sits on. And to the sea that crashes along the shore. It is who you are.*

Those were her mother's words.

And her grandmother's.

Until their last breaths, they'd reminded Audra of who she was and how she was connected to this part of the world.

Her father had always told her the same thing, and for the first few years after her mom's passing, she'd skipped through town as if the stares and whispers still didn't matter.

But they had.

The older she'd gotten, the more she'd understood what they meant. She was the offspring of a crazy man, and she was what legends were made of.

"Stay close," Dawson whispered.

She looped her finger into his belt loop and followed him toward the shack. A million old stories filled her brain. They had never scared her as a small child, but this morning, before sunrise, they terrified her.

"Doesn't look like anyone's here right now," Dawson said. "Come on, let's check out the inside."

"For a second, I thought you were going to ask me to stay here—by myself."

He chuckled. "While I know you can handle snakes and gators all by yourself, it's dark, and well, why risk it?"

Her lips quirked. "Aw, aren't you the gentleman?"

"Liz accused me of being a Neanderthal just because I neglected to open the door for her a couple of times and then didn't bring her flowers after we fought."

"That's pathetic," Audra said. "When we fight, I want good, hard sex. The kind of sex that might include those handcuffs of yours."

"In that case, why don't you stay put and deal with that python over there giving us the evil stare." He waggled his finger.

She shifted her gaze, eyeing the ten-foot python

slithering through the tall grass. "Something tells me you haven't been able to get a girl to let you use them."

He chuckled. "I haven't dated anyone since I became a civilian cop." He glanced over his shoulder. "But the answer is no. Let's just say tying up of any kind hasn't been in the cards."

"If I let you, does that mean I get to use them on you?"

"I think that's only fair." He stepped between her and the snake that seemed oblivious that his morning meal was twenty paces away. He took her by the hand and helped her up onto a platform. "Holy shit," he said softly. "There's another shack over there."

The structure was well hidden behind all the trees and lush vegetation of the mangrove.

"Both are about fifty feet from the waterline at high tide," Dawson said. "There's no way anyone would see them, even if they drove their boat by at a snail's pace."

"Probably not," Audra said, pulling out her cell phone.

Dawson moved closer to her. "Stay right next to me, okay?"

"I hear you. Loud and clear." She glanced toward the sky. Dark clouds covered the moon, giving way to the sun. She tiptoed through the door, and her heart pulsed like a firecracker going off in the center of her throat. "Are those... bundles of cocaine?"

"It sure is." Dawson whipped off his headgear and snagged his radio. "*Chumrunner*, this is *Watchdog*. Do you read me?"

"This is *Chumrunner*. Go ahead," Fletcher's voice crackled over the two-way.

Dawson pointed to the far corner of the hut where a crate hung open.

She inched closer and peered inside.

Guns.

"Jesus," she whispered.

What the hell had they stumbled onto?

A sharp pain filled her skull and rattled her teeth. It vibrated from the back of her head, down her spine, and to her toes. Her legs wobbled, and she crashed to her knees onto the wood floor.

"What the…"

Was that Dawson's voice?

*Thud. Crackle. Smack.*

Nausea circled her gut. It twisted and turned while the searing torture that throttled her brain made it impossible to see.

She opened her mouth, but no words formed. They fell off her tongue as if she were tumbling out of an airplane and free-falling without a parachute.

And then the world went black.

"WHAT THE…" Instinctively, Dawson raised his right hand, stopping the blow to his temple. He ignored the sharp pain rippling across his fingertips and down his wrist caused by metal smacking against his skin.

He reached with his left hand for the weapon tucked in his back holster, but his assailant beat him to it.

"Not so fast." Benson Massey, of all idiots.

Dawson would never live this one down.

And it was made worse by James Huber smacking Audra on the backside of her skull seconds before. The crack had filled his ears as if he'd had a front-row seat to a horror show.

Dawson's jaw hardened. James would pay for that one. Not that Dawson was a possessive man, and Audra certainly wasn't anyone's property, but he'd become… attached.

Damn redheads.

He scanned the hut. One way in, but Eliot had to be around here somewhere. Those two city slickers were attached at the hips.

Three to two odds. Not bad. Only he had no idea how badly hurt Audra was. For now, she wasn't much help as her head bobbed downward, and she moaned.

A hot rage soared through his veins. He hadn't felt that in a long while, and it reminded him he was still a man who knew how to care for another human. It also tugged at his heart in a way that he knew would crush it into tiny little pieces.

However, he had to push that into a little box in the corner of his mind and focus on what he could do, and that was assess the situation. Assumptions were danger-ous, but there was always one that you had to make in these situations—there were always more bad guys.

At least he'd gotten his radio call off before Benson had plucked it from his fingertips and broken the fucking thing.

Time to make a play.

Dawson lunged toward Audra. He had to try.

Benson raised a rather large semiautomatic weapon.

A little overkill, but it got the point across, and bullets were stronger than muscle.

Dawson skidded to a stop. He growled. "Let her go."

James fisted her hair before she could fall to the floor.

She groaned. Her eyes rolled up, then shifted left and right. Another groan, but she wasn't completely out. She caught his gaze and held it for a long moment before her lids grew heavy just as James yanked her hair —a little hard for Dawson's liking.

Her body twitched, and she mumbled something. It wasn't words or anything coherent. But it was throaty, and if Dawson wasn't mistaken, it was a message.

That was a good sign, even as James's fingertips gripped her red hair and jerked her around as if she were a rag doll.

Dawson fisted his hands, rolling them against his thighs. He scanned the hut, mentally noting everything and its precise placement. Mostly drugs, but there were weapons, and he needed to get himself one of those. It wouldn't take but a hot minute for Fletcher and the rest of the gang to understand the situation, but it would be a while before they made it to Coonts Island.

That said, they had a go-to-shit plan in place since they'd met.

If they radioed and went dark, wait five minutes. If nothing happened, come running with weapons loaded and a halfway decent extraction plan. That was if they knew any of the details. If not, wing it, and his team was good at doing that.

However, this time, Fletcher would call Remy. He had to. Dawson carried a badge. It would be protocol, and Remy would have to do things a certain way, and that would piss off the boys.

Dawson couldn't be concerned about that now. He had three things on his mind: Audra and her condition, how to disarm these bastards, and how to ensure he had all the players and enough evidence to make federal charges stick.

"Let. Her. Go," Dawson said, his voice low and menacing.

"No can do." Benson jerked his head toward Dawson. "Give me a hand tying up this asshole."

"I say we just toss them both in the swamp and be done with them." James worked ties around Audra's wrists and ankles. She flopped about, moaning and groaning, but each time she shifted, she managed to raise an eyelid and make eye contact with Dawson.

A signal. She was coherent, hearing everything.

Hope swelled in Dawson's chest. He fought a grin.

Wonderful redheaded woman.

"We wait for my father," Benson said decisively. He dropped into a chair next to a small table and set his weapon between his legs, staring at his goddamn fingernails as if he'd just gotten a manicure. The lazy jerk couldn't even be bothered to get off his ass and strap a zip tie around Dawson's wrists and ankles. That might work in Dawson's favor because he doubted James knew how to ensure he kept his prisoner's wrists tied together. Dawson had half a chance to wiggle his way out, and if they didn't check his pockets, he could use his pocketknife.

"He's going to tell us to kill them." James shook his head. "We can't leave them alive. That's just stupid."

"What's stupid is you questioning me—or my father. We've been at this a hell of a lot longer than you have," Benson said. "So, if I were you, I'd shut the fuck up and do as you're told."

Dawson couldn't believe it. Paul Massey was a drug and arms dealer.

James propped Audra up against the wall. He sauntered over toward Dawson, and all Dawson could do was stare at the man's brand-new boots. Granted, they were the right kind for being in the swamps of the Everglades, but they looked as though they'd barely been broken in.

"Have you ever been inches from a gator in the wild?" Dawson locked gazes with James. "Seen their snot and eyes emerge from the murky, dark water, barely causing even the slightest ripple. Or watch them glide across the top of the water as smooth as butter, searching for prey, searching for something that will hold their hunger at bay for more than a few hours. Days, maybe." Dawson leaned a little closer. "A gator will see you—its meal—and then dip back down where it will blend into the darkness, leaving behind not even the tiniest of bubbles."

James paused. The blacks of his eyes narrowed, then widened.

Dawson chuckled. "Dawn is grazing time for alligators. There are some big ones back here. One that can chew on a grown man's bones and spit them out like toothpicks. That is if they don't first pull you under, twist you around, play with you for shits and giggles, and drown you before they tear you—"

"Shut the fuck up." James cocked his fist and clocked Dawson on the side of his face.

His cheek exploded with a crack. His eyes watered with the faintest of tears.

It wasn't a bad punch, but Dawson had experienced a whole lot worse. He thought about letting James know what a pussy he was but decided it was best to bite his tongue. While he could easily overpower James in seconds, Benson yielded all the power with an automatic weapon that would destroy both him and Audra in a quick pull of his finger.

A tightness filled Dawson's chest. Paul had been one of his suspects, but only because of his son. And even then, he'd struggled with the concept. Paul was the kind of man who followed rules, so at best, Dawson thought maybe Paul could have been covering for something that Benson had gotten his dumb ass involved in.

Not the other way around.

Welcome to the grand illusions of life.

To hear Benson defer to his old man twisted Dawson's gut. It's not like he hadn't been on the lookout for something like this. In that moment, his past failures reminded him of his bad decision.

He couldn't have another one. He couldn't fail Audra.

James cinched the zip ties around Dawon's ankles

and then his wrists. Dawson did his best to keep his hands slightly apart. He wasn't sure he could wiggle them out, but he might be able to access his pocket. Or have Audra do it.

The door screeched open. Eliot Commings strode in, followed by Paul Massey, swinging an automatic weapon over his shoulder like he was the kingpin of a major drug cartel.

Dawson wiggled his wrists. He twisted and jerked his arms in a fast motion, but the plastic ties—the kind that cops, feds, and other law enforcement used— ripped into his skin. He tried three more times. However, he made little to no headway. Warm blood trickled down his hands. He didn't wince. He knew better.

Seconds later, there was another screech of the door.

Dawson held his breath. He thought he'd cleared Silas. He believed the man had…wait. What the hell?

Mo?

Anna's husband.

All the air in Dawson's lungs left in one big flush. It was as if an elephant had flopped on his chest, cracking his ribs and releasing the oxygen. He dared to suck in a breath, but it came in as a pathetic gasp. How the hell had he missed that? As quickly as he could, he raced through the details of the last few days. Mo had gone to visit his mother, and Dawson hadn't seen him around town. Not once. He hadn't really thought that strange, but only because of what Anna had said. And then there were all the conversations he'd had with Anna. They'd been so strapped for money.

It always came down to money.

The only question that remained was whether Anna knew.

Audra stiffened. "Mo?" she whispered so faintly Dawson couldn't be sure it had been an intake of air, or she'd actually said the word.

Paul stomped across the dusty floor and knelt in front of Dawson, staring at him with dark, cold, killer eyes. This wasn't the Paul that Dawson knew.

Dawson's blood chilled. It was as if he gazed into the depths of hell.

And then Paul smiled. It wasn't a sinister grin. It was the same smile that Paul used to greet his guests at the pub, and that's when Dawson realized who he was dealing with. His throat constricted as if a python had curled its slimy body around it and slowly squeezed, constricting Dawson's breath, killing him with a quick flex of its powerful muscles.

Paul snorted. "Looks like you grew a brain much faster than your predecessors did."

When opportunity knocks…take it.

"Predecessors?" Dawson cracked his neck. "I know Trip wasn't involved in this shit. But I'm really starting to question the extent to which Trevor was immersed in all this." Dawson spoke fast so Paul couldn't get in a word. "I say that only because, looking through that young man's files, he was meticulous." A little bit of a lie, but what did Paul know? "His arrest records were decent. And he seemed fair in the way he treated every-one. Almost as good as his old man. So, tell me, what exactly was Trevor's role?"

Paul leaned closer, sucking on his teeth. "Trevor was a wet noodle who thought because he decided to stop snorting the product and slapped on a badge, he was better than the rest of us. Well, it didn't." Paul lowered his chin. "That stupid little shit worked for me when he was a kid. I couldn't have him come back to town thinking he could shut me down or shut down the cartel."

"How did you get him to go along?"

"That was simple." Paul shifted his gaze to Audra. "The cartel let him know what happens to a family when you betray them." He shrugged. "All he had to do was let us do our thing, and we co-existed just fine."

"Why is he rotting in prison?"

"He fucked up," Paul said. "One of our shipments didn't make it through, and we made sure he took the fall. We told him if he didn't confess, his family would pay the ultimate price."

"You are one sick bastard," Dawson mumbled.

"And you're about to find out just how sick I really am."

# CHAPTER 15

AUDRA'S PULSE pounded in her ears. Hearing Paul's menacing words about what he'd done to Trevor burned like acid in her throat.

It also brought back her nightmare, which replayed in her mind like a horror movie stuck on the same loop. However, this time, it was as clear as the lightning flashing in the morning sky.

Two distinct male voices. There was no mistaking who they were now.

Paul and his son Benson. One had hit her over the head… the other had shoved her father into a swarm of alligators.

Tears burned her raw eyes.

Paul rocked back on his heels. "I have to admit, I was a little worried when Fletcher and you boys came to Calusa Cove—my quiet little town. I mean, it's been hard enough dealing with people like Silas, especially after I had to get rid of Trevor. Silas is actually a smart man. I've been dodging him for years, but he's always been a bit like Victor, whether he wants to believe it or not."

Audra sat up a little taller. She jerked her head and blew out a puff of air, but it wasn't strong enough to move the hair from her face. She tried again, huffing, hooting, and howling.

Paul laughed. "Fucking Stigini." He reached out and brushed her hair from her face. "Crazy little wild redhead. You were a freak as a kid, running around town with knots in your hair and dirty feet."

"Kiss my ass." She lifted her chin, staring directly into his soulless eyes. "I know who you are and what you did. I remember." She choked on the last two words.

"You don't know shit." Paul leaned closer. "And whatever you think you know, it was all just a bad dream." He tossed his head back and laughed. "Oh, and I do know you had nightmares. Everyone talked about you screaming like you were dying when you were in that hospital bed. And Silas?" Paul shook his head. "I can't believe he took you in. He felt so bad for you, listening to you toss and turn all night, yelling and crying. It was such a shame. But it was all just one big bad dream."

"You should've killed me the night you killed my father, you douchebag."

The right corner of Paul's mouth turned upward, and if eyes could smirk, his did exactly that. "Perhaps."

"So you admit it." With every intake of breath, her

chest hurt. But she needed the words. Needed to hear *him* say it. "You're going to kill me now anyway, so be a man and admit it."

Paul leaned so close Audra could smell the coffee on his breath. His sinister smile burned a hole in her heart so deep that if she weren't tied up, she could easily coil her fingers around his neck and squeeze until he no longer sucked in breath and his heart stopped beating. "Your father believed in myths. Legends. Conspiracy theories. And pirates. He knew something was going on back here. He had a weird sense about it. All his random jibber-jabber made it easier for me to hide what I was doing. It kept people like Silas and Trip off my ass." He cupped her chin.

"Get your hands off her," Dawson said with a deep, menacing growl.

Paul laughed, squeezing her cheeks. "It's been harder for me without you and your crazy father. I've had to move around from island to island all these years. But I've managed." He gave her cheek a little slap. "Yes. I killed your old man, and I left you out here. I didn't care if you lived or died." He laughed. "I knew if you managed to survive, your brand of crazy would make everyone think you'd killed your father, especially because of that fight."

"Trip believed me." She lifted her chin. "And so did Silas."

"Maybe so. But that didn't last because you slinked away in the middle of the night. It made you look guilty as hell. It gave us more to question. We could all stand around the docks or buy vegetables at the stand and whisper, *She sold off everything. Took the money and ran because she killed him and got away with it.*"

She couldn't sit there a second longer and listen to the bastard. "Only, I'm not guilty. You are." She whipped her lower body around, swinging her legs across the floor, catching his ankles.

He jerked, stumbled backward, lost his footing, and fell on his back. His weapon landed on the floor inches from Dawson.

Dawson inched his body toward the gun.

Benson raced across the room. He kicked the gun away from Dawson and then raised the butt of his weapon, nailing Dawson in the gut.

He groaned, doubling over.

"You're a fucking little cunt," Benson grabbed her by the hair and yanked hard.

She spit in his face.

"Bitch." He backhanded her with brute force. She hadn't thought he had that much power, but she tasted metal. Blood trickled from her lips.

"You're going to pay for that one," Dawson managed to cough out, leaning back toward the wall and pushing himself closer. "You okay?" he whispered, catching her gaze.

"I'll live," she said, glaring at Benson.

Paul handed his weapon to Mo, who wouldn't even look at her or Dawson. He kept his gaze at his feet or on the door.

Coward.

What was he thinking getting messed up with these killers? Poor Anna.

Shit. What if Anna was involved? The thought made Audra shudder.

"We have a small window to get this shit done," Paul said. "That tropical storm is going to be nasty. I heard even Silas is staying home today, so let's wrap this up. Mendoza is expecting this to be distributed today. I'm not about to lose out on any more money. We've been delayed enough as it is." He stood and strolled toward the other side of the room, waving his arms around.

"You're working for the Mendoza Cartel?" Dawson asked.

Paul turned and glared. "None of that matters to you."

"I'm the chief of police. Of course, it matters."

Paul shook his head. "Not for long."

"Wait. What about Hector Mendoza? He died in the Everglades when my dad was young. The story goes that he lived back here until he met his wife," Audra said. "Is he connected to all this?"

"This town and its ridiculous legends," Paul mumbled. "It's all bullshit. Hector betrayed his family, so they killed him. Simple as that." He waved his massive gun. "Mo, you keep an eye on those two."

Mo didn't lift his gaze. Actually, he turned his back, held his rifle, and let out an audible sigh.

Audra shifted and leaned into Dawson. "I can't believe those two bastards killed my dad," she muttered, her chest tight, anger burning a hole in her gut.

She had to get free of the zip ties and take these

murderers down. Audra twisted her hands in an attempt to free them. "My wrists are raw from trying to get out of these things," she said, her voice so low only Dawson would hear.

"I'm close," Dawson said, barely audible. "And I've got a plan."

# CHAPTER 16

"Look at me, Mo," Dawson said once everyone else had left the small hut.

Mo didn't flinch.

"Don't ignore me," Dawson tried again. He didn't know Mo all that well, but he knew their situation. Understood it. And he knew Anna, trusted her, and couldn't believe she knew what her husband was up to. The wife was always the last to know. If she did, well… damn. Either way, he planned on using his connection to his secretary to help get himself out of this lose-lose situation.

The man refused to acknowledge Dawson.

"Do you have any idea what your going to prison will do to Anna?" Dawson said softly.

Mo glanced over his shoulder. "That's not going to happen. It can't happen."

"You're standing there, holding a semiautomatic weapon, while the chief of police is tied up. If Audra dies, that's life. If I die, too, that's two life sentences with no possibility of parole. And even if we don't die, I've got you on kidnapping, possession with the intent to sell, and we're not talking small-town shit here. We're—"

"Stop talking." Mo finally turned. He wiped his hand across his face. "I'm not going to kill anyone. I didn't kidnap anyone. I'm not really part of anything. My job is to drive cars or boats from one point to the other. That's all I do. I don't ask questions. I just do what I'm told, and I take my money. I'm not really doing anything wrong."

"Jesus, Mo. You're a smart man." Dawson lifted his chin. "Holding that weapon while we're sitting here is a whole lot wrong. Now, how about you do the right thing by untying us? Then help us get the hell out of here so I can get backup, and if you are willing to testify against them—"

"Are you kidding me?" Mo inched closer, bending forward. "What about the cartel? It's not just Paul. Why the hell do you think Trevor's sitting in prison with his mouth essentially duct-taped? If he says anything, they'll come after his family. My hands are tied. Like I said, I do my job, and my mom gets a nice cushy nursing home to live out her days, and my wife gets to have her nails done whenever she wants." Tears formed in the man's eyes.

Dawson shook his head. Greed didn't always drive people.

Sometimes, it was simply necessity.

"Have you had any contact with anyone inside the cartel?" Dawson wondered if Paul had driven the point home to Trevor to keep his mouth shut or if someone else had. That little point mattered.

Mo shook his head. "I first started driving crates from Calusa Cove out to Naples and dropped them off. I didn't see anyone. A couple of times, I picked up things out in the Everglades and brought them to drop-off points. I once asked Paul about all this, and he told me if I ever betrayed him, the men he worked for would slit my neck, rape my wife, and—"

"I get the picture," Dawson said. "First, you need to know I've spoken with Trevor."

"Are you serious?" Mo stared at him with wide eyes.

"He hasn't said much, but he's waiting for me to crack the case so he can turn." Dawson nodded. "What I want you to remember is that Paul is in a worse boat than you are, and I can protect you. At this point, the cartel might not even know your name. But they know Paul. They know Benson. You're nothing to them and not worth their time."

"Unless I betray them."

"But you won't." Dawson arched a brow.

"I'm not following."

"We're going to make it look as though you did exactly what Paul told you to do but that I outsmarted you."

Mo sighed. "I can live with that. Paul has a habit of always saying I'm useless anyway."

"How about you reach into my pocket, grab my knife, put it in my hand, and let me do the rest," Dawson whispered. "And when this is over, we'll talk about how I can help you and your family."

Mo blinked. "Why are you helping me when I've so royally screwed up?"

"Because I understand the need to protect those we love and that, sometimes, we'll do almost anything to take care of them—including breaking the law." He cocked his head and raised his hip. "I can't promise there won't be any consequences, but I can promise I will do whatever is in my power to ensure you, Anna, and your family are protected. Everyone will know that you helped me, except the cartel."

Mo glanced around. "My wife believes you're one of the best things that has ever happened to this town. That you're an honest cop with good intentions, even if you do things a little ass-backward." He dug his hand into Dawson's pocket and placed the small knife into Dawson's fingers. "If anything happens to me, please tell Anna I didn't intentionally get involved. I went to Paul for extra work. I didn't know I was moving drugs until it was too late; only, I knew what I was doing couldn't be…legal."

"Nothing's going to—"

Mo raised his hand. "You can't promise that," he said. "Also, tell her that I love her. That she's always been my world, and I'm sorry."

"Okay." Dawson knew better than to argue. "Thank you."

"Now what?" Audra asked.

"I cut our hands out of these zip ties, but we leave our feet bound until I hear the signal."

"What signal?"

"From my team."

"You really think they're coming?" Audra asked.

"I never finished my radio call, so yeah," he said softly as he finished cutting through the plastic. He quickly tucked the evidence in his pocket and went to work on Audra's. "If they aren't here before shit goes south, we have to go for the weapons." He let out a long breath. "Mo, you'll need to choose. Us or them."

"That's an easy choice." Mo nodded. "I won't let them kill you. I do still have a conscience."

AUDRA HATED WAITING. For anything. She had the patience of a toddler. It was made worse by the pounding in her head and the constant swishing of her gut. She'd had enough concussions over the years to know she had another one.

Mild or not, her head felt like a stick of dynamite had gone off.

Thunder no longer rumbled through the hut. It exploded like a bomb. With each thud, a flash of lightning lit up the small structure like it was going up in flames.

The storm was directly over them.

"I can't hear anything outside," Dawson muttered. "If my team is out there, they can no longer signal. We're going to have to make our move." He reached behind her back and squeezed her hand. "Are you up for it?"

"Yes," she whispered.

"Hey, Mo," Dawson called between claps of thunder.

It had been eight minutes since Paul, Benson, James,

or Eliot had come through the hut door. Dawson believed they were moving their base of operation to another location based on the fact they were placing dynamite around the cabin.

She wondered if that was how they planned on killing them, but that would be stupid. It would leave evidence. That was, if anyone came back this far on Coonts Island.

It would be better to feed them to a python or gator.

Mo turned. "Yeah?"

"As soon as someone comes through that door, I'm going to overpower you, and Audra is going for the last of those weapons. Are you good with that plan?" Dawson asked.

"I am." Mo nodded.

"Keep that small pistol tucked in your waistband in case you need it, and don't be afraid to use it. I don't want to have to tell Anna you died a hero. If these jerks don't kill me, she will."

Mo actually chuckled. It was a nice sound cutting through the massive rain pellets landing on the roof.

Dawson cut his feet free and then Audra's. He lifted her chin with his thumb and forefinger. "You protect yourself. If you have to pull the trigger, do it. I don't say that lightly, but—"

She stopped him with a kiss. "I will defend myself and you. Don't you worry about that. I'm not dying out here today."

He grinned. "That's my girl."

Now that had a really nice ring to it. Audra's heart

warmed. Before she could respond, the door opened, and James stepped in.

God, she hated that man. He reminded her of a snake oil salesman—and not even a very good one.

Dawson lunged for Mo, who stumbled backward, dropping his weapon.

"What the hell?" A stunned James stood dead in his tracks like a deer in headlights. He didn't react. Not at all, giving her a chance to bolt forward, snagging Mo's weapon.

She turned, swinging it swiftly across James' face. Metal connected with skin and bone. His body lurched to the side and fell to the ground with a thud. Blood ran from his mouth and cheek.

Unfortunately, she didn't have a chance to find the plastic cuffs before Eliot raced through the doors.

"What the hell is going on in here?" Eliot asked, holding his weapon at the ready.

"Don't move," Dawson pointing a semiautomatic at Eliot's chest.

Audra quickly found a zip tie and slapped it around James's wrists, shoving him to the side. Then, with a little less gusto and more room around the arms, she put one around Mo's wrists. She stared into his eyes and tried to apologize with a glance.

He lowered his lids as if to accept.

It would only be like this until either Dawson's team got here or they completely overpowered everyone on the island.

The only issue with the latter was that they really didn't know how many people were there.

Eliot's eyes shifted as if to assess his options.

Two to one, currently.

Audra inched closer. "Hand it over, asshat." She shifted her weapon, holding it inches from his temple. "I'm not afraid to blow your brains out." She narrowed her stare. "Around these parts, I'm considered an Owl Witch. By day, I'm a—"

"I've heard the stupid stories."

She laughed. "Who said they're stories?" She made a very realistic hooting noise. One she'd learned as a small child. One that she used to make people go away.

Eliot handed over his weapon. "This little coup of yours isn't going to last very long. The second—"

"Don't think. We wouldn't want you to hurt your brain." Dawson literally piled Eliot on top of James but held Mo by the elbow. "Where are Paul and Benson?"

"As if I'm going to tell you," James said.

Dawson shoved his gun into James's gut.

James groaned. Coughed. And groaned again.

"Start talking," Dawson shifted his weapon, aiming it at James's knee. "Or I blow off your kneecap. It's painful. Excruciating, actually. You won't bleed to death right away. It might take days. The gators will sniff out that blood first." He leaned closer. "That is if a big old fifteen- or twenty-foot python doesn't slither in here first—because we'll leave the door open—and circle your body, crushing all your bones, causing a different kind of pain. Then it will—"

"He's at the north side of the island," James burst out, "loading product into the boats."

"He'll be taking them out through Mangrove Bay,

along the Intracoastal Waterway, and then maybe meet up with a ship or something," Audra said. "Or offload onto a different local boat before bringing them inland and up the interstate."

"Agreed." Dawson nodded, his lips curving into a smile. "Are you after my job?"

"Hell, no." She shook her head. "But I might need a job when all this is over," she mumbled.

Dawson cocked a brow. "That's a conversation I'd like to continue. But for now, we need to move through that door. Find something to secure James and Eliot to. We're taking this dipshit with us for security."

"He's nothing. A peon. We'd be more of a bargaining chip," Eliot said.

"You both can burn in hell for all I care," Dawson said as he peered out the door.

Lightning flashed. Thunder clapped.

Audra used to live for nights like this. As a child, she'd sit on the dock and watch storms roll toward her. Now, she wanted to watch this one disappear. Adrenaline surged through her body as she tied Frick and Frack to a pole near the back corner.

*Bang! Bang! Bang! Bang! Bang! Bang!*

Audra hit the deck, covering her head. Her heart pounded in her ears in unison with the rapid fire.

This was it.

Her life was over.

* * *

*Bang! Bang! Bang! Bang! Bang! Bang!*

"Hit the deck." Dawson shoved Mo to the floor and then covered his body with his own. It was his job to protect and serve. That meant it was his job to take a bullet for a citizen of Calusa Cove. Carefully, between gunshots, he lifted his head and checked on Audra.

She gave him the thumbs-up.

The gunfire continued for another two minutes in rapid succession before total silence.

Outside, lightning lit up the night and thunder boomed, shaking the ground beneath Dawson's feet.

He held his breath, motioning to Audra to stay down.

Thankfully, his wild redhead did what he requested.

The door flew open.

Dawson rolled to the prone position, the semi-automatic aimed at the door, his finger on the trigger, poised and ready to fire at whoever came through it.

A man eased around the doorframe, a rifle pressed to his shoulder. "Dawson?"

Dawson let go of the breath he'd held. "Fletcher?"

"Expecting someone else?" Fletcher quipped.

Dawson rolled to his feet. "I almost shot you."

"Is that any way to say thank you for saving your ass?" Fletcher asked. "Again."

"Yeah." Keaton leaned over Fletcher's shoulder, smiling. "We're always coming in and making sure you don't get shot."

Hayes blew through the door, stumbling and grumbling something about always having to tie up the loose ends. "What'd I miss?"

"Only Dawson bitching about us making sure he didn't die today." Fletcher chuckled.

"Jerks." Dawson leaned down, helped Mo to his feet, and cut his ties. "Is Remy here?"

"Yeah. He's dealing with Paul and Benson and trying to get in touch with Agent Pope."

Dawson nodded. He squeezed Mo's shoulder. "Go outside. Don't talk to anyone except Remy. Tell him we have a deal but tell him he has to wait for the details. He'll honor that."

"Thank you." Mo wiped tears from his cheeks. "I'm sorry for what I've—"

"It's all good." Dawson smiled. "We're moving forward." He let out a long breath and made his way toward Audra, who leaned against the far wall. "Are you okay?"

"Yeah." She twisted her long hair with her fingertips. "I have answers. I know what happened. I should be happy."

She dropped her head back and closed her eyes.

Dawson palmed her cheek. He wanted to take away all the pain. All the anguish. But he knew he couldn't.

"They murdered my dad. Fed him to the creatures he loved the most because they're greedy bastards. It was all for nothing."

He pulled her to his chest and kissed her temple. "I wish I could make you feel better, but I know I can't. Just remember, what we did tonight was a good thing. And we saved Mo and his family from a potentially similar fate. Hopefully, Trevor will keep his word, and we'll shut down a massive cartel."

She glanced up at him and smiled weakly. "Can you really keep Mo from going to prison?"

"If it weren't for him, we might've died. So, yeah. I'm going to pull whatever law enforcement strings I can to make sure that the worst thing that happens to him is maybe a few months in county jail or probation and community service." Dawson kissed her sweet, loveable lips. "Mo was trying to make some cash to help his poor mama have a comfortable end to her life where she's already struggling. I can sort of understand that. My nana had some medical issues her last few years, and that guilt of not being there for her has always haunted me."

"You're an amazing man," Audra said softly. "I'm sure your nana was so proud of you."

"She was."

"Good Lord," Hayes said. "This is not the time or place for this mush."

"Besides, doesn't the police chief have work to do like booking drug dealers, coordinating with the DEA, and inventorying the haul?" Keaton asked. "And whatever else it is you do."

"I think our work here is done." Fletcher came up behind Dawson, slapping him on the back. "I'm tired. I'm ready to go back."

"You can leave right after I take statements from all of you." Dawson laughed. "And then you can give my girl here a ride back to my place." He kissed her softly. "I might be a long while doing whatever it is I do. I hope you're not planning on leaving anytime soon."

She smiled up at him. "Not for at least a week."

"I was hoping for more time than that." He cocked his head. "But I'll take that for now."

"Hey, Chief." Remy stuck his head inside the shack. "I kind of need you out here."

"Yeah. I'm coming," Dawson said. "Duty calls."

Audra rested her hand on his bicep. "Guess I'll see you back at the cabin." She slid her hand down his chest. "Thank you."

"For what?"

"For believing me."

He brushed his lips across hers. "That was actually the easy part."

# EPILOGUE

Audra took Dawson's hand, slipping her fingers between his, and followed him up the path behind his cabin toward the main house. The last two weeks had been interesting.

The Python Challenge hadn't been the focal point. Actually, no one cared anymore. Well, not true. Everyone cared about catching the snakes and getting rid of them, and plenty had been removed. Audra didn't know the exact number, but it had been posted, and Keaton had been more than pleased with the results.

But the talk of the town had been the local hero.

The chief of police, Dawson Ridge.

The man who'd brought down a major drug and arms dealing ring and put a damper on the Mendoza Cartel distribution into the United States. Trevor had even stuck to his end of the agreement. The Feds had moved him to a different facility, and his family had been taken into protective custody. All of this because of Dawson.

Dawson refused to take the credit. He attributed it to the great work of his second-in-command, Remy, and the three men he'd retired from the Navy with. And also, some amazing townspeople, including Mo, a man who'd been bullied into working for Paul and his son Benson.

He'd also made it clear that he couldn't have done any of it without the help of Calusa Cove's most notorious Owl Witch, Audra, who, after sixteen years, had been cleared of any suspicion of the murder of her father.

Mo hadn't gotten off scot-free, but he'd been given a plea deal. A good one. Two years' probation. No jail time.

And Anna got to keep her job working for Dawson because he was a good man.

But now Audra had some life decisions to make. She'd already made one by turning in her resignation in her current position. It had been a tough choice. That career had served her well. It had been a dream come true. But she'd used it to hide. To run from her life instead of living it.

However, she had no idea what to do next. Walking down the streets of Calusa Cove, she still turned heads, though not in the same way as before. Her hometown felt more like home again, thanks to Dawson.

"What are we doing?" She'd been given the tour of what Dawson referred to as the "big house" a few times. And it was gorgeous. Spectacular. Now all he had to do was decide what to do with the damn place.

"I want to show you something."

"Shouldn't we get ready for the campfire?" She glanced over her shoulder.

"Hayes and Keaton should be pulling into the cabins right about now. They'll get things started. Fletcher will be by in about ten. I told Baily and Trinity to come in about a half hour. Trinity said she would bring stuff to make s'mores."

Audra laughed. "You know if she's in charge, they will be designer s'mores."

Dawson chuckled. "Oh, I've already had those. I told her if she didn't bring regular shit, not to bother. She promised the cheap stuff. And Baily is bringing ingredients to make margaritas, so we should be set for all the usual fixings."

"Good." She took Dawson's hand, and they navigated the new porch, which had been completed a couple of days ago.

"The inside is coming along nicely. The kitchen doesn't have any appliances yet, but it will by the end of the month," Dawson said.

"You're not telling me anything I don't know."

"Just let me ramble and get through this," he said. "I designed it to be a bed and breakfast. It has twelve rooms. Three of them are family style. But for whatever reason, I did make the third floor fully contained. It has one bedroom, its own bathroom, and a small kitchen as well."

"I know. You could live there if you wanted to."

"I suppose." He opened the door. "But I thought

more of hiring a B&B manager to live here, and since I'm a selfish bastard and don't want you to leave Calusa Cove, but don't think we're ready to live together, I thought maybe you'd like the job."

Audra's heart fluttered as she stood in the middle of the living room. It was spacious and had a big stone fireplace. "What would the job entail?"

"Managing the bookings and the staff, which would include a cleaning service and a cook—unless you wanted to do any of that. The pay isn't great, but it's not awful." He cupped her face and stared into her eyes. "I care about you. I don't want to rush things, but I don't want you to walk out of my life, either. Please stay."

"Could I also work at Everglades Overwatch? Take out a few tours? Tell a few Owl Witch stories?" She wrapped her arms around his waist and waggled her brows at him.

"I'm sure that could be arranged." His arms came up around her. "Is that a yes?"

"That concussion must've really done a number on my head," she said, "but Calusa Cove is home. There are no more secrets lurking in the shadows here. I have nothing to run from anymore. As long as you don't mind me crashing with you until this place is ready, I'll take the job."

He glanced at his watch. "Want to christen the place? We've got a little time, and I don't care if we're late."

"Does christen mean what I think it means?" she asked, cocking one eyebrow.

He grinned. "If you think I'm talking about sex, then yes."

Audra laughed. "Are you always horny?"

He nodded.

She smiled and pressed her lips against his mouth.

This was home.

# PIRATES IN CALUSA COVE

## EVERGLADES OVERWATCH BOOK # 2

*New York Times & USA Today*
Bestselling Author

**ELLE JAMES**

*USA Today*
Bestselling Author

**JEN TALTY**

# PIRATES
*in*
# CALUSA COVE



# ELLE JAMES



# JEN TALTY

# PROLOGUE

*A YEAR AGO...*

TRINITY STEVENSON STEPPED from behind the protective windshield. Her ponytail smacked her face. The wind howled and the seas kicked up angrily as if Poseidon himself was about to emerge from the depths of the ocean floor, waving his trident.

This storm had collided with another system, changed direction, and came at her so fast she barely had a chance to get her bearings. What started as a few hours alone to collect her thoughts, to decide if she would believe him—again—turned into a death grip on survival instincts.

She squinted... searching... scanning the wild waters for the green and red bow lights. Or white the stern light. There had been another boat out there. She'd seen it. And they were charging into the storm, being tossed around by the raging waves like a rag doll. She suspected the small fishing boat to be eighteen to twenty feet long. Way too small to be out here in these conditions. Heck, her forty-footer, while built for the ocean and could handle a good storm, struggled with waves this tall. But Trinity couldn't, in good faith, just leave them out here to be swallowed by the sea gods.

Who was she kidding? She was about to be upside down if she didn't point this vessel toward shore and head in soon. She blew out a puff of air, stared into the darkness, and waited for another flash from the heavens. All she needed was a few seconds of visibility. Something to give her a better gauge of where those red and green lights were bobbing up and down in the open waters.

Thankfully, those lights appeared through the wind, waves, and rain. It rolled down with a massive crest, before turning up toward the sky. Once again, she squinted, focusing solely on the small vessel, struggling to stay above water and losing the battle quickly.

She reached for the radio, glancing at the channel settings already set to sixteen. "Pan-Pan, Pan-Pan, Pan-Pan. This is *Princess Afloat.*"

Pushing down on the throttles, she cut through the top of a massive wave. Quickly, she eased up on the power of the engines, allowing the boat's bow to rise, before giving it more gas to cut through another wave. Salt water splashed across the windshield. It sloshed over the top of the cuddy and landed right on her head. She wiped her face with her forearm and repeated the maneuver, ensuring her boat didn't go sideways.

"This is the US Coast Guard. What's your situation, *Princess Afloat?*"

She rattled off where she believed she was because she couldn't take her eyes off the waves before her to check the exact coordinates. But she knew these waters like she knew the back of her hand. She knew within a quarter of a mile how far offshore she was and in what direction. "There is a boat in trouble about a mile and a half from my location… Oh my God. No." The vessel in question pitched sideways with the wave and rolled. A bolt of lightning lit up the sky. A clap of thunder that sounded more like gunfire rattled her teeth.

A second clap echoed in the night.

Followed by a… flash? Or a spark.

She swallowed her pulse.

"Ma'am. Are you okay?"

"Um, yes. I think so," she managed. "There's a second boat. No lights and the other one, it capsized and it's… oh God. It's sinking."

"Ma'am. We're four miles from your location. Flash your spotlight."

She did as instructed.

"We can see you," the man said. "Look to your port. You'll see us."

*Bang!*

"Oh my God." She crouched behind the steering wheel but not too low. "The other boat fired a weapon," she said as calmly as she could.

The vessel circled—danced—around where the white glow of a stern light disappeared into the dark ocean.

*Pirates.*

That was the only explanation.

*Bang! Bang!*

They must have seen the signal between her and the Coast Guard.

"Ma'am, are you okay?"

"Yes." She sucked in a deep breath, staring at the white water being churned up by the boat heading right for her.

"Ma'am, can you maneuver and head toward the island barriers?" the gentleman on the other end asked. Another voice—a familiar one—muttered a few superlatives in the background.

"Yes. I can do that."

"Trinity, get your ass back to the docks, now," Dawson, the new chief of police, said with real bite laced to his words.

"What about the boat that sunk? I know what I saw."

"You need to be more worried about the one headed in your direction that we need to deal with," Dawson said. "Now head home."

She glanced over her shoulder. She couldn't see anything but waves, rain, and lightning. She couldn't hear anything but the howl of the wind. No boat chasing her. The only other vessel was the Coast Guard less than a mile away now, and racing toward the open ocean. She let out a huge breath. "Heading in." She hooked the mic to the handle and stared at the roller cresting at the top. It wasn't just any crest, either. It was the kind of wave that movies were made about. "Well, crap." She hit the throttle, spun the wheel, and braced for impact.

*Princess Afloat* pitched starboard as a twelve-foot swell crashed into the hull awkwardly. Gripping the steering wheel with one hand, she pushed the throttle down harder because speed was her friend right now. Rollers, she could handle. Waves that turned into surf machines, well, she couldn't risk going sideways. Her boat was too small for that, and she'd surely capsize.

Riding the wave wasn't smart, either. She needed to get in front of it. But the swells were coming closer and faster. She would have to make sure she stayed between the waves as much as she could. Or get on top of one and ride down below before it crest. Not a fun drive.

A clap of thunder rattled the boat right before the evening sky lit up with five flashes of lightning. Normally, she loved a good lightning storm. That was when she was sitting on her front porch, watching the storm roll in from the comforts of home.

The wipers sloshed salty water across the windshield, but it did nothing to help with visibility. Flicking the spotlight on, she found the spot between the grouping of islands that led into Chokoloskee Bay from the north. She'd be protected from the massive waves once she was between the islands and the shoreline.

It was navigating through them, alone, in these conditions, that was the challenge.

She'd been a water baby her entire life. However, to most people of Calusa Cove, she was a spoiled rich girl with servants. It wasn't a falsehood. She'd been born with a silver spoon in her mouth. She'd grown up eight miles from the center of town—in a mansion. The only one in the zip code.

Her mother never worked a day in her life, and that included housecleaning and cooking. They had a staff for that. They had a staff for everything.

Audra McCain once joked that she wouldn't be surprised if Trinity had someone to wipe her ass. Trinity chuckled at the memory. Why did Audra, of all people, pop into her head at a time like this? She had no idea. She hadn't heard of or seen Audra in sixteen years. She wondered what had happened to the local *Stigini*. Poor girl had also gotten the short end of the stick when it came to this town. Lucky her for getting out and staying out.

Trinity had her reasons for coming back two years ago. No one in this town knew. They suspected and some had the story half right.

A man did break her heart. Crushed it. Tore it from her chest and utterly destroyed it. But that wasn't the worst of it. He took her dignity. Her self-worth. And he stripped her of her confidence.

But that was one of the best-kept secrets of Calusa Cove.

However, she had better understanding of her mother. Only, she hadn't wanted to bond with her mom because of it. There was too much pain over her own childhood. She hadn't even told her mother she'd been pregnant. That had been her father. She didn't blame her dad. He'd done what any normal father would in this situation.

Hours after she miscarried, her mother had done the

rarest thing. She'd called. She'd asked to visit and to comfort her in her time of need.

Her mom came to Calusa Cove for a whole week. It had been the worst week of Trinity's life. Not just because she'd ended a relationship with an abusive man, but because she'd lost something she didn't know she'd wanted.

A child.

Her mother had been a miserable woman—and everyone who had met her knew it. The good people of Calusa Cove watched her parents' marriage dissolve. They knew about their loss. Everyone knew that her mother blamed her tragedy on Calusa Cove and they watched her pack her bags and leave the second Trinity graduated from high school. The ink on her diploma hadn't even had the chance to dry before her mom had been on that plane.

Her mother had hated everything about Calusa Cove, and up until a few years ago, so did Trinity. Now, Calusa Cove offered her a sanctuary from her past pains and an opportunity to be the person she'd always wanted.

Another clap of thunder rattled her brain. The boat vibrated, starting at her toes and landing between her temples.

More lightning lit up the night skies. She was a little thankful for the few seconds of brightness guiding her home.

But the waves tossed her cruiser around like a freaking dingy.

Silas had warned her—more like sneered at her—

that a storm was brewing. She'd checked all the weather apps and she knew the seas were ripe today. However, the open water gave her peace and tranquility and after the lunacy of her mother's call this morning, she sure as heck needed it.

But Silas had pissed her off as well. Well, him and Dewey, the mangrove trimmer. Especially Dewey. He was always sitting down at the docks when he wasn't working, staring at her, waiting for her to crash her shiny, expensive boat. He'd waggle his long, crooked finger at her, reminding her that she didn't fit in and that she'd smash her boat one day.

There wasn't a scratch on her baby because she was a darn good boat driver.

But people didn't see her as Monty Stevenson's daughter. The rising star who left on a full ride, started a medical-tech company, sold it for millions after he got burned out, and realized he missed small-town life.

Nope. They saw her as Porsche Stevenson's kid. The one who brought sushi to school for lunch and, at one time, was just like her mother.

As the islands came into view, the waves crashed into them with unrelenting force. She swallowed her pounding pulse. This had to be the worst she'd ever driven in, and frankly, she didn't ever want to do it again.

Easing up on the throttle, she made her way between two stretches of land. It was known as the Ten Thousand Islands. A chain of islands and mangrove islets that stretched from Cape Romano to Lostmans River. This area could be treacherous on a sunny day because of oyster bars and shallow waters. A captain needed to understand the tides and the area.

No matter what anyone said about her, she knew both. But that didn't make this any less dangerous.

She made it through the first set of islands and eased back even more on the throttles, letting out a long sigh of relief. The waves had reduced to four to five, and she could see the inlet leading her to Mitchell's Marina.

Thank God.

No. Thank Poseidon.

But oh, she could hear the crap she was going to catch from Baily, the owner of the marina and now one of her best friends. That was one of the best things about returning to Calusa Cove. She'd never really had girlfriends before. She thought she did, but they had all turned out to be rich, prissy snots.

Kind of like she used to be.

She narrowed her gaze as she pulled down the narrow channel toward the dock she rented. A couple dozen people lined up. Some wore appropriate raingear, others making do with what was nearby, like garbage bags. Most people in Calusa Cove were dirt-poor and the town's population, at last count, was four hundred and twenty-eight.

Silas waved his fist in her direction as he raced across the edge of the shore and toward the docks with the new sexy Fish and Wildlife guy right on his heels.

Wonderful.

This was the last thing she needed. A lecture by one of Fletcher Dane's friends and Silas, the resident grumpy old man who occasionally had a heart of gold if you took the time to get to know him.

She spun the boat, pulling in backward, as she always did. Mainly to show off. To prove she was a master at the helm. It was childish—she knew it—but she wanted respect.

Few gave it to her.

Raindrops the size of mosquitoes pelleted her eyes. As quickly as she could, she tossed the stern line to Silas.

Keaton Cole managed to snag the bowline before she could make her way to the front of her vessel.

"I warned you," Silas said, taking her hand. "Why didn't you come in sooner?"

"Because someone needed help," she managed above the roar of the wind whipping and swirling through the marina. The palm trees bent over. "I tried to help, but I couldn't get to them. Pirates did and unfortunately, they sank." She steadied her bare feet on the dock, holding her wedges in her other hand. "I radioed the Coast Guard. And before both of you lay into me, I already got barked at by Dawson and ordered back to the docks."

"Not sure what to think of that man." Silas shook his head. "You're crazy, you know that? You had us all worried. I was sitting here enjoying a beer and watching those two systems collide, but there was no Trinity. I stood out there for over an hour while I watched that storm turn into a nightmare and no Trinity. Waves like that will take even a boat your size."

"I'm well aware of what the sea can do." She blinked.

"Are all the boats from this marina back? Do we have any idea who could've sank out there?"

"You were the only one we've been waiting on," Silas said.

She shifted her gaze toward Keaton, who had served in the Navy with Dawson Ridge, the new chief. "Why was Dawson with the Coast Guard?"

Keaton arched a brow. "He asked if he could because that's what he does when one of his townspeople didn't come in and there were reports of pirates in the area."

"Oh." Wonderful. Here came another flipping lecture.

Keaton jerked his head toward the main building. "Let's get you inside and warmed up. You looked like a drowned rat."

"Gee, thanks. Just want a girl wants to hear." She figured she had mascara running down her cheeks. Some habits died hard, and she was still a vain woman, even if she wasn't trying to impress a man. At least not this man.

She had a man. It was a new relationship. They'd only been dating for two months and she thought Fenton would be different.

Well, at first he had been. And he didn't bark at her like Keaton did.

While Fenton worked at one of her father's many car dealerships, he didn't see her for her bank account. Fenton made good money. Perhaps not the kind she'd been born and raised with, but enough to shower her with some very nice gifts.

Though, not too many. He was a man who believed

everyone should live within their own means, which sometimes caused a few interesting discussions. She made good money as a data scientist, a career that allowed her to work from home and live anywhere. But again, old habits died hard and she wasn't about to give up the things she enjoyed.

Shoes, handbags, and designer clothes.

She no longer paid full price because that was just stupid. She didn't have to have top-of-the-line everything. Nor did she have to have... everything. But yeah, she liked her BMW.

To say she lived within her means was a bit of a stretch. Daddy bought her boat, so there was that. She understood this made it harder for her to get the one thing she wanted more than anything—respect from the people of Calusa Cove. She did want them to see her in a different light.

Fenton didn't seem to care about her princess status or her father's money. But earlier today, she'd picked up his cell and found a weird text on it. It was from someone named Al. Just Al. At first, she didn't think anything of it, but when it dinged in her hand and a second text came over that was sexual in nature, her heart stopped.

Fenton got defensive at first. But he softened, saying it was just some guy he knew being a dick.

She struggled to believe it, though she wanted to and it was why she'd gone for a late-night boat ride when she hadn't planned on it.

Keaton pressed his hand on the small of her back.

Her body responded and that annoyed her on more

than one level. "I have a boyfriend." She wasn't sure if that was for her benefit or for Keaton's.

"I'm well aware. His name is Fenton. He drives a flashy Range Rover." Keaton did not remove his hand. "Only he doesn't deserve you and he doesn't come around much."

"He works a lot." She glanced over her shoulder. Silas turned and headed toward the parking lot. The gathering of people had dissipated, but not without muttering a few nasty little whispers. This town always had to have something to gossip about.

Lately, it was her.

The hum of car engines filled the air as vehicles pulled out into the street.

"While it was mighty nice of you to try to help whoever's out there, you should have just radioed and come in." Keaton nudged her closer to the main building. "I heard they fired a few shots at you."

The front door opened and Baily stood in the entrance, holding a tall mug of something.

"Not sure it was at me," she mumbled. "And I didn't even see the pirate boat at first. Once I did, I had no intention of staying out there. Once I got ahold of the Coast Guard, and they were on the way, I turned around and came home."

"It's the part where you stayed until you saw the Coast Guard, even though you were in danger, that concerns me." He stepped aside, letting her enter the marina first.

"Oh my God. You do not listen. I didn't know I was in danger at first. Once I did, I turned around. I'm not stupid." She took the mug of steaming coffee that Baily offered and smiled. "Thanks. I really need this."

"I put a shot of something else in, too," Baily said with a sweet smile, which quickly turned into a frown as she suspiciously eyed Keaton.

Trinity knew the history. They'd spoken of it—though not at great lengths—and while she more than understood why Baily felt the way she did about Fletcher, his friends, and what that meant, she didn't agree.

"I wouldn't mind of cup of that," Keaton said. "Especially when chatting with this one is like talking to a brick wall." He lowered his chin. "You were in danger the second those storms collided."

"Anyone ever tell you you're a bully?" Trinity asked.

"You. Every time we find ourselves in a discussion." He pointed toward the far counter. "Coffee?" he asked Baily.

"You can help yourself." Baily glared. "Feel free to make a donation to the coffee fund."

"As if I'd take a free one." Keaton shook out his coat, stomped his muddy boots, and strode past.

When it came to the Baily and the guys, Trinity bit her tongue. This wasn't her battle. She had her own problems—not that she'd shared them with anyone. Not even Baily. It wasn't about the shame. Not anymore. It was about taking back control. Being in charge of her own destiny.

The radio behind the counter crackled to life.

She and Baily raced to it, staring at it as if it yielded great power.

Dawson had only been chief for a few weeks. But he'd been one of Ken's best friends. It didn't matter if she wanted to blame Ken's military brothers for his death—she did have a heart, and no one wanted to see a storm take one of Calusa Cove's finest.

"Lost visual of pirate ship. No visual of wreckage at sea, halting search," a male voice boomed over the radio. "Heading back to port."

"This is heartbreaking," Trinity whispered. "I feel so bad for whoever was out there."

A strong hand came down on her shoulder.

She flinched.

"That could have been you." Keaton's hot breath tickled her neck. "Don't you ever pull a stunt like that again."

She whipped her head around. "Excuse me?"

He stared deep into her eyes. A hint of anger was etched into his dark brown irises. "Dawson went out there with the Coast Guard to look for *you*. We were all worried that something happened to *you*." Keaton exhaled through his nose and a second later, he inhaled sharply. She hadn't known him all that long, but she didn't have to. From the moment they'd met, they'd been like oil drizzled on top of water with a lit match dropped on top.

The instant heat—instant attraction—had been palpable. And she knew it hadn't been one-sided. No. He looked her over like a tongue licking a Popsicle on a hot summer day. They had stared each other down like a couple of sex-starved teenagers. Then one of them opened their mouths and the next thing she knew, they were fighting.

Every day it was the was the same. She did something that he found offensive. Reckless. And he was overbearing and opinionated.

It didn't matter that he was sexy as hell. He drove her crazy.

Besides, she had a boyfriend, something she constantly forgot about whenever she was in Keaton's presence.

She pursed her lips. "If I needed help, I would have radioed. I'm not stupid."

He cocked his head. "But you didn't think to radio anyone to tell them you were safe. What you were doing. Or that you were helping someone or even heading in until after you'd been in that storm for a good forty minutes to an hour." He jerked his thumb over his shoulder. "Do you think those people were standing out there to watch you back your pretty toy into the dock? No. They were worried something bad happened to you. We all were. I would have hated to have to call that boyfriend of yours to tell him you'd been lost at sea." He turned on his heel and marched his sexy ass right out the door.

"Jeez, that was totally unnecessary," she mumbled.

"I can't believe I'm going to side with him, but no, it wasn't." Baily sighed and leaned across the counter, taking Trinity's hand. "I tried to radio you. But you never answered."

"Crap. I put it to sixteen when the storm hit and the

reception was spotty anyway with all that rain and wind. Why didn't you try me on—"

"That's for emergencies. Two is what we use for marina chatter. You know that."

"You're right. You're right. I'm sorry, Baily. It won't ever happen again. I swear." The old Trinity would have gotten her panties in a twist and huffed out. But not the new and improved Trinity. No, this version valued and respected her friends and their feelings.

She could admit when she was wrong.

And this time, she could have been dead wrong.

TRINITY RACED out her front door and flew down the porch steps, flinging herself at Mallary. She pulled her friend into her arms and hugged her tightly. "I'm so sorry, Mallary." Tears poured out of her eyes. "If I had known that was Jared out there, I would have..." A guttural sob filled her throat, choking off the rest of her... what words? There were no words to express the horrible guilt and the terrible sadness that swirled around in Trinity's soul.

"I can't believe he's gone," Mallary whispered. Her shoulders bobbed up and down. Her body grew heavy as she collapsed to the steps.

Trinity sank with her friend, clinging to her, wishing she could take away all the pain, but not even time would do that. She cradled Mallary in her arms, stroking her hair, letting her friend purge all the emotions. No amount of caring and kind words would ever make this okay.

She stared out over the ocean. Barely a ripple on the water as the calm seas gently lapped against the shore. Not a single cloud in the sky as the bright sunrays stretched its long fingers, warming her skin. She blinked. So many questions that might never be answered.

But Trinity knew what she saw... a boat lost to the sea.

She was told that Keaton, Dawson, Hayes, and Fletcher had volunteered to scuba dive in the area where the vessel may have gone down—but no one was sure of the exact location. They were trained Navy SEALs. If anyone could find the boat—and Jared —it would be those four men. She glanced at her watch. They would already be a hundred feet down by now.

But Trinity, a certified deep scuba diver herself, knew how hard that would be. She knew how deep those waters could be. How the currents and the wind from the storm could have taken Jared's body farther out to sea. It might be a futile attempt. Even the boat could have twisted, turned, and landed in a very different location. However, she was grateful they were good enough men to go out there and try.

That included Keaton.

No matter how much they clashed, she couldn't rid herself of the attraction. And she tried.

"I don't understand why my brother was out there alone. He said he was taking his new friends. I hate those guys. Especially that Ralph idiot. He's bad news." Mallary pushed from Trinity's embrace.

Trinity had never met Ralph or his friends. But she'd heard all about them from Mallary and how Mallary believed them to be a bad influence on her little brother. How they were using Jared and his kindness. His generosity and his desire to be liked and accepted by his peers was something Trinity understood all too well.

"I know taking a gap year isn't a bad thing," Mallary said, swiping her cheeks. "Jared wanted to stay and work with our dad. He loved fishing. They talked about taking over Daddy's business all the time. He thought he should spend a year seeing how things were done in all facets of the charter business before spending four years in business school. I supported that idea. I mean, I took a gap year, and it was the best decision I ever made." Mallary spoke so fast, it was amazing she managed to choke up a few sobs. "His mother hated everything about that idea. She bragged about how she finished her four-year degree in three and a half years and had just turned twenty-one. Of course, I reminded her that she ended up pregnant by a man twice her age. I know my dad loves her, though I can't fathom why. She's a brainless twit and not half the woman my mother was. I'm not bitter, but I miss my mother so much right now. Her death was so pointless and I don't understand it. She had so much to live for."

"I know. I know." Trinity had met Mallary years after her mother had died by suicide. She swallowed a bunch of pills that no one had known she'd been taking for anxiety and depression. Not even Mallary's father. It had all been a shock, and Mallary had been so close to her mom. She shared pictures of them going to get their hair and nails done—always with big, bright smiles.

"I wanted to like my stepmom, but she tried too hard to be my mother. It was gross." Mallary sniffled. She tilted her head and smiled. "I did, however, adore my half brother. He was sweet and pure and didn't deserve to be lost at sea. Do you think he still be alive?"

What a loaded question. There was always the possibility. Stranger things had happened. But she didn't want to give her friend false hope, especially since that storm had rumbled on till four in the morning, twisting and turning the ocean with waves uncharacteristic for this time of year. Trinity looped her arm around one of the few true friends she'd managed to make—and maintain—from her years at university. She held Mallary's gaze.

"I know it's crazy to hope for a miracle, but I reached out to an old charter buddy friend of my dad's and he said he's heard of people being found days after their boat went under."

"No, it's not crazy. If I had a brother, I'd be doing the same thing and Jared was a good captain. He would have done all the right things."

"Only you watched his boat capsize." Mallary sighed.

"We don't know it was his vessel," Trinity said. "There are two other missing boats from nearby coastal towns. It could have been one of them."

"But you told me you witnessed a boat go down. One that looked similar in size. You also said there was a possible pirate ship in the area." Mallary hiccupped.

"You heard gunshots. The Coast Guard said all the same things and my brother never came home. Why? Why my brother?" Mallary shot her hand up. "That was a rhetorical question. I'm not expecting an answer."

"Do you have any idea what he was doing or why his friends didn't go with him?"

"All I know is my dad said Jared asked if he could use one of the charter boats to go fishing with his friends. My dad reminded him that a storm was brewing off the coast and to be mindful of the weather. He never worried about Jared on the water." Mallary shook her head. "He trained us both to handle ourselves out there. The lessons were sometimes tough, but Jared really knew what he was doing. He loved the ocean so much than I ever did. I could take it or leave it. Growing up, we used call Jared *baby Aquaman.* If there was rough weather coming, Jared would have come in. He didn't take chances. He knew how devastating the sea could be."

"I can tell you it was bad out there and Jared's little fishing boat could easily capsize."

"You're not helping." Mallary glared, blowing out a puff of air. "Bethany babied that poor kid. She wanted him to be an overachieving pencil pushing nerd—sometimes I swear she wanted him to take over that flower shop, as if that were a place for Jared."

"I'm not saying this for any other reason than flowers could have gotten him laid," Trinity said, desperately needing to lighten the mood. She pushed down her aversion to the concept of receiving such a thoughtful gift, reminding herself that somewhere, there was a man who presented a woman with flowers for no other reason than that he cared.

Mallary dropped her head back and burst out laughing. "At least I can be happy he got to experience sex before he died."

"No. Seriously?" Trinity jerked her head. "Little Jared? With who?"

"This marina babe. A girl by the name of Valerie. A real looker too." Mallary heaved in a breath and let it out with a big woosh. "I miss him so much already. When I was his age and my friends would all complain about their pain-in-the-ass little siblings, I didn't understand. He was just a baby back then and I couldn't get enough of him."

"I remember when we met in college. I first thought you were a teenage mom."

"I thought of myself that way with him," Mallary whispered. "What am I going to do? My dad is dealing with so much because Bethany has completely lost her shit. The worst part is she's blaming me—and my dad— for what happened. As if we told him to go out there… alone. Now everyone believes he might have had something to do with the jewels stolen from Ralph's parents."

"I heard that." Trinity nodded. "Dawson, you met him, the new chief of police of Calusa Cove. I overheard him telling his buddies that they believe either pirates heard Jared must have had the jewels from the *Flying Victoria* or that he was meeting pirates out there to sell them."

"That's utter crap. My little brother would never." Mallary's face hardened. She stared at Trinity with daggers shooting from her unwavering gaze. "I bet it was Ralph who stole that jewelry. That kid is a no-good little twit. But it still doesn't explain why Jared went out there alone, and my ugly stepmother will never forgive either me or my dad."

"Oh my God. That's so unfair. Neither of you were even out there."

"Doesn't matter. My dad handed him the keys, and once again, I took my dad's side. She's always feeling ganged up on by us. It's my fault he deferred college for a year, and now she's going to blame his death on me for as long as she has breath in her lungs."

Trinity understood a little something about blame. Totally different situations, and she wouldn't compare. Not out loud. But her mother blamed her very existence for her misery. If Trinity hadn't been born, her father might have never thought to move back to Calusa Cove. He would have never wanted to share this part of his life with his precious daughter. To show her something other than the station to which she'd been born.

And Porsche would have never lost their second child.

"Right now, all you can do is allow yourself to grieve. You have to do that. You have to let the emotions in— and out. Don't fight it. Plus, your dad is going to need you. His heart is breaking just like yours. So is Bethany's, even if she doesn't empathize with anyone other than herself. Remember, I'll be here every step of the way. Whatever you need."

"Do you mean that?"

"Of course I do."

"My dad wants to have a memorial. I think it's too soon, but I won't argue with him. He asked me to help him plan the memorial. You know how much I hate things like that."

Oh boy, did Trinity know that. When they'd been in college, a friend—not a close one—but someone who lived in their dorms had died in a horrible accident. They had all been drinking that night, but Amber had been a hot mess. They all drew straws, and Mallary got the short one. But when she went to go collect Amber, she'd disappeared. They all searched for her for over an hour. No one could find her. The next day, the police found her body. She'd stumbled into someone's backyard and fell into their pool. They'd all been utterly heartbroken.

"My dad also wants me to speak at this…thing… He believes Jared would have wanted me to, but I haven't a clue as to what to say."

Trinity squeezed her friend's shoulder. "We'll figure it out together."

"I don't know what I'd do without you."

"Ditto." Trinity's phone vibrated. Quickly, she pulled it from her pocket and glanced at the text. She'd ignored Fenton since their fight yesterday, other than to let him know she was fine. That she'd made it in safely. She'd neglected to tell him anything about her adventure at sea. He'd learn about it soon enough.

Though, it appeared by his worried text, he might have already been told.

She frowned.

"What's wrong?" Mallary asked.

"Nothing." Trinity tucked her cell back in her pocket. She'd deal with Fenton later.

"Come on. I need something to distract myself from what's happening. My brain can't stop going back out there." Mallary pointed to the open ocean.

Trinity sighed. While Mallary could be high maintenance as friends went, and she wasn't always there when Trinity needed her most, she was a good person. She was kind and decent, and if she needed a distraction, Trinity could give her that. "It's Fenton. We got into a fight yesterday. It's why I went out on the boat instead of going out with him."

"Oh. I didn't know that." Mallary brushed her hair from her face. "What happened?"

"I saw a text. He says it was from some dude, but the words on the screen screamed some girl he was sexting with. Not some random old buddy sending him sex jokes. I'm not stupid. It was dirty talk, and I can't do another cheating man again."

"Seriously?" Mallary jerked her head back. "Fenton? No way. That man adores you. Worships the ground you walk on. I can't believe he'd be chatting with another chick. He wouldn't do that. No way. You totally misinterpreted that text."

Trinity wanted to believe that. She really liked Fenton. He was normal, if there was such a thing. He wasn't needy. He didn't demand all her time. The only thing he did was occasionally get jealous.

Of Keaton.

Granted, she did find Keaton sexy as hell—in the looks department. But his personality was sometimes a little too rough around the edges—at least toward her.

"I don't think so," Trinity admitted. "And this isn't the first red flag." Only, this was the first time she was talking about it with anyone.

"What do you mean?" Mallary crinkled her nose.

"I found an earring in his car a week ago."

"What did he say about it?" Mallary's eyes went wide. She swiped at her cheeks.

"He told me he let one of the girls in the office take his car to get lunch."

"Well, there you have it." Mallary lowered her chin. "I get you're wounded. I know you have some trust issues. I would too. But come on. Fenton is a keeper. He's supersweet. He's kind, and generous, and he's good to you. He wouldn't cheat. He's so not the type."

He was a man. He had a dick. That made him the type in Trinity's book. But she wasn't about to argue with Mallary. That woman thought Fenton was the perfect man—for Trinity.

For a hot minute, so did Trinity, but she wasn't so sure now.

"Call him back." Mallary nudged her. "Make up with him. Life is too short."

Jeez. How could she argue with that?

So, Trinity yanked out her phone and texted Fenton, letting him know she'd meet him later.

Maybe her friend was right. Maybe she was reading too much into all this.

# ABOUT JEN TALTY

Jen Talty is the *USA Today* Bestselling Author of Contemporary Romance, Romantic Suspense, and Paranormal Romance. In the fall of 2020, her short story was selected and featured in a 1001 Dark Nights Anthology.

Regardless of the genre, her goal is to take you on a ride that will leave you floating under the sun with warmth in your heart. She writes stories about broken heroes and heroines who aren't necessarily looking for romance, but in the end, they find the kind of love books are written about :).

She first started writing while carting her kids to one hockey rink after the other, averaging 170 games per year between 3 kids in 2 countries and 5 states. Her first book, IN TWO WEEKS was originally published in 2007. In 2010 she helped form a publishing company (Cool Gus Publishing) with *NY Times* Bestselling Author Bob Mayer where she ran the technical side of the business through 2016.

Jen is currently enjoying the next phase of her life...the

empty nester! She and her husband reside in Jupiter, Florida.

Grab a glass of vino, kick back, relax, and let the romance roll in…

Sign up for my *Newsletter (https://dl.bookfunnel.com/82gm8b9k4y)* where I often give away free books before publication.

*Join my private Facebook group (https://www.facebook.com/groups/191706547909047/) where I post exclusive excerpts and discuss all things murder and love!*

Never miss a new release. Follow me on Amazon:amazon.com/author/jentalty

And on Bookbub: bookbub.com/authors/jen-talty

*Deadly Secrets*

*Murder in Paradise Bay*

*To Protect His own*

*Deadly Seduction*

*When A Stranger Calls*

*His Deadly Past*

*The Corkscrew Killer*

*First Responders: A spin-off from the NY State Troopers series*

*Playing With Fire*

*Private Conversation*

*The Right Groom*

*After The Fire*

*Caught In The Flames*

*Chasing The Fire*

*Legacy Series*

*Dark Legacy*

*Legacy of Lies*

*Secret Legacy*

*Emerald City*

*Investigate Away*

*Sail Away*

*Fly Away*

*Flirt Away*

*Hawaii Brotherhood Protectors*

*Waylen Unleashed*

*Bowie's Battle*

*Colorado Brotherhood Protectors*

*Fighting For Esme*

*Defending Raven*

*Fay's Six*

*Darius' Promise*

*Yellowstone Brotherhood Protectors*

*Guarding Payton*

*Wyatt's Mission*

*Corbin's Mission*

*Candlewood Falls*

*Rivers Edge*

*The Buried Secret*

*Its In His Kiss*

*Lips Of An Angel*

*Kisses Sweeter than Wine*

*A Little Bit Whiskey*

*It's all in the Whiskey*

*Johnnie Walker*

*Georgia Moon*

*Jack Daniels*

*Jim Beam*

*Whiskey Sour*

*Whiskey Cobbler*

*Whiskey Smash*

*Irish Whiskey*

*The Monroes*

*Color Me Yours*

*Color Me Smart*

*Color Me Free*

*Color Me Lucky*

*Color Me Ice*

*Color Me Home*

*Search and Rescue*

*Protecting Ainsley*

*Protecting Clover*

*Protecting Olympia*

*Protecting Freedom*

*Protecting Princess*

*Protecting Marlowe*

*Fallport Rescue Operations*

*Searching for Madison*

*Searching for Haven*

*Searching for Pandora*

*Searching for Stormi*

**DELTA FORCE-NEXT GENERATION**

*Shielding Jolene*

*Shielding Aalyiah*

*Shielding Laine*

*Shielding Talullah*

*Shielding Maribel*

*Shielding Daisy*


*The Men of Thief Lake*

*Rekindled*

*Destiny's Dream*


*Federal Investigators*

*Jane Doe's Return*

*The Butterfly Murders*


*THE AEGIS NETWORK*

*The Sarich Brother*

*The Lighthouse*

*Her Last Hope*

*The Last Flight*

*The Return Home*

*The Matriarch*


*Aegis Network: Jacksonville Division*

*A SEAL's Honor*

*Talon's Honor*

*Arthur's Honor*

*Rex's Honor*

*Kent's Honor*

*Buddy's Honor*

*Aegis Network Short Stories*

*Max & Milian*

*A Christmas Miracle*

*Spinning Wheels*

*Holiday's Vacation*

*The Brotherhood Protectors*

*Out of the Wild*

*Rough Justice*

*Rough Around The Edges*

*Rough Ride*

*Rough Edge*

*Rough Beauty*

*The Brotherhood Protectors*

*The Saving Series*

*Saving Love*

*Saving Magnolia*

*Saving Leather*

*Hot Hunks*

*Cove's Blind Date Blows Up*

*My Everyday Hero – Ledger*

*Tempting Tavor*

*Malachi's Mystic Assignment*

*Needing Neor*

*Holiday Romances*

*A Christmas Getaway*

# ABOUT ELLE JAMES

ELLE JAMES also writing as MYLA JACKSON is a *New York Times* and *USA Today* Bestselling author of books including cowboys, intrigues and paranormal adventures that keep her readers on the edges of their seats. When she's not at her computer, she's traveling, snow skiing, boating, or riding her ATV, dreaming up new stories. Learn more about Elle James at www.elle-james.com

Website | Facebook | Twitter | GoodReads | Newsletter | BookBub | Amazon

Or visit her alter ego Myla Jackson at mylajackson.com
Website | Facebook | Twitter | Newsletter

*Follow Me!*
www.ellejames.com
ellejamesauthor@gmail.com

Maliea's Hero (#4)

Emi's Hero (#5)

Sachie's Hero (#6)

**_Bayou Brotherhood Protectors_**

Remy (#1)

Gerard (#2)

Lucas (#3)

Beau (#4)

Rafael (#5)

Valentin (#6)

Landry (#7)

Simon (#8)

Maurice (#9)

Jacques (#10)

**_Cajun Magic Mystery Series_**

Voodoo on the Bayou (#1)

Voodoo for Two (#2)

Deja Voodoo (#3)

Damned if You Voodoo (#4)

Voodoo or Die (#5)

**_Brotherhood Protectors Yellowstone_**

Saving Kyla (#1)

Saving Chelsea (#2)

Saving Amanda (#3)

Saving Liliana (#4)

Saving Breely (#5)

Saving Savvie (#6)

Saving Jenna (#7)

Saving Peyton (#8)

Saving Londyn (#9)

***Brotherhood Protectors Colorado***

SEAL Salvation (#1)

Rocky Mountain Rescue (#2)

Ranger Redemption (#3)

Tactical Takeover (#4)

Colorado Conspiracy (#5)

Rocky Mountain Madness (#6)

Free Fall (#7)

Colorado Cold Case (#8)

Fool's Folly (#9)

Colorado Free Rein (#10)

Rocky Mountain Venom (#11)

High Country Hero (#12)

***Brotherhood Protectors***

Montana SEAL (#1)

Bride Protector SEAL (#2)

Montana D-Force (#3)

Cowboy D-Force (#4)

Montana Ranger (#5)

Montana Dog Soldier (#6)

Montana SEAL Daddy (#7)

Montana Ranger's Wedding Vow (#8)

Montana SEAL Undercover Daddy (#9)

Cape Cod SEAL Rescue (#10)

Montana SEAL Friendly Fire (#11)

Montana SEAL's Mail-Order Bride (#12)

SEAL Justice (#13)

Ranger Creed (#14)

Delta Force Rescue (#15)

Dog Days of Christmas (#16)

Montana Rescue (#17)

Montana Ranger Returns (#18)

Brotherhood Protectors Boxed Set 1

Brotherhood Protectors Boxed Set 2

Brotherhood Protectors Boxed Set 3

Brotherhood Protectors Boxed Set 4

Brotherhood Protectors Boxed Set 5

Brotherhood Protectors Boxed Set 6

### *Iron Horse Legacy*

Soldier's Duty (#1)

Ranger's Baby (#2)

Marine's Promise (#3)

SEAL's Vow (#4)

Warrior's Resolve (#5)

Drake (#6)

Grimm (#7)

Murdock (#8)

Utah (#9)

Judge (#10)

## *Delta Force Strong*

Ivy's Delta (Delta Force 3 Crossover)

Breaking Silence (#1)

Breaking Rules (#2)

Breaking Away (#3)

Breaking Free (#4)

Breaking Hearts (#5)

Breaking Ties (#6)

Breaking Point (#7)

Breaking Dawn (#8)

Breaking Promises (#9)

## *Hearts & Heroes Series*

Wyatt's War (#1)

Mack's Witness (#2)

Ronin's Return (#3)

Sam's Surrender (#4)

## *Hellfire Series*

Hellfire, Texas (#1)

Justice Burning (#2)

Smoldering Desire (#3)

Hellfire in High Heels (#4)

Playing With Fire (#5)

Up in Flames (#6)

Total Meltdown (#7)

***Take No Prisoners Series***

SEAL's Honor (#1)

SEAL'S Desire (#2)

SEAL's Embrace (#3)

SEAL's Obsession (#4)

SEAL's Proposal (#5)

SEAL's Seduction (#6)

SEAL'S Defiance (#7)

SEAL's Deception (#8)

SEAL's Deliverance (#9)

SEAL's Ultimate Challenge (#10)

***Texas Billionaire Club***

Tarzan & Janine (#1)

Something To Talk About (#2)

Who's Your Daddy (#3)

Love & War (#4)

***Billionaire Online Dating Service***

The Billionaire Husband Test (#1)

The Billionaire Cinderella Test (#2)

The Billionaire Bride Test (#3)

The Billionaire Daddy Test (#4)

The Billionaire Matchmaker Test (#5)

The Billionaire Glitch Date (#6)

The Billionaire Perfect Date (#7)

The Billionaire Replacement Date (#8)

The Billionaire Wedding Date (#9)

**The Outriders**

Homicide at Whiskey Gulch (#1)

Hideout at Whiskey Gulch (#2)

Held Hostage at Whiskey Gulch (#3)

Setup at Whiskey Gulch (#4)

Missing Witness at Whiskey Gulch (#5)

Cowboy Justice at Whiskey Gulch (#6)

**Boys Behaving Badly Anthologies**

Rogues (#1)

Blue Collar (#2)

Pirates (#3)

Stranded (#4)

First Responder (#5)

Cowboys (#6)

Silver Soldiers (#7)

Secret Identities (#8)

Warrior's Conquest

Enslaved by the Viking Short Story

Conquests

Smokin' Hot Firemen

Protecting the Colton Bride

Protecting the Colton Bride & Colton's Cowboy Code

Heir to Murder

Secret Service Rescue

High Octane Heroes

Haunted

Engaged with the Boss

Cowboy Brigade

An Unexpected Clue

Under Suspicion, With Child

Texas-Size Secrets